Christmas

IN CHESTNUT RIDGE

ALSO BY NANCY NAIGLE

Christmas Joy

Hope at Christmas

Dear Santa

The Christmas Shop

Christmas Angels

A Heartfelt Christmas Promise

The Wedding Ranch

CHESTNUT RIDGE NOVELS

And Then There Was You

Visit www.NancyNaigle.com for a list of all Nancy's novels.

Christmas
IN CHESTNUT RIDGE

Nancy Naigle

ST. MARTIN'S
GRIFFIN
NEW YORK

First published in the United States by St. Martin's Griffin, an imprint of St. Martin's Publishing Group

CHRISTMAS IN CHESTNUT RIDGE. Copyright © 2024 by Nancy Naigle. All rights reserved. Printed in the United States of America. For information, address St. Martin's Publishing Group, 120 Broadway, New York, NY 10271.

www.stmartins.com

Designed by Omar Chapa

The Library of Congress Cataloging-in-Publication Data is available upon request.

ISBN 978-1-250-79415-4 (trade paperback)
ISBN 978-1-250-79416-1 (ebook)

Our books may be purchased in bulk for promotional, educational, or business use. Please contact your local bookseller or the Macmillan Corporate and Premium Sales Department at 1-800-221-7945, extension 5442, or by email at MacmillanSpecialMarkets@macmillan.com.

First Edition: 2024

10 9 8 7 6 5 4 3 2 1

To my neighbors in Patrick County, Virginia:

In a town where most folks have generational roots, you welcomed me like one of your own. I've tried to capture the sense of community found in Patrick Springs in this series. I hope these characters warm your heart as you have mine. You've uplifted and inspired me and this series. Thank you.

Christmas

IN CHESTNUT RIDGE

Chapter One

Sheila Aldridge leaned back in her desk chair, considering how to answer. She glanced over at her empty desk calendar, although she already knew she didn't have plans over the Christmas holiday, but the "what's your calendar look like" question always made her freeze, feeling like a mouse getting ready to be pounced on by a cat. Real estate slowed this time of year, making it one of her least favorite seasons, especially since her divorce. But this wasn't just anyone asking, it was Natalie. "My schedule is fairly flexible. What are you thinking?"

"I want you to come stay with me for the holidays. I miss my best friend," Natalie said. "Please say yes. I promise it'll be fun."

Natalie had moved from Richmond to the tiny mountain town of Chestnut Ridge last year following a devastating loss. Sheila understood that Natalie needed to get back on her feet, even take time to lick her wounds, but she never thought she'd stay up there.

I'd have guessed she'd last three months. Tops.

"Why don't you come here instead? We could do the lights at Lewis Ginter Botanical Garden. It'll be like old times." Sheila could never get Dan to go see them, so for six years running, it had been her and Natalie going together. *Good riddance, Dan.*

"You know I can't. Randy is here, and it's our first real Christmas together."

"Which is probably why I shouldn't be there. You don't need a third wheel while you snuggle-bunny your way through the holidays."

"Oh stop. You're never a third wheel. Plus, the town has this huge festival called the Christmas Tree Stroll. It'll be fun."

"Exactly how huge? There aren't but a couple thousand people in the whole town." It came out a little snarkier than she'd intended.

"Everyone will be there. If it's one thing about Chestnut Ridge I've learned, it's that folks enjoy getting together. The Christmas Tree Stroll is supposed to be the party of the year," Natalie explained.

Sheila had thought Natalie's move into her late husband's hunting cabin was a big mistake for a girl used to all the conveniences of living in the city. But the joy in Natalie's voice was undeniable. She was making a new life for herself in the small town of Chestnut Ridge, and it warmed Sheila's heart that Natalie sounded like her old self again.

Natalie was still rambling. "And it's held on the high school football field," she explained. "So, it might not be the lights and festivities at the Lewis Ginter Botanical Gardens, but rows and rows of Christmas trees will line the whole field, and each tree is decorated in a different theme. I've seen pictures and this year it's going to be even more spectacular."

"If you've never been to this Christmas Stroll, how do you know that it will be even *more* spectacular?"

"Because I just entered." Natalie's excitement was contagious.

Sheila grinned while shaking her head. "Of course you did. I knew there was more to this invite."

"Go ahead, make fun," Natalie said. "Not only do I want your help, but I'm also counting on the festival inspiring new ideas for next year's card collection. Technically, it's work and play, and that's always more fun when you're around. Come on. Please? You're so good at decorating. I need you."

"And you want to win." This was the enthusiasm Sheila had missed since Natalie left town.

"I do, and with your help I know we can create something magical."

"Mm-hmm. What are we going to win?"

"Bragging rights for next year and a banner."

"A banner? High stakes. How can I say no?" Sheila couldn't contain her amusement, but she didn't want to disappoint her friend, either. "Okay, fine. What would I have to do?"

"Does it even matter?" Natalie's voice bounced with excitement. "We're decorating for Christmas. It'll be festive. And festive is fun."

"Fun for you, and your sweetheart. Everything is fun when you're in love. That leaves me the third wheel, and that's about as fun as a flat tire." Sheila stared at her empty calendar.

"Again with the third wheel? Tricycles are cool. It's better than being a unicycle sitting at home by yourself."

That pinched. "You've got a point, but I do like to know what I'm being roped into. I have my limits. I refuse to dress up as an elf."

"At the most, we might wear those cute light-up antlers, but even that's negotiable. You can help me decide."

"This better not end up like the time you tricked me into landscaping from dusk to dawn on a ninety-degree day for Habitat for Humanity."

"You enjoyed that," Natalie reminded her.

"Not the sweating part. I'd have at least dressed more appropriately if you'd told me I was going to be up to my armpits in dirt and compost."

"You wouldn't have come if I'd told you."

It was true. She wouldn't have. She'd never been the get-your-hands-dirty kind of gal, but it had been a rewarding experience. She'd volunteered again since then. "I had fun that day despite the heat and dirt. More to the point, I'd do anything with you."

"So you'll come?"

"Yes," Sheila said with a sigh. "But I reserve the right to complain about it later." She knew deep down that spending Christmas with Natalie, even in Chestnut Ridge as the third wheel, was going to be wonderful. Natalie's beau, Randy, was a good guy, and now that things looked pretty serious, she was glad to be spending more time with them, always having Natalie's best interests at heart.

"You won't have any reason to complain. It's going to be great."

"I know it will. I miss you. Christmas wouldn't be the same without you." Sheila twisted her long ponytail in front of her shoulder. "I guess now that Randy has relocated up there, this move is a forever thing, isn't it?"

"There are days I still can't believe it, but here I am living in Chestnut Ridge and happier than I could have ever imagined. I love living here."

"You *love* Randy," Sheila said, and the joy in Natalie's lively response made Sheila hopeful.

"I do. So much. He's so good to me. I'd live in a tent to be with him," Natalie said. "And you know how I feel about sleeping on the ground."

"Okay, okay." Sheila picked up the rose-gold pen with her company logo on it and poised it over her calendar. "When do you need me?"

Natalie clapped and squealed. "This is great."

"Don't act so surprised," Sheila teased. "You know I can never say no to you."

"But I'm not usually asking you to go out of town," Natalie said.

"True."

"Okay, so the festival kicks off with a Holiday Warmup that Orene hosts. I know she'd be thrilled if you could make it for that."

"Absolutely. She's incredibly sweet."

"Good. So, that would mean being here by the evening of the thirteenth for the party—"

"You do realize that's a Friday the thirteenth?"

"Oh stop! That's a silly superstition, but if you want to come on the twelfth to be safe, that's fine by me, and stay through the New Year, but if that's too long, then at least stay through Christmas day."

"Let's take one holiday at a time. That's two whole weeks." She couldn't even bring her hand to the calendar.

"Oh come on. You make your own schedule. Now that you have four real estate agents working under you, you can take time off. You need a break once in a while. Money isn't everything."

"It sure makes life easier, though."

"You know better than that. You and Dan were rolling in the big bucks when you two split up."

"I know. You're right. I'm just playing. Okay, I'm blocking the dates, but on one condition."

"Anything."

"Let's see if Orene will put me up while I'm down there so you and Randy can have your time together too. No arguments."

"Fine."

"And I do have to go to Virginia Beach to see Mom the weekend before Christmas. I'll drive back to Richmond that night to check my mail, then come back for the Christmas Tree Stroll and spend Christmas with you."

"Perfect!"

Sheila slid the broad-tip marker across the dates. "You'll check with Orene for me?"

"I'll talk to her today and give you a call back. We're going to win that banner for sure with you on my team."

Sheila's thought flowed right out of her mouth. "I wonder how they'll feel about an out-of-towner and the newest resident of their little town winning the coveted banner?"

"Hadn't really considered that, but I guess that's for us to find out," said Natalie. "They'll be fine. You'll see."

"Let me know what I can bring from the city to hedge our bets."

"Oooh, excellent idea." Natalie picked up a pen. "I'll start a list."

Sheila could almost hear the ideas pulsing through Natalie's brain.

"I'll send you the flyer from last year," Natalie said. "It's hard to explain over the phone. The short version is each team adopts a tree. Then, we have to pick a theme, and a name for our entry. If there's something similar, they make you come up with another plan, so I want to get ours in early. Oh, and after the stroll awards are announced, they distribute the competition trees to families in need across two counties. Isn't that awesome?"

"It is. Oh gosh, there are a million ideas already floating through my head." Sheila jotted down a quick brainstorm of ideas, including snowflakes, antique toys, rose gold, stockings.

"Mine too. Orene has scrapbooks from every single year. I'm going to check them out this afternoon. I'll send pictures so you can see."

"Okay, yeah, I'll think on it too." But Sheila knew Natalie was off and running. "You've already been on Pinterest, haven't you?"

"Maybe. A little. And Instagram, and TikTok, and you don't even want to know all the time I've wasted researching this already," Natalie admitted. "We need something original. Nothing much store-bought if possible."

"Well, then I won't bother with doing a bunch of shopping here," Sheila said. "We'll come up with something spectacular! I'll bring my glue guns."

"In the past, some winners based their tree designs on holiday movies or songs. The local seamstress did one that looked like a winter wedding gown last year. The garland was shimmering fabric with pearls and beads. It was drop-dead gorgeous."

"I've seen those Christmas tree dresses. Do you need me to bring my big pre-lit tree. It's a really nice one. It looks totally real?"

"No. The town purchases the trees from the Christmas tree

farms here in the county. It's part of the entry fee. We get to pick the height and type though."

"I like the look of long needles, as long as they aren't in my house," Sheila said.

"True. The short-needled trees seem sturdier, though. Depending on what we decide to do, we might need that. We get the whole business week to decorate, not that it'll take that long, but it gives us some flexibility to do other things while you're here too."

"Which is why you want me to come for two weeks."

"Exactly. I'm going to warn you, this town grows on you fast," she said, as if tempting her.

"You don't have to worry about that. I'm a city girl from my salon-touched roots to my pedicured toes." Sheila jotted a note to get her nails done before she went.

"I'll let Orene know we'll both help with the Holiday Warm-up," Natalie said, "but everyone pitches in. That's just how folks are around here."

"Chestnut Ridge sounds like a fairy-tale town."

"In the best possible way, and everyone is genuinely nice. If you're lucky, it'll snow. There's nothing more breathtaking than these mountains blanketed in fresh snow."

"It's been a long time since I've seen a white Christmas. Do you want me to bring my tree for your cabin?"

"No one does fake trees up here."

"If you spritz a little pine smell on it no one could tell the difference."

"Christmas tree farms are how our neighbors make a living, and everyone supports the local businesses here. These tree farms make a production of picking out your Christmas tree. You're going to love it."

"We'll see about that." Unexpected excitement coursed through her. "I barely remember the last time I decorated a tree. I guess I'll be getting my fill." Sheila tapped her finger on her desk pad, where she'd been scribbling notes. "I have to ask. White lights or colored lights?"

"That entirely depends on the theme," Natalie said, "but I'll admit, I prefer the big colored lights."

"Me too. It just seems more festive."

"Get ready. These two weeks in Chestnut Ridge are my Christmas gift to you."

"Thanks, Nat. I'm ready for a Christmas worth remembering."

Chapter Two

The Sunday before Thanksgiving, Sheila gathered her things to set up for her last scheduled open house of the year. The Carrolton Estate was a stunning home in a sought-after neighborhood. Houses in this area didn't come up for sale that often, and she'd sold this one to a newlywed couple just four years ago. Unfortunately, they'd already outgrown the house and were eager to find a new perfect place to call home.

She fussed with fresh flowers until they looked perfectly welcoming on the entry hall table. Luxury listings were what she was known for and, frankly, closing out the year with a commission of this size would be a wonderful way to wrap it up.

Humming Christmas carols as she arranged freshly baked cookies on a platter in the kitchen, she realized she was excited about her holiday plans in Chestnut Ridge.

Sheila was thankful for Natalie's newfound happiness after the difficult path she'd traveled the last few years. First she'd lost her husband, Jeremy, and then, just as she was climbing out of the depths of grief, Marc Swindell popped into her life and conned her out of just about everything she owned. Then again, if that hadn't happened, Natalie might not have met Randy. *Who's to say the right path to happiness is always a smooth one? Lord knows, I've had my rocky roads. Isn't it time to bring on my joy yet?*

Thank goodness Detective Randy Fellowes had been assigned to Natalie's case when Swindell swindled Natalie. Not only for the justice that was finally served, but for the happiness Randy brought to her. A joy that Sheila hadn't seen in Natalie's eyes since Jeremy passed away.

We've both been through a lot over the past five years. I hope my happy days are ahead too.

She heard the front door open, and straightened, assuming her best friendly Realtor demeanor.

Not every visitor who came to an open house was a prospective buyer; she'd learned that a long time ago. But as she gave this couple the once-over, she saw that they had *interested buyers* written all over them.

"Welcome. Thanks for coming out today." The opulent Richmond house would draw a lot of people, even on the busiest travel weekend of the year. There'd be lookie-loos, but she was certain she'd get at least one good offer today. It was just too special a property for the right buyer to pass up.

Sheila handed the couple a glossy booklet with all the details about the house. "Make yourselves at home. It just might be your next one. I'll let you mill around."

The husband looked impressed with the pricey marketing material. It was one of her secret weapons. These high-end properties deserved the extra touch, since the commissions were extra big.

The woman peered over her husband's shoulder. "I've got to see that kitchen."

Sheila had staged special pictures, opting to use different ones from the online listings, for the fancy booklet. Photos staged specifically for this showing, with an eye to the demographic right down to the artwork inserted into the picture frames. Photoshop was one incredible invention. Not that she knew how to use it, but she was smart enough to hire a whiz kid who did.

"Look, hon!" The woman's blue eyes danced as she looked up from the brochure, and then she turned to Sheila. "I've *always* wanted a fancy spa bathroom."

"Me too. It's a beauty. When you walk in, the relaxation will practically lift you off your feet. Feel free to enjoy the champagne and strawberries." Sheila had set them up in a shiny silver ice bucket and crystal flutes. Who could resist that?

"I can't wait," the woman gushed, and she hooked her arm through her husband's, practically dragging him down the hall. "This way, right?"

"Yes, ma'am, but I'd start in the kitchen. Don't miss the pantry. It's definitely a chef-quality space."

The husband's eyebrows cocked in appreciation.

"And there's an outdoor kitchen too." Sheila knew how to pick up on the subtleties of body language to pitch the right perks.

A family came in right behind them with an adorable little girl with blond ringlets and wearing a powder-blue dress that matched her twinkling eyes.

"Welcome." She offered a children's version of the pamphlet to their daughter. One with a picture of a kitten on the ottoman and a puppy in the backyard. The little girl had adorable Shirley Temple dimples when she smiled.

"There are some fresh-baked cookies on the kitchen counter," Sheila whispered to the parents as they accepted the brochure.

"We've been waiting for something in this neighborhood to come up for so long," the woman said. "It's honestly a stretch on our budget, but we couldn't resist checking it out."

Sheila dove in. "Well, interest rates are low right now. There are so many advantages. Walking distance to the academy, which makes this a highly sought-after neighborhood for families with school-age children." Sheila noticed the way the wife shot a glance to her husband. That was clearly something they'd discussed before. "It's a lot of house for the price point. Take a look around. The HOA is lower than other similar neighborhoods, which is a real plus because it keeps those monthly additional expenses down, and this house has one of the highest efficiency ratings I've seen," Sheila added.

"That *is* helpful," her husband said.

"I'll answer any questions you might have," Sheila said. "My card is in the booklet, and I have a wonderful team that can help you navigate any challenges. Home buying requires looking at the long term, especially when you're raising children. We're familiar with this area. We're here to help you with this house, or find the perfect one in your price range."

"Thank you so much."

For a moment, Sheila's mind wandered as she watched the little girl tug at her mom's hand toward the kitchen.

She'd always thought she'd have children by now, but she and Dan had never been blessed that way. No matter how many times Dan swore it wasn't the reason for their separation, the fact that he was married less than a year after their divorce to a new wife who was already pregnant left her aching.

She took comfort in helping families find the perfect home to raise their children. That would have to be enough.

She could so easily picture herself walking her children to school on pretty days. She'd cut back on the hours she worked in a heartbeat for something like that. *If I had a daughter, I'd have snatched this house right up.*

People came in a steady flow, giving her plenty of time to talk with each of them. It was really a perfect open house.

During a lull of activity, she checked her emails. Natalie had sent the details on the Christmas Tree Stroll. A photograph taken from above showed how many trees there were, and she couldn't begin to count them.

Sheila recognized Orene in one of the pictures. Smiling broadly, she was standing with a woman holding a sign that read DUCK THE HALLS WITH A CHRISTMAS SONG THEME. Their team had decorated their long-needled pine with colorful decoys wearing festive wreaths, and a garland of shiny red and green shotgun casings and colorful feathers. A handwritten note below the picture said, "'Deck the Halls' performed on quacking duck calls played from the tree skirt." Sheila had to admit that was innovative.

She scrolled to the entry form. Each team could have up to eight people on it. All decorating would be done on a tree of pre-selected type and size. There were lighting requirements, which also included a "no open flames" clause. *That sounds like a rule that must've come from a prior incident.*

Each entry should include a sign no larger than twenty by twenty inches with a name that helped describe the theme of the entry.

TREES WILL BE JUDGED ON [A] UNIQUE DESIGN AND CRE-ATIVE USE OF LIGHTS AND DECORATIONS; [B] STORYLINE

OR THEME; [C] DISPLAY AND PLACEMENT OF DECORATIONS;
AND [D] OVERALL PRESENTATION.

Sheila went back to the email, to which Natalie had attached about ten pictures. Each tree was more unique than the last. *We're going to have our work cut out to come up with something better than these.*

"Excuse me?"

Sheila looked up, surprised she hadn't heard the customers walk through the living room on the walnut hardwood floors. It was the first couple she'd greeted, at the very beginning of the open house. They'd left earlier; that they'd come back was a good sign.

Sheila stuffed her phone into her pocket. "What do you think?"

"This house is perfect," the wife said. "You're right about that master suite. It's amazing. And that tub. Oh my gosh."

Sheila had draped the thirsty white robe she'd treated herself to on her last visit to the Greenbrier over the freestanding, fully jetted tub.

The champagne and fresh berries and a copy of *The Shell Collector* positioned just so on a table with turquoise and real gold in the acrylic overlay couldn't go unnoticed.

"Buy the house, and I'll throw in the champagne bucket and robe," Sheila teased.

"We'll hold you to that!" the woman said. "Where did you find that table? It's stunning."

"A local craftsman makes those. I can give you his information." She owned three of them. This one, another with sapphire-like gems and silver inlays, and one with tiny pine cones floating in acrylic in a wide knot right in the middle. They didn't go with anything in her house, but she hadn't been able to resist them.

Now they'd found their place in her open-house arsenal of tricks, and she was pretty sure she was keeping that guy busy with all the cards she handed out.

Sheila tried to resist celebrating before the deal was done. "Any questions I can answer for you before I close up shop here?"

The husband and wife looked at each other, and then he spoke up. "We'd like to make an offer."

"Wonderful." And there it was. What a way to end the year. "We can do the paperwork here, or meet at my office."

"We're ready to work it up now."

"Just let me take down the Open House sign, and we'll get this taken care of." Sheila jogged out to get the sign and balloons and tucked them in the back seat of her Mercedes. It only took a moment, and she was back, locking the door behind her. "Okay, this is so exciting. It's a magnificent home."

Three hours later, she'd presented the sellers with the offer and they were tickled pink, and since the buyers had a prequalification letter, there wasn't much worry that things wouldn't go smoothly. She called to congratulate the couple and discuss the next steps.

It had been a long day with the open house and the deal, but well worth it.

She unlocked the door to her house and walked inside, kicking off her shoes and hanging her purse on the coat tree. After a quick shower, she pulled out a mason jar of salad from her refrigerator, added a few cooked shrimp, and sat in front of the television to eat dinner with a glass of chardonnay.

In a couple of weeks, she'd be in Chestnut Ridge. This would be one of the last quiet evenings she'd have until the new year, since she'd moved the holiday party for the office to next week. That would keep her busy.

She picked up her phone and started typing in a list of things to pack. A gift for Orene. Two probably. A thank-you for letting her stay and a Christmas gift. She'd seen the cutest teapot in an antique store a few weeks ago while she was looking for a new punch bowl for the open house. She'd immediately thought of Orene then. Too bad she hadn't made the purchase. She hoped it was still there.

I'll stop by there tomorrow.

Her phone rang and wasn't that perfect timing. Orene's name displayed on the screen.

"Hello, Orene. I was just thinking about you."

"Wonderful, because I have your room ready for you. I'm so delighted you're going to come join us for the Christmas Tree Stroll this year."

"It sounds like fun."

"Oh, it is. You'll never want to spend the holidays anywhere else," Orene said. "Now, I had a couple of questions for you. What's your favorite Christmas cookie?"

"I haven't met a cookie I didn't like, but if I had to pick a favorite, I'd say gingerbread. The thin crispy ones."

"Perfect! I just so happen to make the best gingerbread around," Orene bragged. "And what's your favorite color?"

"That's easy. Red."

"Excellent, dear. I can't wait to see you. It'll be a little chaotic the first night with the Holiday Warmup in full swing, but I promise you a quiet stay the rest of the holiday. I hope you plan to relax while you're here."

"I do. I've got all my work covered here. I even ordered a

couple of new Christmas novels to read. It's going to be all Christmas, all the time, while I'm in Chestnut Ridge."

"As it should be," quipped Orene. "I can't wait for you to arrive."

"Thank you so much for letting me stay with you. I'll see you soon." Sheila hung up the phone, feeling like she'd just received a warm hug. It had been too long since she'd had one of those.

Chapter Three

Tucker parked his red Ford F-450 pickup in front of the firehouse. Tonight everyone, volunteer firefighters and his paid staff, would come together to celebrate a job well done, honor those they'd lost, and plan for the following year.

He walked around to the passenger side of the truck and opened the door. He slid a box to the edge of the seat and hoisted it out. It was heavy, and the thin cardboard sort of dipped under the weight of the contents. He slid one hand under the middle to support it, and headed through the parking lot filled with mostly pickup trucks and a few minivans.

The community had worked hard to raise the funds to move the fire station into this new building to position them for success.

Hickory smoke filled the air. The Newton brothers had been tending the barbecuing of the whole hog since the wee hours of the morning.

Lights glowed through the huge glass-panel doors, and friendly banter echoed out into the night. Pride coursed through him as he walked inside to the large group he considered his second family.

Good folks. All of them.

Tables set up earlier this afternoon were now filled end-to-end with casseroles, side dishes, fresh bread, and baked goods that would be enjoyed alongside the barbecued pork.

Tucker walked in and rang the bell that hung next to the front entrance door. "Hey now! How is everyone?"

Cheers and whistles were followed by the shuffle of people turning their attention to their fire chief as the room began to quiet a bit.

Refreshments filled the long table next to the microphone platform, which was mostly used for bingo nights to raise money, but tonight it was Tucker onstage. He set the box down, then grabbed a cup of sweet tea before walking up the steps to take the microphone. "Everyone ready to get this business taken care of so we can eat?"

"Yes!" Everyone gathered around.

"Thanks for coming out," Tucker said. "To my full-timers, thank you all for keeping it safe for every one of us. It's a team effort, and you are continually teaching and learning from each other."

A whistle came from the back.

"We are fortunate to have such a strong group of volunteers," Tucker said. "When I go to the state meeting, I'm really proud that we don't have the problems that so many departments across this state are facing. They struggle to find people with this work in their heart. Our recruitment and training numbers have been outstanding. Give yourselves a round of applause."

As everyone clapped, Tucker looked at the faces in front of him, feeling like a lucky man. "We made it through the year with no critical injuries, and I'm grateful for that."

"What about when Sully burned off his eyebrows?" someone shouted from the back.

"That was a cooking incident. I'm not counting that one. The bananas Foster was still good, and I'm still convincing myself the crunchy topping was toasted coconut and not his red eyebrows."

His comments brought lots of laughter, and playful ribbing rose among the group.

"Yeah. Yeah, well, those things happen. But tonight is for serious business. First of all, over seventy percent of fire stations across our country are staffed entirely by volunteers. For a county the size of ours, it's an honor that we have support from our county to staff a small but mighty and dependable team. But these bays are darn near full of people." He swallowed hard, controlling the emotion threatening to turn his words to a tremble. "Volunteers. You are critical to this equation. We don't take any of you for granted. Even those who may have only come out on a very limited basis. You went through the training and you are here for us. Thank you."

He clapped his hands together, and everyone joined in.

"Thanksgiving is this week. You know, I don't remember a single year that we didn't have an incident on Thanksgiving Day. Every fire and rescue is important, but those around the holidays just seem to be harder to take. We need to keep our community on their toes. Be sure to pass on safety information to family, friends, your church pastors, anyone who you talk to. The more knowledge and awareness we can raise, the better off we'll all be. We'll be hosting a Thanksgiving dinner here on Thanksgiving Day. Pop in and out as you like. The Trout and Snout is providing all the side dishes, and a big thank-you to the Newton brothers for bringing the barbecue tonight and always. Despite the loving nickname of the Pig Newtons, they will be smoking turkeys on Thanksgiving for us."

"Tom is a turkey, so that sort of works," someone said.

Tucker shook his head. It was like a family reunion every time they got together. "Any families you know of who might need any assistance, give Tommy the name and addresses. Anything we don't consume, we'll be sure gets into the right folk's hands that evening."

Tommy held his clipboard over his head. "See me, or there's another sign-up sheet over on the bulletin board."

Tucker went through the rest of the agenda. Finally, with all the business at hand done, he picked up the box he'd placed near the mic earlier.

"Now, my favorite part. Another thank-you letter, and it came with this huge box of cookies. Think y'all can quietly pass this around while I read it?" He handed the cookie box off to someone and it started moving around the room.

"It turns out Mrs. Davenport works for the bakery over in Galax. Her family made these. They are almost too pretty to eat."

"No such thing as a cookie too pretty to eat." Luke's voice rose above the others as he reached for the red and white candy-cane-shaped cookie on the top.

"Coming in," said Bob, as the decorated Christmas tree cookie caught his eye.

And then it was a free-for-all of hands and elbows until the box was down to a single sparse row of cookies.

Tucker lifted a card in the air. "This is from the Davenports. You'll remember we got called out in the wee hours of the morning on this one about two months ago when that thunderstorm plowed through here. Lightning struck their house."

Heads nodded.

"Keep in mind whether you were there that day or not, you are part of this team and these thanks go to every single person in this building. Listen up."

Tucker pulled the card out and began reading it.

Dear Men and Women of our Chestnut Ridge Fire Department,

We want to take a moment to express our heartfelt gratitude for all of your efforts during the recent house fire at our home. You were all incredible and we are forever grateful.

We never imagined we'd experience such a tragedy and the thought of losing our home and everything in it was absolutely devastating. However, the quick response and efficient actions of your team contained the fire and minimized the damage.

We were impressed by the professionalism and compassion of each one of you. Seeing how you worked together as a team and put your lives at risk for the safety and well-being of our family was truly inspiring.

We know that we will never be able to fully express the depth of our gratitude. Our family will forever be indebted to you for your bravery, dedication, and commitment to serving our community.

We hope that our small words of thanks will offer you some sense of the appreciation that we feel. We made these Christmas cookies for you as a small token of our appreciation.

Again, thank you from the bottom of our hearts.

We are forever grateful,

The Davenports

"Thank you for your service." Tucker was as proud of them and the work they did together as he could imagine any father would be of his children. "Well done. We make a difference."

"He's getting all mushy up there. See. Happens to the best of us."

The voice came from the middle of the crowd, and as folks stepped away, Tucker spotted who had yelled that. The old fire chief who had retired and promoted Tucker into the position.

"Chief Bowers," Tucker yelled out. "Thanks for coming out tonight."

The man walked forward, a slight limp on his right side. "No. I'm not the chief anymore. That's all you now, Tucker. You make me proud." Bowers shook Tucker's hand.

Then, he turned to the group of people who stood shoulder-to-shoulder in front of them. "You've done such a great job. Every person in this room helped this kid become a great leader." Bowers clapped and everyone joined in. "Who knew me having faith in this kid, the youngest volunteer I ever allowed to go on the front line, would someday result in him becoming the youngest captain, and then the youngest chief. Well done, boy."

"Thank you, sir," Tucker said.

"Hats off to all of you. You are all heroes in your own right." A round of thank-yous came from the group. "I didn't come to just bluster some attaboys to y'all, I have another reason to crash this party."

Tucker had no idea what he was talking about.

Everyone got quiet.

"The food," he said, raising his hands in the air. "This guy's taken enough of your time. Let's eat."

"Grab your plates and then gather around," Tucker said. "I

want to go over the Christmas Tree Stroll with y'all and get a committee formed tonight. If we're going to win this year, we have to really bring it."

"We got robbed last year."

"We did good, but you have to admit the winning tree was pretty awesome." Tucker defended the winner, then went to the front of the line so he could eat first, then talk about the Christmas Tree Stroll while the others ate.

The noise climbed to a gregarious level in a hot hurry as the metal chafing dish lids clanked back and people chatted while filling their plates.

Once everyone had gotten their food and the room quieted down, Tucker took the mic again. "The Christmas Tree Stroll. Y'all listen up. I think we can just do a quick raise of hands on the type and height of the tree. I say we stake claim to the tallest short-needle tree available this year. All hands in favor?"

If every hand wasn't in the air, he couldn't tell whose wasn't.

"Good. Looks like we're all in agreement. Lessons learned from last year?" Tucker asked.

"We need to be careful with how heavy the ornaments are this year. Lighter ornaments, or wire them in place better. Last year we spent a ton of time picking up ornaments off the ground and trying to rehang them while people were coming through for the stroll. It was a nonstop effort, and it looked sloppy."

"Good point. Others?"

"If we're going tall again, we need to get the tree topper up first. Once everyone gets in there to decorate their trees, we can't position a good-sized ladder to do it."

"Good feedback. Any others? Or ideas for themes. We can go broader than fire trucks, you know."

The ideas started blasting him from all sides.

"What if we did something with water?"

"A great big bonfire?"

"Yeah, and kids could roast marshmallows over it."

"Sending the wrong message y'all," Tucker said. "No way."

"How about transportation in general?" Dixie Rogers said. "Trucks, cars, planes, and trains. I have my granddaddy's train set in the attic. It's too big for us to use around our tree. It's a shame no one is putting it to good use. Even has the little steam puffs."

"Now, that's an idea."

"If we do that, we could use real toy trucks, and let that be part of the gift giving at the end," said Tommy Newton.

"And add those Breyer horses. That's transportation too. Maybe a pink Barbie Corvette or two?"

"I like it." If there was one thing Tucker could be confident in, it was that this group of people were never short on ideas. "I really like the idea of the ornaments doing double duty. And we definitely want to make it for boys and girls with that in mind. Maybe even somehow add a couple of scooters or bicycles into the design? Or is that too much?"

"No! I like that," said Danny, who also owned the bike repair shop. "And I can order a case of shiny bicycle bells and streamers. They'd be festive. How's that sound?"

"This is great. I think we have a plan. What kind of tree topper is going to at least get us an honorable mention this year?" Tucker scanned the group. "Come on. Get creative."

"I still can't believe we didn't get one for the station helmet. That bedazzled thing glowed for a mile."

Tucker had to agree. It had taken Doris a long time to put

together too. "Maybe we can still tuck that bedazzled helmet in the tree. Put a partridge or two turtledoves in it or something."

Doris looked pleased with the idea.

"How about we rig up Santa on a sleigh cruising around the top?"

"North Star?"

"Snow machine?"

"If we're doing transportation, we could do checkered flags or stop lights."

"Santa on a tiny trike? I have one in the back of the store we could use," said Danny. "Not sure what it would take to prop it up there, though."

"How big is it?"

"It's a push deal, for a tiny tot. Plastic. It doesn't weigh much."

"Can we paint it?"

"Sure."

"How about brightly colored balloons instead of Santa on the trike?" someone hollered out.

"Maybe the tricycle underneath the tree with eight tiny fire trucks pulling it?"

"I like that a lot. I can help work on that," said Tommy Newton.

"Great. Santa on a trike isn't something I've ever seen. Eight tiny fire trucks each with a name across the windshield like we have Bull Mountain Boys on ours. Either way seems we're on the path to a cooler idea than whatever the flower shop comes up with this year. I think GG's is our biggest competition."

"We need something electronic on it."

"Josh and I can help with that. We could make the whole thing spin, or since we have the train around the bottom, maybe we do some kind of chasing lights down the tree that give the impression the train is chugging through it."

"Okay, I need two people to head up the committee and get y'all all scheduled to help out."

"I can help," Doris said.

"Me too," said Tommy.

"Great. So y'all see Tommy or Doris before next week to get your names on the schedule. We need eight team members for on-site decorating, but like last year we can have people prefab things here at the station before they go over to assemble. We'll need more hands on deck to wrap gifts after the trees are judged if we decide to make every ornament an actual gift."

"I like that idea," said one. "Me too," others agreed.

"Got that, Tommy and Doris? Extra hands the night following the awards."

Doris said, "We're going to win this year!"

Enthusiasm spread through the firehouse.

"Now we're thinking," said Tucker. "We'll email out a sketch once the team has a plan pulled together in case anyone has any other suggestions to add. That's it. Good night."

Chairs screeched, and everyone pitched in to box up leftovers for distribution and the firehouse freezer for the next potluck.

Once the station cleared out, Tucker flipped all the light switches and secured the building, grabbing the Styrofoam trays, one with food and the other with goodies, that Doris had put together for him like she always did. He walked outside to his truck at the far end of the now-empty lot.

He could picture the transportation-themed Christmas tree. Bright yellow construction trucks, a multitude of tiny shiny race cars, trains, planes, horses, and scooters could pull double duty as decorations. Shiny handlebar bells and neon streamers to add some whimsy, and wouldn't it be fun to rig up small battery-operated spinning tricycle wheels with cards in the spokes for sound?

Tucker felt his excitement build. They might not even need any regular colored balls on this year's entry. This idea also happened to fit right in with his favorite song, "I'll Be Home for Christmas."

Each team created a sign to post next to their tree, and he could use a router to etch the words "99 Ways to Get Home for Christmas" on theirs. Ninety-nine toy vehicles or modes of transportation should be enough to fill the biggest tree in the competition, which was always theirs. Since some of the items were big, if they couldn't fit all ninety-nine on the tree, a few under the tree would work too.

Ninety-nine gifts for kids in our county.

Public safety in Chestnut Ridge was the most important thing in his life, but knowing there'd be ninety-nine more smiling faces on Christmas morning, thanks to the generosity and kindness of his team of firefighters, was overwhelmingly precious.

Chapter Four

Sheila spent Thanksgiving Day alone. She didn't have to. Her sister had invited her to come to Virginia Beach to spend the day with her family, but the nursing home had asked that they keep Mom's visitors to a minimum during the holidays, with Mom being so confused, so Cassie and Sheila had split them up. Cassie got Thanksgiving and Sheila would be there for Christmas.

Being that close to Mom and not seeing her just didn't feel right, so Sheila declined Cassie's invitation. Besides, ever since Cassie insisted Mom needed be under twenty-four-hour care, that had been a sore spot between them, and had made Christmas hard for Sheila.

When Sheila told Natalie about declining Cassie's offer, Natalie begged Sheila to come to the mountains for Thanksgiving too. But Sheila didn't want to wear out her welcome before her planned visit even started.

And the idea of spending a lazy Thanksgiving at home in her pajamas with a novel had sounded so appealing.

Only the weather had turned dreary. She spent the rainy and windy morning watching the Macy's parade, then curled up with one of the new novels she'd just bought.

As she got to know the characters in the first few chapters, her interest built, wanting to know what was going to happen next, and cheering on her new friends in their quest for romance.

The novel had her remembering funny things that happened at Thanksgivings past, like the first time she hosted the big family dinner. She'd been so thankful when the turkey came out of the oven, golden brown and juicy, that she'd run to grab her phone to take a picture. When she walked back into the room full of pride, her perfect bird was missing a huge bite from one leg. Under the table, Dan's dog licked his paws, looking quite pleased with himself as he lapped up the remaining morsels from the floor. She cried. Dan laughed, and together they amputated the one leg the dog had mutilated and told the guests that Dan hadn't been able to keep his hands off of it. She wondered if he'd ever fessed up to what really happened that day.

For a fleeting moment, she considered calling Dan to wish him Happy Thanksgiving.

That's a horrible idea. Not only because he didn't deserve the time of day from her, but because it would make her look pitiful, and likely cause a rift in his otherwise perfect holiday with his new family. Dan had a new wife and new life now. He was just a map dot on her journey. One she was happy to leave in the past.

At three in the morning, she finally turned the last page of the novel. Despite the problems that seemed insurmountable, she found herself filled with hope following the happily-ever-after.

She closed the book, exhausted, with a tear in her eye and

joy in her heart. It was such a satisfying story, but it made her feel lonelier than ever.

She let out a long sigh. Looking at the chair that she'd refused to let Dan take, even though he'd picked it out and she'd always hated it, she regretted being petty about it now.

Cool it with the pity party, Sheila.

Kernels of popcorn fell to the ground as she forced herself to get up from the couch. She'd absently eaten her way through the whole bowl while she read.

I'll pay for all that salt content tomorrow.

She went to the kitchen and downed a glass of water, hoping to head off some of the bloat, then crawled into bed.

She woke up the next morning in the mood for a little retail therapy, but there was no way she was braving Black Friday shoppers. Not even for a cute new sweater to wear to the mountains.

That was one shopping day that she felt quite comfortable leaving to others to navigate. People fighting for the last electronics bargain or twenty-dollar leather bag was not her idea of a good time.

She spent the day working on lists. Presents to buy. Ideas for the Christmas Tree Stroll. She squandered nearly four hours on Pinterest, just looking for ideas and getting sidetracked by holiday decorations, recipes, how to make bows, and, somehow, a tradition of fruitcake-tossing events.

Sheila couldn't say for sure if she'd ever tried the holiday cake with the bad reputation, but she knew they were heavy. No doubt you could fling one of those round ones for a good long way. Just the thought of that made her burst into a fit of giggles, and before she knew it she was ordering not only one fruitcake, but three different flavors after reading a whole article about the history of fruitcake and the circle pans it was baked in. Who knew it wasn't baked in a Bundt pan? It seemed completely logical to her that if it was a cake with a circle cut out of the middle, it would be. Oh no, because Bundt pans are meant to be flipped over to get the cake out, and you don't do that to a fruitcake.

She grabbed her credit card and set the cakes to ship to Orene's house the week of the fifteenth. The order would serve double duty. They could eat the cakes for dessert, and if they were terrible, they could fling them like those people in Manitou Springs.

She picked up her phone and dialed Mom's room at the Hilltop. Two years ago, Sheila and her sister had to make the difficult decision to move Mom to a memory-care unit. Alzheimer's and balance had been an ongoing concern, but when Mom got confused and wandered away from the house one day, the police called Cassie to tell her they had picked her up. Cassie met the policeman at Mom's and the real truths began to unravel. Mom lived alone back then, and she'd seemed fine. But the police had been called several times by neighbors, and even by Mom calling to report someone was moving her plants while she slept. But upon investigation, the neighbors said she was as busy as a bee planting and replanting the same plants all over that yard.

It was harder on her and her sister than it was on Mom. The schedule and being surrounded by caring people had helped Mom get into a routine, and most of the time she was in a happy frame of mind. Some days she was sharp, and others she didn't recognize anyone. The latter were coming more often.

"The Hilltop. Annie speaking."

"Hi, Annie. This is Sheila. I wanted to check in on Mom. How's she doing today?"

"Cloudy, with a chance of rain," the nurse said.

Sheila winced, knowing that meant Mom didn't recognize anyone today. These were quiet days, but her sweet spirit exuded no matter what that nasty disease did to her brain. She'd toddle around in a daze, sweetly smiling and nodding, on those days that Nurse Annie reported her as "cloudy."

"Can I just tell her that I love her? Do you think it will upset her?" Sheila's heart ached.

"She won't understand that it's you, but no harm in it. Give me just a minute. I'll put her on."

In the background, Sheila heard Nurse Annie talking to Mom. "Miss Cynthia. Someone is on the telephone for you. Can you take a listen? Yes, for you."

"Hi, Miss Cynthia," Sheila said. "This is Sheila, and I just wanted to call to wish you a blessed day, dear."

"Sheila." The words came out as a statement. It was clear to Sheila that Mom wasn't sure who she was speaking to today. Again. "That's nice of you to call," Mom said. "What is today?"

"It's Friday. I hope you had a delicious Thanksgiving dinner yesterday. Did you have turkey?"

"I think so. The pie was my favorite." There was a long pause. "Were you here?"

"No, I wasn't, but I'm glad you had a wonderful day. Did you have a nice visit?"

"I think so." Silence on the other end was broken by a slight muffle. "Maybe."

She could picture Mom's blue eyes, wide with wonder. "You are loved." Sheila gulped back the last syllable. "Always."

"Thank you, young lady. Happy Thanksgiving."

Sheila hung up the phone and swallowed back tears. "I miss you, Mom."

When Sheila woke up the next morning, she was still on the couch in yesterday's pajamas. No one in their right mind was house-hunting or doing open houses on Thanksgiving weekend, but next week would be intense, so she needed to get some things done. They had open houses set Friday, Saturday, and Sunday, and she had a long list of things to gather in preparation.

She jumped in the shower and got dressed in jeans and a winter-white corduroy shirt over a taupe turtleneck, taupe woven belt, and boots. She always liked to look nice, even casually. A quick twist in the mirror, and she opted to keep it simple. No earrings today.

She picked up her purse and keys and headed outside. The sun was bright, but the wind had a bit of a nip. Even so, she opted to drive her new car, rather than the big four-door Mercedes. The Tesla had been a splurge, but when one of her clients offered it to her for way under the value it was too good to pass up. In the divorce, his wife was making him sell it so she could get half the money. According to him, he'd rather lose money on the car than give her half what it was worth. And the deal was made.

So, until she sold the vehicle, she drove it on weekends and was loving it a lot more than she'd expected.

She went through her list of things for the last open house of the year. She was in pretty good shape, and it was still a week out, so she headed downtown to the antique shop where she'd seen that pretty teapot. It would be perfect for Orene.

At least Small Business Saturday was a more civil day to shop.

Luck was on her side when she spotted a parking spot right in front of the store. She went inside and made a beeline for the intricately carved vintage wood and glass trolley cart that it had been sitting on. She stopped short. Neither the cart nor the teapot was there. She spun around, looking to see if she'd misjudged the location by an aisle or two.

"Can I help you?" a pretty brunette asked.

"Hi. Yes. I was in here a couple of weeks ago. I saw a really pretty carved wooden cart right around here somewhere."

"Oh gosh. Wasn't that a beauty? I'm sorry. It sold."

"Well, that's fine, because I was really interested in the teapot that was sitting on it. Is it, by chance, still around?"

"The Tiffany-style one?"

"Yes, that's the one."

"Actually, that was a lamp. I know what you're talking about. I put it over here with a few other teapots I have." She hooked her finger and led the way toward the front of the store.

"Oh gosh. I have a friend who collects teapots. It was so unusual. I'm disappointed that it's not a real teapot."

"I moved it over here. There are several teapots."

There it was. The memorable stained-glass teapot. "It's a lamp?" She reached around back and found the cord. "I'll be."

"If your friend collects teapots, she would probably enjoy it."

"True, but I kind of had my heart set on giving her one to add to her collection as a Christmas gift." Sheila looked at the other teapots displayed. "I don't see anything that's really grabbing me."

"Well, I do have another one. It's sort of playful, but I really like it and it has a Christmas theme."

"You've got me interested." Sheila followed the woman over

two aisles to a section filled with glass-front hutches. The clerk pulled out a small teapot from a cabinet, cradling it between her hands like a precious baby bird.

"This," she said, "is so sweet. See the scene with the man selling chestnuts on the street, and the Merry Christmas wish on the top?"

"Did you say chestnuts?" Sheila couldn't believe her luck. "It's perfect. Sold."

"Wonderful!" The woman closed the cabinet. "I can take it up front for you if you'd like to look around."

"That's all I need today, and this is the perfect gift. Did you know there used to be like a billion American chestnut trees up in the Blue Ridge Mountains of Virginia until the turn of the twentieth century? They were abundant and huge, like the great redwoods out West until blight wiped them out."

"I've lived here my whole life and I've never heard of that."

"I know," Sheila said. "I just learned about it over the summer. I have a friend that moved up there." She was glad she'd listened as Natalie droned on and on about the local lore of Chestnut Ridge. "Chestnuts used to be the main cash crop there."

"I had no idea." The clerk wrapped the teapot in decorative tissue paper. "Do you need a box for this? I think I have one in the back that this would tuck right into."

"That would be so helpful."

The woman went to get the box, leaving Sheila to mill around the collectibles and primitives near the register.

Sheila picked up a mercury-glass Christmas ornament piled with others in a big glass bowl. There were a few scuffs on it, but it wasn't a reproduction. Her family used to have ornaments like this on their Christmas tree when she was growing up. The funky magenta, turquoise, and gold paint all joined in the middle of the deep inset with the mica stencils looked vintage.

"Here we go. It fit perfectly." The woman carried a shiny white box with gold trim on the edges to the counter.

"That'll do the trick. Thank you." Sheila picked up the bowl of ornaments. "Are these vintage? It's so hard to tell."

"I can give you a couple of key pointers on that. First, check out the cap. See how small the opening is? Most of the mass-produced ornaments have a wide cap. These early blown-glass ornaments from Germany and Poland have a much narrower opening. Second, the cap won't have any decoration. It'll have a plain metal cap. And third, if there's glitter, it's not vintage. It should be mica, which is a stone product that glistens like glitter, but is actually fine irregular-shaped dust. These look like the real deal to me." The woman sifted through the box, removing two of them. "I'd skip these two. This one is cracked and I'm not so sure that one is vintage. I can give you a deal on the rest."

"I'll take them too, then." Sheila was delighted with the buys.

She drove home in a much better mood for having checked off everything on her shopping lists. The exercise probably helped too.

When she got home, she wrapped Orene's gift in a pretty red toile-patterned paper she'd bought from the neighbor kids in a fundraiser. A bit overpriced, but for a good cause. It was solid on one side and decorative on the other, and the texture was thick and sturdy. She fluffed the bow on top of Orene's present. Not wanting to waste the remnants, she pulled up a DIY on her phone on how to make a gift bag out of the scraps. It wasn't that difficult. In fact, the bag turned out so cute, she fashioned three more just like it.

You can never have too many bags for Christmas.

Last week, she'd purchased spa-day-escape gift cards for her agents at the salon in the opulent Hotel Jefferson. These bags seemed the right size for those. She hopped up from her chair and ran into her office to see if they'd fit. Each had been tucked into a fancy gold envelope with a glittery snowflake sticker seal. The envelopes fit right inside the red toile bags.

"So cute!"

She couldn't wait to hand them out at the office party. Time was going to go quickly with everything going on.

Countdown to Christmas fun in Chestnut Ridge: Thirteen days.

Chapter Five

Sheila wished she'd trusted her instincts and planned to go to Chestnut Ridge on Thursday. She knew Friday the thirteenth was not worth tempting. First, she hadn't made it halfway down the block before she had to stop and put the seat belt across her purse and laptop in the passenger seat to stop the insistent warning sound. Apparently, anything over a certain number of pounds, whether it had a heartbeat or not, required a seat belt. And now it wasn't even ten o'clock in the morning yet and she was in standstill traffic on a two-lane road with nothing but open fields around her. Stuck.

She craned her neck, trying to figure out what the holdup was, but she was behind one of those big eighteen-wheelers and couldn't see a thing.

The minutes clicked off on the clock.

Sheila glanced in her rearview at the piled luggage and gifts for her two-week trip. Shiny foil wrapping paper gleamed in the sunlight from the Jenga-stacked gifts.

She affectionately tapped the steering wheel of the fire-engine-red Tesla Model X. Thank you, Dr. Tanning. She still couldn't believe the deal. Extravagant? Absolutely. Impulse buy? Definitely. But as it turned out, the sweet ride had also been the ticket to soothe the what's-missing-in-my-life mood she'd been battling lately.

Frustrated, sitting there behind the big rig in traffic, she tried to call Natalie. Unfortunately, there was no phone service.

Finally, after another four minutes, the cars started moving.

It took some time for the truck in front of her to shift through gears and get up some speed, but as she slowly moved forward, she saw the culprit of the gridlock.

She was thankful it hadn't been an accident, but what were the odds of seeing a farmer wearing a bright orange hat following a Border collie herding goats across the street?

That's a first.

The animals meandered along the side of the road nibbling and exploring, proving the whole grass-is-greener-on-the-other-side thing. The farmer calmly ushered his herd toward a red pole gate, while the dog did his job running behind them, nipping and barking, to get them to move. One big white goat with a red head wasn't ready to give up the brushy foliage so easily, though. Instead of moving, she lowered her head and then rose up on her hind feet. The Border collie didn't seem concerned, making a wider circle and coming back around until the goat finally moved on with a big hunk of greenery hanging from her mouth.

As Sheila got closer, she noticed that one of the other goats was wearing a Christmas sweater.

She chuckled to herself and gave the farmer a wave as she drove by. The image of the goat wearing the red and green Christmas sweater stuck with her all day, bringing a smile to her face every time it popped into her mind.

The rest of the drive to Chestnut Ridge was pleasant enough, and although the trees had shed their leaves weeks ago, it was pretty. The lazy bluish haze hung over the mountains like a watercolor. She could see why Natalie appreciated these views.

Sheila pulled into the driveway at Orene's house at four o'clock, only an hour and a half after she'd planned to be there. The Mountain Creek Inn, which wasn't an inn at all, truly was a grand old house, and a lot of it. The Colonial Revival–style country farmhouse with its wraparound porch was inviting. Even on these cold days, she could imagine sitting in one of those rocking chairs. The last time she was here, the hanging baskets were overflowing with vivid raspberry-colored bougainvillea.

Today each basket had red and white poinsettias, variegated ivy, and a big candy-striped bow that matched the one on the door wreath, which also sported a single white ice skate in the center of the circle of pine. Colored balls and pine cones gave the wreath a playful beauty that had her imagining an afternoon on the ice spinning like an ice skater in a flowing short skirt.

Before she could get the ice dancing out of her mind and get out of the car, Orene stepped out on the porch.

Natalie came out behind Orene, and jogged past her and down the driveway as Sheila got out of the car. "It's so good to see you. I was starting to worry," she said as she pulled Sheila into a hug. "Let me help you with something."

"I was going to call, but I didn't have a signal half the drive. I even got stuck in traffic for a goat crossing. Don't even ask." Sheila lifted her hand. "I can hardly believe those words came out of my mouth."

"Well, forget about the goats. Tell me how the car drove. Did you let it do the driving for you?"

"Heck no. I'm not trusting a car to be smarter than I am."

"We're going to try that hands-free driving while you're here. I can't wait."

"Fair warning. This car is pretty cool, but enjoy it now, because I plan to sell it for a healthy profit to treat myself to something else, like a fun trip somewhere."

"You always say that but you never go anywhere. You're a workaholic. Admit it."

"Until they create a twelve-step program for that, I'm not considering it a problem."

"Fair enough," Natalie said. "Come on."

Sheila got her bags from the passenger seat, and she and Natalie walked up to the house.

"Hey, darlin'. Welcome!" Orene spread her arms and hugged Sheila tight. "It's good to see you. Thank you for staying with me. You have no idea how happy I am about this visit."

"I appreciate you letting me stay with you in the real house." Sheila shot a look in the direction of Natalie, who knew full well she was teasing. "Natalie offered me the cabin, but I'd rather hang out with you."

"Honey, you are welcome here any time you like," said Orene. "I might even put your name right on that door."

"I'd be okay with that," Sheila said.

"Come in and relax. We can get the boys to bring in your stuff later," Orene said. "Some say chivalry is dead. I say not as long as Orene Fischer is around. I make sure those men remember where the term 'gentleman' came from. They need to know how to act. I tell 'em so."

"Excellent. Who am I to argue?" Sheila said.

Natalie led the way into Orene's kitchen. "We were just setting out the food for tonight."

"It smells like heaven in here." Sheila closed her eyes and inhaled deeply. "Sweets. Savory. Citrus?"

"Yes," Orene said. "Made my famous orange sherbet punch. It's a favorite. Careful now, sometimes those boys spike theirs with a little moonshine."

"Do they really still make that stuff?"

Orene's hands hooked to her hips. "You better believe it. Moonshine started up here in these mountains, and some of those families are busy as ever. Some of them are even pretty good at it."

"Don't tell me you drink it. Doesn't it taste like kerosene?" Sheila's face twisted in disgust.

Orene nudged Natalie. "One would think, but no ma'am. When it's done right, it's very smooth."

"She's telling the truth." Natalie shrugged.

"Really? You tried it?" Sheila couldn't believe it. "You don't even drink, Nat."

"Hey, I had a cold a few months back, and Orene hooked me up. I swear it kicked that cold to Colorado." Natalie smiled broadly. "Can't deny good old-fashioned hometown cures."

"That might've been a coincidence."

"Could've been, but I wasn't complaining at the time," Natalie said. "I'd been miserable for a week by the time Orene came over to see me. I slept for two days and woke up feeling ready to roll."

"Laugh all you want," Orene said. "Everything in moderation has its place. It's overindulgence that becomes a problem."

They walked into the dining room, where the entire length of the table was filled with appetizers.

Sheila stopped, thinking about how much time and effort her

little office party had taken. "You didn't make all of this food by yourself, did you?"

Orene grinned. "Most of it."

"I made the sugared pecans," Natalie said. "Of course, Orene taught me how to make them. And she helped."

"You must have started weeks ago."

"No," Orene said. "I've done this for as many years as I can remember. Helped my momma and grandma host too. It's fun, and it really doesn't take as long as you'd think. I enjoy it."

"Well, tell me what all this stuff is," Sheila said. "Can I taste any of it?"

"Sure. There's plenty."

Sheila picked up a triangle of toasted bread and took a bite. "Pimento cheese?"

"My family recipe. It's good, isn't it?"

"It is. Oh my goodness." She picked up a deviled egg. "These are my favorite picnic treats."

"Mine too," Natalie said. "She adds bacon and chives. Are they to die for?"

"Yes." Sheila rolled her eyes. "This food goes on forever."

"And this is just the appetizer stuff. The sweets are all on the sideboard. Go look." Orene was about as relentless as that Border collie trying to move her along toward the other room.

Colorful cookies were piled high on raised Christmas plates. A coconut cake—at least four layers tall, with pretty red-and-green-frosting holly piped on top—was as professionally done as one in a bakery. "Even a bûche de Noël?"

"Don't be so surprised. We do get the Food Network on satellite TV here, you know," Orene said. "I just call it a Yule Log. It's easier to say."

"Sheila thinks we're using rabbit ears and talking through tin cans and strings," Natalie quipped.

Orene's laugh was contagious.

"I don't think it's that bad, but there's no high-speed internet. I checked the last time I was here. I was willing to buy it for y'all if it was available," said Sheila.

"It's not. We barely get decent cell service," Natalie said as Sheila's phone rang.

Sheila glanced at the screen. "Sorry, I need to take this."

She answered, turning her back on Orene and lowering her voice to talk to her associate. When the call had concluded, she apologized again and said, "Just something quick they needed me to confirm."

"I hope you're not going to be getting calls the whole time you're here." Orene pursed her lips. "Bad cell service and slow internet may test your patience while you're here, but I promise you . . . slowing down is good for the soul if you give it a chance."

"I don't think I'll be here that long." Sheila sat in one of the chairs next to the table. "It would take months for me to actually slow down."

Orene gently squeezed Sheila's neck muscles as she walked by. "You are as tight as a slingshot. I'm not going to give up on you, though. I've taken a liking to you this past year."

"Thank you. I think the world of you too. In fact, I have a wonderful Christmas gift for you. I'm going to go get it from my car. I can't wait for you to open it." She got to her feet.

"No, ma'am." Orene wagged her finger. "You can sit right back down. No presents will be opened until Christmas Day. I have a strict rule about that."

"Oh come on," Sheila complained. "I can't wait that long."

Orene looked over at Natalie. "Is she always like this?"

"Ever since I've known her. She always insists I open my present early. Then I end up getting two presents, because she wants me to have something to open on Christmas Day too. She's festive like that."

"We'll work on that, Sheila," Orene said. Then, with a click of her fingers, she waved her hand for them to follow. "You can put my gift under my tree. You've got to see it. I'm so proud of it. Come look." Orene darted toward the living room, her pint-sized figure swishing with each step. She turned and reached her arm in the air in a flourish in front of her Christmas tree.

Natalie and Sheila stopped dead in their tracks.

"I can smell the fresh-cut evergreen from here," Sheila said from the hallway.

"That's because it's a balsam fir. My favorite."

The extravagant tree filled the whole corner of the room. "I think we have a winner. We may as well not enter the contest, Natalie."

"Orene!" A shocked Natalie walked over for a closer look. "You have been holding out on me. I've been here all day, and you didn't show me this? You did this all by yourself?"

Orene cocked her head and grinned, pride pouring from her tip-to-toe. "Always do."

"How did you put the topper on? And the tinsel. How tall is that tree?"

"I have no idea. The ceilings are eleven foot. I make sure Jesse has his brother, Joe, cut me a tree just the right height for it to be on the stand and have room for the angel. I don't care if he has to prune it six ways to Sunday. He knows what I need, and he always comes through."

"Okay, that explains where you got the tree, but were you up on a ladder?"

"I was. I'm quite capable."

"But . . ."

"Oh, quit fussing. I've been doing this forever. My sweet husband, God rest his soul, built me a ladder with railings on it like those librarians use for the tall shelves. It's big and heavy, but the firemen come over and bring it in for me. It beats rescuing kittens from trees. They really don't mind."

"Amazing. Well, this is the most elegant tree I've ever seen," said Sheila. "And the most tinsel I've ever seen. Where did you even buy all of that? You hardly see silver tinsel in the stores anymore."

"I put each strand on the limbs one piece at a time, and take it down the same way. Some of that tinsel is older than you are."

"Tell me you're kidding," Sheila insisted.

"No. Cross my heart. My daddy did it that way, and I've carried on the tradition."

"I can't believe you did all this by yourself."

"Tucker helped me with the lights and the topper. It's been our tradition for years. The chief assigned him to help me when he was first a volunteer. The joke was on them, though, because Tucker and I hit it off and he's helped me every year since." Orene seemed quite tickled over that.

"I still don't think you need to be on a ladder," Sheila said.

"I come from hardy stock," Orene insisted. "As long as you continue to do what you do, you'll do what you do until you don't."

"I haven't started decorating and my cabin isn't even the size of this room," said Natalie.

"Absolutely stunning." Sheila walked closer. "Some of these ornaments look like Fabergé eggs."

"You have a good eye." Orene's chin tipped with a mischievous tick.

"Really?" Sheila spun around, but Orene wasn't joking. "You have Fabergé eggs on your tree? Do you know what they are worth?"

"Well, not worth anything if you don't enjoy them. They were gifts to my family from someone who once stayed here in the house. Years ago. They do look pretty, don't they?"

"Gorgeous."

"Wait a minute," Sheila said. "Natalie, please tell me Orene is on our team for this contest."

Orene giggled. "Sorry, but I am not. Everyone wanted me on their team, and I'm too impartial to be a judge. We finally just had to make it a rule that I'd be on everyone and no one's team."

"Well, that should work in our favor," Sheila said. "So, who all is coming tonight? It looks like you have enough food to feed the whole city of Richmond here."

"Darn near everyone who lives in Chestnut Ridge will probably stop in even if just for a quick nibble. You'll have to represent Richmond on your own. This Holiday Warmup is as big a tradition around here as that glittery ball drop in Times Square is to New York City. When the day comes I'm too old to pull this off you better start kissing me goodbye, but there's no need to worry about that yet."

Orene would be ninety next year. Sheila knew because even in the short time she'd known her, she was well aware of Orene constantly reminding everyone that she expected a big surprise party to celebrate her ninetieth and planned to live to see a hundred.

Sheila prayed she and Natalie would age as well as Orene did.

"Excuse me." Sheila left Natalie and Orene talking by the Christmas tree, and walked out to her car and got the rest of her things. Balancing the large bag of Christmas gifts in one hand and suitcase in the other, she climbed the stairs to the second floor. She'd stayed here only four times since Natalie moved to Chestnut Ridge, but she felt at home here. Then she carried the carefully wrapped gifts for Orene downstairs.

Orene's eyes lit up when she saw it. "Is that my Christmas present?"

"One of them is! Want to open it?" Sheila couldn't wait for her to. She wondered where Orene would place the teapot in her huge collection.

"Did you hear a word I said earlier?" Orene pursed her lips.

"Fine. I'll just shove it under your Christmas tree. But if you change your mind—"

"I won't, but thank you, and the box is so pretty. Set it right in front of the tree. It's as if you knew exactly how to match my decor."

Sheila tucked the gift under the tree. Somehow all that tinsel made it look as if it could sway like a ballerina.

Silver tinsel dripped from every single tiny needle on the tree, yet somehow it didn't look overdone. Like jewelry, blown-glass ornaments and old mercury-glass ones in vibrant gem tones accessorized it perfectly. She reached out to touch one of the Fabergé eggs. "I've only seen these in magazines before. This brilliant blue is eye-catching."

"There are three eggs on the tree. That one there is the Theo. Inside there is a silver and gold Neptune, King of the Oceans. See the rubies in the seahorse eyes. It's five of a Limited Edition of 250. That's not my favorite one, though. Look over to the left."

Sheila scanned the tree. "Here we are at Christmas doing an Easter egg hunt."

"Why yes. Sort of."

Sheila spotted the other egg, which was a rusty red that the gold had dulled to over the years.

"That's the Springtime Lily egg. Can you find the secret?"

Sheila gently took it from the tree to see if she could open it, and finally realized that the crown-shaped knob at the top pulled up to reveal three small black-and-white pictures. "Who are these people?"

"That's my baby picture, my mother, and my grandmother."

"How special. I hope you keep this displayed somewhere year-round."

"I do. It usually sits on the piano."

"You are full of surprises," Sheila said.

"Every visit is like a field trip," Natalie said.

"When you've lived as many years as I have, you've done a lot of things, met a lot of people, and can remember only about half of it."

Orene grabbed Natalie's hand and marched over toward the tree. "Come on, you two. Let's take some pictures of everything before we get started so we can put them on the town's website."

With a clunky digital camera, Orene took a picture of Natalie and Sheila together.

"Let's get a couple with all of us," Natalie said, taking out her phone and getting one of Sheila and Orene together.

Sheila lifted her phone. "I'm an expert with selfies. I've got longer arms than you. We can all be in this one." She stretched her arm way in front of her, then dipped down a little, with Orene tucked right between her and Natalie, and hit the button.

"Let's see it," Orene said.

Sheila turned her phone around for them. "Oh my goodness. If I were ever blessed with two daughters, I'd have wanted them to be just like you two!"

A rush of joy flowed through Sheila. How was it that this woman she barely knew could suddenly give her the feeling of home? Maybe there was something special about Chestnut Ridge. She glanced at Natalie and Orene, arm in arm, smiling at the picture. She was so grateful for these ladies. Sadness cloaked her in an odd tangle; she was grateful for this moment, but missing the moments like these with her own mother.

Chapter Six

"I'm headed to Orene's. Anyone want to pile on?" Tucker's truck had a flatbed, one of those diamond-plate jobs, making it easier to throw stuff on the back and get on the move when timing mattered most. Which was often in his line of work.

Half a dozen guys ran out and hopped on.

"Shotgun," yelled Doris, as she lagged behind. The rest of the guys squished into the back seat of the crew cab.

Tucker rolled down the window. "Hang on!"

It wasn't but a couple of blocks to Orene's, but just in case there was a call, Tucker never walked anywhere he could drive.

When Tucker pulled to a stop at the curb in front of Orene's, the guys tumbled out of his truck like elves on too much eggnog, laughing and bantering all the way inside.

Tucker followed along behind the rest of them, carrying a four-foot-tall red stocking that he'd filled with individually wrapped portions of homemade turkey and venison jerky. Green bags contained turkey jerky, and red ones, the color of Rudolph's shiny nose, were for the venison.

On the white band at the top of the stocking, Tucker had glued a gift tag:

TAKE ONE—NAUGHTY OR NICE
Homemade Jerky by Tucker

Orene's place was already teeming with activity when he walked in.

Kids raced around the yard, in and out of the colorfully lit shrubbery, in a rambunctious game of tag. Amped up because it was the last day of school until the new year, they were probably supercharged on cookies and cupcakes too if he had to guess.

The huge magnolia tree looked nice. Tucker and his guys had brought over the ladder truck to string thousands of white lights all the way to the tippity top, then spread big red, green, and silver balls nearly the size of soccer balls on it for Orene.

Inside, the house smelled of savory and sweets.

Stretch, owner of the Trout & Snout down the block, carried in a towering stack of to-go boxes and placed them on the entry table.

"Thanks, Stretch," Tucker said.

"Figured maybe there'd be fewer leftovers at the end of the night if we gave folks an easy way to take some home."

"Good thinking." Jesse, who ran the company that supported the senior care center, patted Stretch on the back of the shoulder. "I'll take some over to the seniors. We've got quite a few residents who won't even have a visitor. A nice packaged meal or dessert will make their day."

"That's unfortunate. Let me know how we can help out over

there, Jesse." Tucker's heart went out to those whose families seemed to forget them. "I can send the junior firefighters' club over to visit. They are logging hours at the station house over Christmas break."

"That'd be great. Maybe have them change the batteries in the smoke detectors and check the fire extinguishers, and just spend a little face time with the residents while they are there."

"Sure thing. Consider it done."

"Hey, Tucker." Randy, the newest resident of Chestnut Ridge, walked over and joined him and Jesse. "Just the man I was looking for."

"Me?" Tucker asked. Randy was a good guy. It had taken Tucker a minute to get used to the idea of Natalie finding interest in someone. After all, she'd been married to his best friend, Jeremy. It was still hard to believe Jeremy was gone. But Randy fit right in here, and if he had to guess he'd probably end up the next sheriff in this town. And they were starting to become pretty good friends.

"Yes," Randy said, lowering his voice. "I was wondering if I could get you to help me with a surprise for Natalie."

"Of course. Name it."

Randy looked over his shoulder. "I don't want to take a chance on her overhearing, so I'll stop by the station if that's okay."

"Sure. Stop by anytime. I'll be helping the team get our Christmas Stroll tree started Monday and Tuesday, but I'll be at the firehouse the rest of the week."

"We'll be decorating Monday night, too," Randy said. "I've been reduced to the role of resident mule. Lifting, hauling, and toting."

"You'll get paid in cookies. It's not too bad a gig."

"I'll stop by on Wednesday. Don't let Natalie know we've talked. It's a surprise." Randy waved as he slid between two people and worked his way back toward the living room.

"Hey there, Chief." The New Orleans twang still lingered in Nelle's accent, even though she'd been in Chestnut Ridge for years.

Tucker turned to see Nelle holding two huge plastic containers stacked one on top of the other. Tucker greeted Nelle with a hug. Paul Grandstaff stood beside her.

"Mr. Grandstaff, you're looking well, sir," Tucker said.

"Thank you. Merry Christmas." He leaned his weight on the ornate shiny silver handle of his cane. "My, there are a lot of people here. I guess I didn't realize what I was missing all these years."

"Tried to tell you, boss." Jesse wrapped an arm around Nelle's curvaceous waist. "Not good to be alone *all* the time."

Paul Grandstaff didn't look so convinced, but he forced a smile.

Tucker had heard that Jesse and Nelle had become chummy over the past year, but this was the first time he'd seen them together.

"You can't tell that man anything," Nelle teased Jesse about Paul.

Tucker nodded to Nelle with a wink. "What'd you bring?"

She gave him a playful smirk. "What's your favorite?" She laid on that Cajun accent heavier than usual.

Tucker shifted the stocking to his other hand, trying to ascertain what she might have in the semiopaque containers. "Don't make me guess from all of your wonderful dishes, Nelle." Tucker narrowed his gaze, twisting his lips into a silly pucker. "I'm hoping for jambalaya."

"You just made Santa Nelle's nice list, boy. It *is* my jamba-laya!"

Tucker fist pumped the air. "Let's make it mine! I'm off to hunt down a bowl." He shot forward, then spun around. "Don't you take that lid off until I make it over to the table!"

"Can't promise you won't be the only one banging their plastic spoons for my jambalaya." Nelle's hearty laughter was turning heads. "Go on now, but hurry on back."

He jolted for the kitchen, but only made it two steps before he slammed right into someone with an *oomph.* "Oh gosh. I'm so sorry. I didn't—" He dropped the stocking to steady her by the shoulders as she went off-balance.

"Sorry!" the woman squeaked out. "I wasn't paying attention to where I was going," she said, nearly breathless. Her shiny auburn hair swung over her shoulder as she regained her footing, and then she brushed away drops of Orene's orange sherbet punch from the front of her top.

"It was me. Forgive me. Look what I did." He swept at the droplets that had spilled from her punch cup, then withdrew. "You should probably do that yourself." He pulled a bandanna from his back pocket. "Here. Use this."

"Thank you." Her emerald-green eyes connected with his; then she took the square and dabbed. "It's fine. No harm done." Her glance fell to the ground, where the bag of jerky lay between them.

"What's with that?" She pointed to the stocking. "Don't they usually make Santa wear a furry red suit?"

"Well—"

"Wait a minute. You're not the Grinch, are you? Did you steal that? I was just in the other room where ours were hung by the chimney with care." A playful glint sparkled in her eyes. "Uh-huh. I've caught you red-handed."

He leaned down and snagged the stocking. "I promise I brought this one with me."

"Sure you did. Who doesn't travel with a giant red stocking? Which looks to be quite heavy," she noticed. "Suspiciously so!"

"It's full of homemade turkey and venison jerky."

"Like salty dried meat?" She shivered. "Sounds like a heart-attack sack if you ask me."

"May not be elf-approved, but it's good, and contrary to popular opinion, aside from the salt content it's pretty good for you. Don't knock it until you try it."

"I'll try to withhold judgment." Realization crossed her expression. "We've met. You're Tucker. Right?"

"I am. You . . . ?" He couldn't place her for the life of him, but he never forgot a pretty face, and this woman was worth remembering.

"It was brief. I didn't expect you to remember. I'm Sheila." She stuck out her hand. "Natalie's friend. I'm staying with Orene while I'm here to help Natalie with the Christmas Tree Stroll."

"She said she had a secret weapon. I didn't know it was a who and not a what."

"What can I say?" She shrugged.

"What would it take for me to buy you over to my team?"

"I can't be bought."

He wasn't so sure of that, but he really didn't need any more help on his team. He was just enjoying the banter at the moment. "Everyone has their price."

"Not this girl."

"Hmmph. We'll see about that." He liked a woman with some spirit.

"What? Are you just going to run me over again if I don't?"

"No. Sorry about that. It really was an accident. I can't believe I didn't recognize you. Your hair? It's longer. A lot longer."

She ran her hand through it. "No. It's the same, but the last time I saw you was in the middle of the summer and the humidity was as high as the temperature. If I had to guess, I was wearing it up."

"Yeah." He nodded slowly, now remembering. "The ballerina bun."

She cocked her head and laughed. "Never really thought of it like that. But okay."

"I like it this way." He reached out and touched the curling tendril hanging in front of her shoulder. "Very pretty."

She reached her hand to where he'd just touched her. "Thank you."

The sweet floral smell of her perfume teased his nose. He wanted to lean in for another whiff, but he held himself together. "Maybe you could share a few ideas with me."

"Are you digging for insider information for the most important competition in Chestnut Ridge over the holidays?"

"Would it work?"

She cocked her hip. "Never."

"I thought as much. Well, you might feel differently after I share this with you. Nelle"—he nodded over his shoulder at the New Orleans–bred woman behind him—"she brought her homemade jambalaya. You do not want to miss out on this. I was just rushing off to get a bowl when I bumped into you. A happy accident it seems. Come on, we'll find two." He grabbed her hand,

and she let him lead her to the kitchen. In a few seconds, they were on Nelle's heels before she unsealed the lid on the container.

When Nelle picked up the ladle, Tucker had two bowls set out.

"Boy, you've got better manners than that," she scolded him.

"I'm serving Sheila first," he said, looking for approval. "She's a guest."

Nelle's lips pulled into a thin line, and then with a hearty heap she filled the bowls. "Oh, well, that's entirely different."

"See," he said to Sheila. "Nelle likes me. You will too."

"We'll see." Sheila raised her brow.

He handed her one of the bowls. "Come on, let's go sit on the front porch and enjoy this under the Christmas lights. Did I mention I was the one who hung those twenty thousand lights in the magnolia tree?"

"That sounds like a lot of lights. Are you always this helpful?"

"I try to be."

She laughed, but he hadn't meant for it to sound like a joke.

They stepped outside and Sheila immediately hunched her shoulders. "It's freezing out here."

"The temperature has dropped, hasn't it." He waved her to follow. "Come on. The jambalaya will warm you up." He ushered Sheila to the rockers at the far end of the porch. "Sit." Here the wind was blocked.

"Thanks." Sheila took a bite. "Oh my gosh. I'm so glad you persuaded me to cut in line for this. I didn't think I liked Cajun food, but this is really good, and perfect on a chilly night."

"Nelle is an amazing cook. She takes over the lunch counter a few days a week in the back of the hardware store on Main Street."

"In the hardware store?" She dropped the spoon in her bowl and pushed her hand into her pocket to keep it warm.

"Well, years ago it was the pharmacy and there was a soda fountain. Now it's a hardware store. And Nelle's lunch counter. She's open for lunch—Monday, Wednesday, and Friday."

"Nice schedule."

"You should get Natalie to take you. I'm sure she's been. It's a local favorite."

"I'll do that. What do you suggest I order?"

"There's no menu. Which is kind of the beauty of it. No choices to make."

"There are days I wish I didn't have to make one more choice."

"I know. You're having whatever Nelle is cooking. No one has ever complained about it once she started doing that."

"Count me in." She took another bite. "I can't believe how many people are still coming and going. Oh my gosh. Look over there, those people are all wearing matching sweaters! It's like a parade."

"That's the Mullaney family. Looks like all six kids and the cousins are with them." Their sweaters were bright green, with a reindeer on the front and a blinking red nose bobbing from the center. Bells on the felt antler headbands jingled as they filed inside in a chorus of Merry Christmases. "Never a dull moment at this party. Are you enjoying it?"

"I am."

Softly spoken, the words seemed sincere, and it was as if her green eyes were looking straight into his heart.

Dang, Nelle, is there some kind of Louisiana Cupid spell in this jambalaya?

He gave his spoonful a suspect glance, but then took the bite anyway.

It wasn't a bad feeling. Just a little unexpected.

Chapter Seven

Sheila couldn't take her eyes off of Tucker, and that was weird because she didn't remember having any thoughts about him at all the other times they'd met. They were brief interactions. But how had she not noticed his wide shoulders before? Or the kindness in his steely blue eyes?

The last thing I need to feel is attraction for a man, no matter how good-looking or nice he is, who lives this far from home.

"I can't believe how many people are here." She hugged her cup for warmth.

"It's an annual tradition. If someone doesn't show up, then it's cause for a wellness check." Tucker pretended to puff up. "As fire chief of this town, I take that very seriously."

"Of course you do." She pointed her spoon at the big Christmas stocking. "Are you going to give that jerky away or just haul it around so you can brag about it all night?"

"I really do need to pass this stuff out. Thanks for joining me for the jambalaya."

"It was great. Thanks. I'm glad I didn't miss this."

"I'll carry your bowl inside for you." He took her empty bowl. "You'll excuse me?"

"Sure thing." She watched him walk away. His laughter wafted out into the night air as he shouted offers of homemade jerky to the guests. She'd never met such a confident yet humble man. It intrigued her that he'd have gone to the trouble of making mounds of jerky just to give away to people for the holidays. His thoughtfulness touched her.

I should have acted more interested in his jerky instead of just teasing him. I'm out of practice. I don't even know how to flirt anymore.

She shook off the thought and rocked back, staring off into the thousands of tiny lights in the magnolia tree. *You did a good job, Tucker.* The hum of joyful chatter coming from the house was comforting. Her thoughts drifted, the lights blurring, as she wondered what living this way must be like for Natalie and Randy. She'd thought for sure Natalie would move back to Richmond to be with him, but instead he'd taken a leave of absence and moved up here to give the relationship a go. They both seemed completely fulfilled.

Sheila sat listening to the others talk. One man was telling someone that he'd been trying to talk Orene into opening up the Mountain Creek Inn as a teahouse a couple of days a week to help defray the cost of upkeep of the older home. It wasn't a bad idea, and apparently, according to what she was overhearing, it had once been a dream of Orene's to do that.

She could imagine Orene fussing over couples, and mothers and daughters, for high tea on fancy place settings. Towers of fancy little pastries and dainty sandwiches.

Wouldn't it be nice to plan a fancy high tea one day while she was in town?

"There you are." Natalie walked outside and sat in the chair next to her. "I've been looking for you."

"Sorry. It's just so peaceful out here. I didn't want to be a hanger-onner to you and Randy."

"You're not. I want you to meet these people."

"I guess I'm just feeling a little tired after the drive," Sheila said.

"I understand. You can go upstairs whenever you like, but I have a feeling it's going to be loud for quite a while." Natalie lifted a green baggie and a red baggie up in front of her. "Which do you want? Turkey or venison jerky?"

"Tucker's homemade jerky," Sheila said with a smile. Somehow, he'd walked off and not even offered her any.

"It is. How'd you know? Did you already get some?"

"Surprisingly I did not, but he was carrying that huge stocking around like it had money in it."

"Just jerky, but it tastes like a million bucks."

"I'll take the turkey." She took the green bag from Natalie, opened it, and put a piece in her mouth. "Oh? I thought jerky was supposed to be dry and tough. This is tender." She chewed, pausing only to say, "And really good."

"He's known for making the best around." Natalie tucked the venison jerky in her pocket. "I'm going to save this one and put it in Randy's stocking. He could make a meal out of this stuff. I think he'd be fine if it's all I served for dinner."

"Santa Claus Is Coming to Town" echoed from inside.

"Come on. This is my favorite Christmas song." Natalie got up and Sheila followed her. They wound their way through the kitchen and dining room and through throngs of people to the living room, where two kids sat side by side on the piano bench, pumping the piano's pedals with their feet to keep it playing. "The old pianola has been in Orene's family since the 1920s," said Natalie. "It plays paper rolls. I'd never seen a player piano before moving here."

"Me either." Sheila watched with interest. "The history in this house is amazing. Everything has a story. It's like a museum."

"It is." Natalie and Sheila joined in on the second part of the song.

Orene shouted out to the room, "Trivia time! Who knows how old the song 'Jingle Bells' is?"

"A hundred years old," said one of the kids on the piano bench.

"Written in 1857. It's over a hundred and fifty years old. Let's sing that one!" Orene switched out the song roll on the pianola and then grabbed a set of jingle bells from the mantel and shook them while the kids went to work again, pumping the piano until the unmistakable song began to play. Orene led with "'Dashing through the snow . . .'"

And everyone joined in, bouncing to the upbeat tempo. Sheila imagined what it might have been like to have lived in a time where a suitor would bring his horse and sleigh over to take his sweetie for a ride through the snowy drifts under the stars. It must have been a romantic time.

The singing continued.

Sheila excused herself. "I'm going to get some air." She edged herself through the caroling crowd and made her slow way out to the front porch, where she could still hear the words to the song clear as day. Until all of a sudden, alarms were sounding, and the singing stopped.

Tucker swept past her. "Let's go!"

Confused, she swung around and jumped out of the way as

men and women rushed past her out the door and down the side-walk.

Randy and Natalie came outside.

"What's going on?" Sheila asked.

"You don't hear the wail of the siren?" Randy asked.

Sheila listened intently. Yes, just above the volume of every-one scampering and frantic conversations, she could hear the rise and fall of the alarm. "I do now."

A moment later, the fire truck came down Main Street, diesel engine rumbling, siren blaring, and lights flashing, followed by a line of pickup trucks.

Sheila noticed lettering across the front windshield of the hook and ladder truck. "What's that say?" she asked Natalie.

"Bull Mountain Boys."

They walked out into the yard, watching the fire truck rum-ble down the street.

Randy pointed over Orene's house into the distance. "You can see the smoke back that way."

Thick black smoke lifted into the air. Even in the evening sky, it was a dark billowing cloud.

Orene walked outside with a dish towel over her apron strings. "Not exactly how I had this party ending." She followed everyone else's gaze toward the sky. "I sure hope it's not some-one's home." She pulled her arms tighter. "Doesn't look good."

Sheila could smell the smoke in the air already. "Is everyone in this town in the fire department?" It sounded like a stupid statement when she said it out loud, but that fire alarm really emptied the place.

"Just about," Orene said. "There aren't too many people who are still capable that don't volunteer in some way."

Paul walked outside. "Anyone have any news on what's up yet?"

"No. We were just talking about that," said Natalie.

"That being said," Randy injected, "I'm going to check in with the sheriff to see if he needs my help and see if I can get some details."

Natalie reached up and pecked him on the cheek. "Let us know."

He jogged down the sidewalk toward the spot where he'd parked earlier.

"I didn't realize Tucker was the fire chief until he mentioned it," Sheila said.

"I never mentioned that?" Natalie shrugged.

"I think I would've remembered that. I knew he was Jeremy's best friend growing up, and helped with the cabin." Sheila didn't mean to sound so interested. With a flip of her hand she said, "Not important."

"Oh, it's very important, and he's very good at it," Orene added.

Sheila felt bad for her comment being taken the wrong way.

"Hopefully, this is just an overzealous husband trying out his new Black Friday sale fryer," Orene said. "I swear we have more incidents because of people trying to fry turkeys. When did that even become a thing?"

"It's really tasty," said Sheila. "I have to say I'm a fan."

"Well, it's dangerous. I wish they'd put some kind of training or licensing in place for people to cook like that." Orene pulled her hands to her hips. "Last year, we had a turkey fryer incident that shot that raw bird twenty feet in the air. It landed in a dry tree, and that sparked another fire. It was a mess. All that was left was the charred carcass hanging from a branch. Horrible."

"You have to admit that's a funny image." Sheila couldn't contain the giggles.

"It was," said Natalie. "You should hear Tucker tell that story. He's a great storyteller, but fire isn't funny business."

Natalie wrapped her arm around Paul. The old man, who had turned out to be Natalie's late husband's grandfather, had become real family to Natalie.

It made sense that Natalie would want to stay close to the only family she had, now that Sheila thought about it. Natalie and Paul had formed a special bond, and knowing Jeremy had grown up here had to have been some kind of comfort.

"How about I take you on home, Paul?" Natalie suggested. "Nelle and Jesse are going to stay and box up stuff for the seniors."

"That would be great. I am a little tired. This is a lot of excitement for an old man." He turned to Orene. "A wonderful evening, Orene. Thank you for having Jesse trick me into coming."

"Well, since you turned down Natalie, I had no other choice," Orene said sharply. "You old bird. You aren't going to be the recluse on that mountain anymore if I have anything to say about it. Natalie's like family to me, and that makes you family too."

"Thank you." He bowed. "Note taken. Shall we?" He hooked his arm for Natalie.

Sheila watched them leave, then turned to Orene. "Let's get out of this cold. You're not even wearing a coat. What are we thinking, standing out in the weather like this?"

"Don't treat me like an old lady. You know better than that."

"You're right. I do. I'm cold."

"Well, then let's get you out of the cold," Orene said. "Wouldn't hurt for us to say a little prayer for our neighbors."

It had been a long time since Sheila had turned to prayer automatically. She reached over and squeezed Orene's hand. "Yes, I'm thankful for this warm and welcoming home."

She and Orene raced inside, where it was still warm and toasty. Orene pulled up an app on her phone, and a moment later they were listening to the online streaming of the fire on the mountain.

"Is that the fire Tucker's team is working?" Sheila asked.

"Yes. They got a grant for this last year. It's very interesting." She leaned in toward her phone, listening. "It sounds like they've accepted the other counties' help. It must be a big fire." Orene shook her head. "So close to Christmas," she said. "How awful."

They prayed for the fire fighters and the situation at hand. Following the Amen, Orene looked to Sheila. "We've got all this food. I've got an idea."

"Uh-oh. You've got that look in your eye," Sheila said to her.

Chapter Eight

Tucker flipped the emergency lights on in his truck as he sped toward the fire. Every minute counted, and any information he could provide ahead of the fire truck arriving could save lives. The smoke was thick on this side of town, making visibility difficult already.

When he turned down Old Mill Road, it got worse.

4450 would be on the north side of the street.

He leaned in, heightened awareness pushing him to go faster. His heart raced as it always did under these circumstances, and at the same time he was praying there'd be no casualties. But lifesaving wasn't a zero-sum game.

Tucker had a couple of hunting buddies who lived on this side of the mountain, both trained as volunteers. With any luck one of them would be on location when he got there.

The houses were far apart on this side of the mountain, which could be in their favor to contain the fire to one structure, but the weather was tricky tonight. Winds had been kicking up for the past two weeks, and a pattern of dry air had made them post an alert to the county about fire hazard. With so much dense forest in the area, if the wind didn't cooperate, things could get out of hand fast.

"Aw, man." He pulled off the road at the address, immediately recognizing the house Diane and Jack Jacob had been working on for nearly three years to fix the old place up. It had been in Jack's family. His grandfather's place. Empty and neglected for a generation, it was a huge undertaking.

Another truck was parked on the street. He hoped it was one of his volunteers.

Tucker jumped out of his truck and pulled on his gear, talking into his radio the whole time.

"Two-story fire fully developed on arrival. We're going to need the following equipment: extra tankers, stagger arrival. Rescue immediately, foresters and ground crew for possible spread to natural areas."

Flames from the back of the house licked the night sky. The Christmas tree still stood in the front window, every colored light twinkling in celebration of the holiday.

One of the volunteers came running from around the back of the house. "Chief! Jack Jacob is in the backyard trying to fight it with a garden hose. He said it started back there."

"Cut the power, and get Jack out of there," Tucker said. "Trucks are two minutes out. Clear the vehicles. Get ready for their arrival."

"Yes, sir!"

Diane came running from the far side of the yard, young children in tow. "Tucker! It's spreading so fast. What do I do?"

"Is everyone out of the house?"

She nodded. "Yes. The kids. Momma. Check on Jack!"

"Doggy!" the little girl at her side screamed.

"Family pet inside?" Tucker asked.

"I don't know." Tears streamed down her face, clearing soot in a path down her cheek. "Maybe? I thought I saw him out here."

"Stay back." Tucker had no sooner gotten the words out of his mouth than the fire truck swooped to a stop in front of the house. "Keep the children over by the picnic shelter. Don't worry. I'll get Jack. We're here now."

Diane swept her family up like little ducklings and rushed them out of the way.

Tucker radioed further instructions to his team, including having someone pick up the family and take them somewhere warm and out of view of their home ablaze.

Doris would handle that. She was a lifesaver that way.

Tucker radioed the latest update: "Everyone is accounted for, except possibly the family dog. Not sure if it was inside or out. Keep an eye out."

Jack was putting up a fight, determined to save his home.

The oldest rig in Tucker's fleet, the one with THE BULL MOUN-TAIN BOYS across the windshield, rolled up.

"Pull the two-and-a-half-inch hose, Bull Mountain Boys." It was the biggest hose they had on that truck, and they needed to squelch this fire before the wind kicked up again.

The team dropped from the truck and spread out to evaluate and begin taking control of the situation.

An update came over the radio that they were bringing Jack around for medical attention.

Tucker watched two suited-up firefighters supporting Jack be-tween them. He was coughing and desperately trying to catch a breath, but in desperation, Jack pulled away, attempting to turn back to save his home.

EMTs raced to his side and checked his airway following exposure to the thick, dense smoke. Shortly thereafter, he was given oxygen while the rest of the team prepped him to be loaded in the ambulance.

Soot covered Jack from head to toe. He had to have taken in a lot of smoke. Running on adrenaline, he didn't know how much danger he was in. These were dangers Tucker's team was trained in.

It only took a moment for the EMTs to confirm his suspicions. "Possible thermal damage. Burns on his hands and neck. We're taking him to Roanoke."

Tucker jogged back around to the front to direct the other units that had come to help. That was one thing about being in a small county. All the neighboring counties were ready to back you up.

Hoses stretched from the tanker truck through the yard, and another tanker was on the way to wet down the surrounding areas. In these dry conditions, the last thing they needed was the mountainside to ignite.

It was a hot fire. The old wooden house was crumbling as fast as they could soak the flames.

Firefighters rotated in and out as they continued to try to drown the fiery embers.

Sheriff Brothers walked over. "What can we do?"

"Keep the roads clear. Two other counties are on the way for backup. It's going to be a long night."

"We've got it." He turned on his heel and hopped back in

his car, flipping his blue lights on and heading back down the mountain.

Tucker checked in with Doris and her team on the status of getting the family moved to the station if other arrangements hadn't been made yet. Being here was too much for anyone to watch. Especially with the added stress of children and the holidays for the Jacobs, and Tucker couldn't allow any distractions to put his people in danger.

He walked toward the family, still under the canopy of the picnic shelter, which was the first thing Jack had built. They'd parked an RV under it, and that's where they had all lived for the first year as they began work on the old homestead.

Betty Jo, Diane's mother, cried, grabbing his arm as he got closer. "How can we tell the children there won't be Christmas?"

The EMTs rolled a weary Jack Jacob to the ambulance, which made Betty Jo become even more emotional.

"They're taking him to Roanoke for treatment. It's precautionary," he tried to reassure her. He'd thought he could instruct her to communicate to Diane, but Betty Jo was nearing hysteria. He moved past her. "It's okay," he said to Diane. "Jack took in a lot of smoke. It's not something to mess around with, so we're taking him to get checked out, but don't worry, I don't think he's in any critical danger. We'll be moving you to the fire station."

"My keys are still inside. My purse. Everything." She sucked in a breath. "I—"

"We're going to take care of you. Just let us lead you through this, okay?" He spoke slowly, trying to comfort her. "I'll keep you updated every step of the way. I promise."

Over his shoulder, Tucker saw an SUV slide to a stop across the street.

Natalie hopped out of the driver's side. His heart hitched when he saw Sheila come around from the other side, excited to see her, but this wasn't the time. People meant well, but the last thing he needed was another person to watch over during an emergency.

Before he could address Natalie, Orene had joined her and Sheila.

The fire department van blocked his view of them as it pulled in front of the picnic shelter.

Doris got out carrying bottles of water. "We've got it from here, Chief." She, along with a couple of her blue-helmetted volunteers, swept in to help the family. Doris flipped her hand as if to dismiss him. That always tickled him, the way she'd do that.

"Thank you." Tucker checked back in with each of the teams. Gathering and imparting information. Keeping everyone on task, and making sure progress was communicated, so they stayed safe, which was his priority.

He walked over to his truck and typed an update in the computer.

Across the way, a volunteer handed out blankets to the members of the Jacob family. One of the boys was running with his like a Superman cape, oblivious to the danger or that their home was going up in smoke around him.

Another volunteer carried the creature-comfort box filled with the handiwork of the seniors: hand-crocheted bears, bunnies, dinosaurs, and even firefighter dolls with the Bull Mountain Boys badge stitched to the hats, which always put a smile on the kids' faces. Doris stooped down, although it wasn't necessary. She was barely five feet tall herself, but she got right down at their level with the basket of assorted crocheted toys. The kids seemed to calm down.

Each of the Jacob children was bent over picking out a sooth-
ing something to cling to. Doris tucked a small one in the arms of
the youngest, whom Diane had on her hip. His tiny chubby arm
flapped in the air, and then the toy went straight into his mouth.
A little yarn never hurt anyone. Least of her worries.

Back at the fire station, each of them would get a box that
the women's auxiliary put together for this type of emergency.
Essentials, like water bottles, electrolyte packets, minor first aid
items, snacks, wet wipes, toothbrushes, and some things that were
specific to men, women, or children. They had a whole shelving
unit of them. Blue boxes for the men, pink for the women, and
polka dots on the kids' boxes.

He watched Doris and her team escort the family, wrapped
in blankets to fight the cold, to the van in which they'd transport
them to the fire station, to stay until they determined what the
next steps needed to be. Shelter was a certainty already. This
house wouldn't be habitable anytime soon, if ever.

Thank God for an angel like Doris to come out of retirement
to be a part of his team. She'd been married to a firefighter for
forty years, so she knew the ins and outs from real-life experience.
Having been a teacher in the community, she had the people
skills and know-how to organize and act quickly. Plus, she knew
everyone in town.

Tucker's radio was active with standard updates and check-
ins. He didn't allow idle chatter on the airwaves during an emergency. Scanning the area, he noted that the number of yellow
helmets, indicating rookie members or those on probation, were
appropriately distributed among the black helmets, worn by more
experienced team members. Safety came with experience that
you couldn't teach in a classroom.

Then he heard the message he'd been dreading.

"Wind shift, we've got fire on the east side of the structure in the woods, about forty feet."

It wasn't unusual. And in the winter, when the air was drier, the trees and fallen debris made like kindling. It was almost expected, but he'd hoped for the best tonight.

"Bravo team, set up for water from the pond. We need a ground team on the east side of the structure."

A second tanker truck, from Dobyns, had just arrived. "Dobyns, unit twelve, pull to the front. You're on the forest fire with Bravo."

"Ten-four."

The diesel engine rumbled up the street, and the Dobyns firefighters piled out. Bravo team captain was already on it.

Keep these men safe.

A gust of cold wind kicked up, and sleet pelleted his helmet.

Chapter Nine

A gust of wind blew so hard that Sheila turned her back to stave off the icy blast. She pulled the hood of her jacket up over her head. Sneaking a glance, she saw that Orene and Natalie were huddled together doing the same as they stood across the street from the burning house. Maybe coming to bring food to the fireman wasn't such a great idea, but Orene was pretty convincing when she had her mind set on something.

Another gust of wind shook her hood, causing it to flap loudly.

The last of the dry, brown leaves swooped through the air to the ground, and tall trees with thick limbs swayed as if they were only twigs.

Creaking branches arched in weird ports de bras like giant unsteady ballerinas in a panic.

Until this moment, Sheila had never actually heard wind howl, and quite honestly she wasn't sure if it was the wind howling or the fire moaning. Either way, the sound crawled up her skin.

Something snapped, and she swung toward the house just as blinding flames shot through the roof.

Shattered glass lay scattered on the ground around the house, glinting in an eerie orange glow.

It was a brutal realization of the power of nature—wind, smoke, freezing temperatures, and a fire burning so hot that it blanketed the area in a haze.

Her throat burned, and her eyes stung.

Natalie yelled to her. "I'm going to see if I can help them."

Sheila saw the people being rushed across the street. "You stay with Orene, I'll check." She was closest to them anyway, and they almost got to her before she could get to them.

"How can we help?" Sheila asked.

"I'm Doris. I'm with the Chestnut Ridge Fire Department. I need to get them to the fire station to warm up. Can you stay with the Jacobs family while I bring the van closer?"

"Absolutely."

"I'll be right back." Doris race-walked away.

Huddling in blankets, dirty and scared, they looked lost.

"I'm so sorry." Sheila didn't know what else to say to the mother and her frightened children. Another woman, probably her mother, stood shivering despite the blanket wrapped around her shoulders.

In shock, certainly, they looked like their world was crashing in. And it was. Literally just yards away.

Sheila let out a breath, wishing she had words to comfort the woman, and her children with eyes as wide as saucers. It had to be confusing.

A sharp snap came from the house as something collapsed, shooting glowing embers into the air, spinning and rising as if they might never fall, but they would as they turned to ash.

Firemen called out to one another. Moving quickly, almost

effortlessly, despite the thick hoses and heavy equipment on their backs.

They were doing a lot more than just hosing water on the house fire. Some swung axes into the exterior, wood splintering with each crashing blow, to allow water to get inside and slow down the raging inferno, she supposed.

It was hard to not think they were doing as much damage as the fire.

Even if the fire stopped at this very moment, answering her silent prayers, there'd be so much damage it'd be a wonder if they could ever make it livable again.

It was overwhelming to witness, and it wasn't even her house.

The woman's hand shook as she let go of a toddler's hand to sweep the hair from her face and gulp for a breath of air.

"We're going to get you through this. Just breathe," Sheila said, and then Doris pulled up in the fire department van.

Sheila followed as the volunteers shuffled the family toward Doris. Once they were getting into the van, Sheila ran over to Natalie and Orene, who were passing her a stack of Styrofoam containers of leftovers from the party for the family.

"I knew this would come in handy," Orene said.

"You better get back in the van, Orene. It's too cold to be standing out here." Sheila ran the food over to the fire department van and handed it to the woman inside.

"We've packed up some food for you. They're going to take you to the fire station, where you'll be comfortable and warm." Sheila felt ridiculous handing the woman food when there were larger problems staring them right in the face. "You might not feel like eating right now, but you'll need this to keep your strength up."

"Thank you," the woman said. "I'm Diane. I don't think I know you."

"I'm visiting. I'm a friend of Natalie and Orene's. My name is Sheila."

Diane attempted to smile, then leaned forward, nodding as if she recognized Orene's SUV. "Thank you for your kindness."

Orene waved a bony wrist in the air. "Honey, this is awful. I can't believe it," she hollered from across the way.

"We were just getting on our way to your house for the party when the dog started barking nonstop. Something on the back porch caught fire. I have no idea what could have started it."

"Oh darling. Thankfully, you are all here and safe." Orene pressed her hand to her chest.

"I don't know where the dog is." Diane's eyes darted around. She hitched the chubby red-faced crying baby on her hip. One look back to the house and tears fell to her cheeks.

"Let me take him for you." Sheila held out her arms, and the baby reached for her. She cradled him in her arms, and he grabbed her shirt and smiled. A little snot bubble formed as he giggled against her warm wool peacoat. With nothing in hand to use, she wiped his nose with her fingers, saying, "You are a big boy. Everything is going to be okay." Holding him tight to her body, she could feel his tiny heartbeat rabbiting in his chest. "It's going to be all right."

Diane shook out her arms. "He gets heavy."

"He's a healthy baby. That's a good problem." She bobbed him up and down. His tears were quickly replaced with giggles and coos.

Doris helped the last of the Jacob family on board.

"Your husband is on his way to Roanoke, and I just got an

update that he's stable. Don't worry, Carter says he's griping that he's okay. That's got to be a good sign." Doris laughed.

"He always says he's fine," Diane said, "even when I know he's not. I'm glad they made him go." Diane took in a stronger breath. "I can rest easier knowing he's getting checked out."

"Yes, ma'am," Doris agreed.

Sheila tucked the baby in Diane's arms. "Here you go. He's so precious. Is there anything I can do for y'all tonight?"

"Keep an eye out for our dog."

"We will. What's his name?"

"Bananas." Diane rolled her eyes. "Kids named him. Don't ask."

Sheila reached into her pocket and touched a lone business card. "I'm in town for two weeks. Here, my cell phone is on this card." She pressed it firmly into Diane's hand. "Use it if there's anything I can do. Even if it's just to come and hold the baby or watch the kids so you can lock yourself in the other room and catch your breath."

"Really?"

"Yes. Really. You are safe, and there are people here who want to help you and your family." It surprised Sheila as much as it did Diane. Surprised that she was reacting like a lifelong resident of Chestnut Ridge. *Maybe there's something in the air here that opens hearts a little wider.* An overwhelming need to help had come over her, and it felt good.

"Thank you so much." Tears streamed down Diane's face. "I'm sorry."

"It's okay, Diane. This is an emotional situation. I'd be more worried if you weren't upset."

Diane squeezed her arm. "You're an angel."

Sheila stepped back to close the door on the van, then waved to the children as Doris drove away.

Sheila turned and looked at Natalie in disbelief. "This is heartbreaking. I've never seen anything like this."

"It's terrible," Natalie said, "and with it so close to Christmas. I wonder what caused the fire." She climbed into the vehicle.

Orene had overheard the whole thing, responding with, "Could've been wiring, a candle, who knows, but does it matter? So many things can go wrong. That house was so old. They'd been working on it to bring it up to date. Doing what they could as they could afford it. Too bad that it fell into such disrepair. It was a nice place when I was a little girl, but it had been left empty for longer than is good. Things break down over time."

Natalie watched a firefighter run across to the EMTs. "I think that guy is hurt. Look at how he's holding his arm. No matter how hard they work, will they be able to save the house?"

"It's the lives that matter, and the forest and preserving nature here on the mountain that drives all these folks to volunteer to help," Orene said. "There's so much more than a structure to protect."

"Thank goodness for homeowner's insurance," Sheila said. "But finding temporary housing isn't easy, even in the city. I can imagine it will be even harder up here."

"Maybe, but folks around here don't mind disrupting their lives to help others." Orene lifted her chin. "I've taken in quite a few over the years. Some folks I knew from church. Some I'd never even met. I treated them all the same. It's what we do in Chestnut Ridge."

"That wouldn't happen in the city. They'd be more likely to

raise some money to put you in a hotel than open their home to a stranger. No one wants to be inconvenienced."

Natalie grinned. "You are experiencing firsthand the beauty of Chestnut Ridge. It's not all just the landscape. It's so much more."

Sheila was beginning to believe that. "Let's pick up some of the immediate needs for them tomorrow," Sheila said. "With all those children, nothing will be easy or cheap. Just diapers and pajamas could break the bank. I can't even imagine. Orene, do you know someone who can help us get the sizes so we could help them?"

"Doris will already be gathering that information," Orene said. "She's Tucker's right hand on that administrative stuff and her heart is bigger than Alaska."

Tucker walked over to the vehicle. "I know you mean well, but I need to ask you to vacate the premises. We have more trucks coming in."

"We wanted to see if we could help," Orene said. "Plus, we have all this food. If it's going to be a long night, I'd rather keep your guys and gals going strong."

"As you can see, the weather is not cooperating, but we've got plenty of manpower. The homeowner was taken to the hospital, and the rest of the family is now safely evacuated. Hopefully, the family dog will turn up."

"Maybe he's just hiding. He has to be scared," said Natalie.

Sheila could tell she was thinking about Buzz, that little dog of hers. Natalie treated that beagle like a child.

"Doris will work on finding a place for them to stay. Hopefully, we won't have to split them up, but that's a lot of people," Tucker said. "The structure fire is contained. We'll be working hot spots for hours, but we're more concerned about this shifting wind and the woods right now."

"So, you're in for a long night," Sheila said.

"Definitely."

Orene lifted her chin. "We'll set up food and drinks over under the picnic shelter. If it doesn't get eaten, that's fine. We can come clean it up tomorrow."

"That's not necessary, and it's going to end up everywhere in this wind," Tucker said.

"We'll leave all the food, plates, and paper towels in the big boxes, so nothing will blow away. If nothing else, it'll let everyone know they are appreciated. And then we'll be out of your hair."

Tucker stepped in front of Sheila, blocking her from the flying embers as the roof fell in on the house, sending sparks swirling.

She ducked her head into his coat.

"I've got to get back. Y'all should leave. It's getting dicey."

"We'll go as soon as we set everything up," Orene said.

Sheila pressed her lips together, trying not to laugh at Orene's won't-take-no-for-an-answer attitude. Clearly, she was willing to throw around her weight when she saw reason to. She caught the half smile on Tucker's face. He knew he was beat.

Tucker caught her gaze and shook his head.

She couldn't help but smile. "I promise we'll be out of your way in a second."

"Thank you. I'd appreciate that. I've got to get back to this." He stepped toward the business at hand. He wasn't happy about them being there. "You ladies please be careful and watch yourself over these hoses. I don't mean to sound ungrateful. I do appreciate you thinking of us, but it's my responsibility to keep you safe as well."

And the craziest thing ran through Sheila's mind at that moment.

I'm not going to be able to think of anything but you after this.

The fire chief's smile practically melted her sensibilities.

"I thought he'd never leave," Orene said. "Come on, let's get this stuff over there and skedaddle."

"No. You stay put, Orene," Sheila said. "It's too messy out here, and if you fall, that's one more thing they have to deal with. Nat and I can move the boxes."

Orene's nose wrinkled, pushing her glasses up in a way that magnified her eyes strangely.

"We'll be quick. We've got this."

"Okay, fine. I'll get the boxes sorted and mark them on the outside," Orene said.

Natalie grabbed a box of cookies and brownies, and Sheila carried the five-gallon jug of sweet tea and followed her.

When they got back to the SUV, Orene had marked the side of each box with the contents, a big smiley face, and THANK YOU in big block letters.

"That looks great." Natalie lifted a box. "Pile on another. They aren't that heavy." Sheila helped her with the other, and it only took a few trips to get everything moved over.

"Did you hear that?" Sheila dropped the last of the boxes on the picnic table. "It's like a squeaking noise."

"I thought I heard something back there too, but it's so noisy with all the equipment. I wasn't sure."

Sheila stooped next to a row of stickery overgrown holly bushes. "Natalie! I think this is the family dog."

Natalie raced to her side, dropping to all fours. The scruffy mixed-breed dog cowered beneath the pointed green leaves and berries. "Come on, pup. It's okay. All this noise must be terrify-ing." She reached out and clicked her fingers, but the dog just whimpered.

"Is he stuck?" Sheila asked. "Here, Bananas. Where's that good puppy?"

"He's terrified. Get some of the roast beef for me."

"I'd crawl out from under just about anything for that. Hang on, let me find it." But Orene's neat handwriting made it easy to put her hands on the box with the carved roast beef. She grabbed a slice from the foil tray and handed it to Natalie.

"Bananas, look what I've got for you. Yummy. C'mon, boy."

His ears perked, then swiveled like satellite dishes before he lowered his chin and cha-cha'd forward and back, and then fi-nally belly-crawled to Natalie for a taste.

"That's a good boy."

Sheila couldn't believe their luck. "Do you know how happy that family is going to be to hear this little guy is okay?"

"I can only imagine," said Natalie. With one quick swipe, she caught the dog by the collar and pulled him to her. He didn't put up a fight, but then Natalie was still hand-feeding him roast beef at the moment.

"Hurry, let's get him in the SUV before we run out of bait." Sheila ran to open the door. Natalie swiftly dropped the canine into the seat next to Orene and slammed the door.

"Hot dog!" Orene shouted. "We found the missing pup."

"That's a horrible pun, Orene." Natalie spun around in her seat with her mouth agape.

Orene's hand slapped over her mouth. "I promise I wasn't making a joke about the dog and the fire."

But all three of them needed that laugh at that moment.

"Let's see if we can't get the rest of the family a few smiles." Sheila was grateful for the laughter that relieved some of the heaviness in her heart for this family. She and Natalie got in the vehicle still laughing at Orene's slip up.

Natalie turned the key and pressed the accelerator.

"To the fire station!" Orene shouted as Bananas bounced from seat to seat as they headed down the mountain.

Chapter Ten

It took all night to get the fire to the stage where the situation was considered stabilized. The team would monitor for hot spots with the thermal imaging equipment and watch for any sparks the wind might reignite.

Tired and filthy, Tucker was relieved that only a small area of the woods had been burned, and thankfully once the underbrush quit fueling it and the wind died down, the activities were enough to suppress it finally.

Weary from the all-nighter, Tucker showered at the firehouse, then met with fresh team members to brief them to take over through the day.

Work would continue to keep hot spots under control, and investigators controlled access while they collected evidence to identify the point of origination for their reports. The home-owner, Jack, had said the fire started on the back porch.

"Good morning. I'm sure you've heard that we were called out in response to a fire at the Jacobs' home up on Old Mill over-night. In training, you hear that a fire can double in just fifteen to thirty seconds. We all witnessed that firsthand on that call. Weather conditions can turn a small fire into something out of control in a flash, especially with how dry the air has been. Stay on your toes."

He didn't like any injuries at all, but thank goodness those sustained were minor. "We have one shoulder injury and Douglas twisted an ankle. I need you all to be sure you're inspecting all of your equipment. We need to learn from every incident. Small things like worn-out boots, and I know they are expensive, but that is a risk of an injury that can be mitigated. Who here has taken the time to really look at the tread on their boots lately?"

Only a couple of hands went in the air. "Yeah, me either, and this is a good time for us all to do that today."

He leaned forward, lowering his voice. "The Jacobs lost everything in that house. They are upstairs in the community room until we get them moved somewhere."

"Was it the Christmas tree that caused the fire?" someone asked.

"No. It was not. Their tree was still so fresh it didn't ignite for a long while, but remind folks to keep those trees watered. This time of year it's a big factor. Ground crews from not only our house, but our neighboring counties, and our new volunteers from the national parks division brought expertise to the table, taking charge of the edges of the forest at risk, prepping fire circles on the outer bands, while we fought the main fire."

A hand shot up. Tucker acknowledged the older man in charge of the junior firefighters' club with the school.

He stood. "This is the kind of project that's perfect for our junior firemen to replant that area. We've got that allotment of trees, and it'll be a good learning opportunity for them to see where the fire jumped from the house to the woods, and how the preventative trenches were dug to contain it to a controlled area."

"Excellent. Take lead on that." Tucker jotted a note in his book. "Yeah, that opportunity doesn't arise that often. Thanks for bringing that up."

Tommy stood. "We may need some backup volunteers for the Christmas Tree Stroll. Some of the team were out last night and will need some rest. Others are shifting into active participation on the fire that we hadn't planned on." He ran his fingers down his dark horseshoe mustache. A nervous habit. "So anyone with some extra availability, let me know today if you can. Spread the word. I'll update the staffing list for duty and the Christmas Tree Stroll on the app and bulletin board for everyone by lunchtime tomorrow."

"Put me down for whatever you need," said one of the volunteers.

"Much appreciated. Y'all can see me after the meeting. Thanks, Chief."

"Thanks, Tommy. I know Doris will get the Jacobs added to the county list for help with the holidays, but this family is going to need the support of the whole community for more than two weeks. Let's see what we can do to get the word out." Tucker scanned the room. "That's it. Go out and be safe."

Tucker left the station house filled with thanks for these people he considered family. It wasn't always easy to check the emotion at the door. A mixed blessing.

"Tucker?"

He turned to see who was calling his name.

"Hey!" A woman was yelling from the window of a vehicle as bright red as the fire truck.

He walked over, realizing the closer he got that it was Sheila.

"Hey there. Nice car." He stepped back, taking a better look. "One of those electric jobs. Read about them. Never have seen a Tesla like this in person, though."

"Long story. A deal too good to pass up. I'll tell you about it someday, but I wanted to catch you to see if there's a list of things I can get for the family."

"There's one started. I could email it to you, or you're welcome to go on up. They are in the community room."

"Would it be okay? I spoke to Diane last night. I wouldn't mind checking in with her, maybe just give her some encouragement that she's not in this alone."

"Can never give too much of that. Sure." He pointed to the far side of the building. "If you park over there, you can take the stairs straight up."

"Is it okay that I brought a few things for them?"

"Yeah. That's really thoughtful."

She got out of the car. For a short girl, she had legs that seemed to go on forever as she stretched them out to stand. She draped her arms across the top of the door. "I can't tell you how moving it was for me to see all that last night. The way everyone worked together against the power of that fire. I never realized just how hot and fierce a house fire could be." She swallowed. "I . . . it just never really dawned on me. Anyway, I hope you weren't upset with us showing up. Orene was insistent."

"Oh, I know Orene, and there's no stopping her when she has her mind on something. She does stuff like that, and trying to chase her off takes me off task. She knows to stay out of the way."

"Good. I was worried we'd upset you."

"Don't you worry about that." He had a feeling it would be

hard for her to set him off, especially the way her wide smile reached her eyes. He found it hard to pull his gaze from hers, and his mouth went a little dry. "I'm headed home for some rest. You go on up." He lifted his hand in a wave and started to walk away.

"Umm—"

He stopped and turned back.

"Once you're rested up, I'd like to pick up on our conversation, ya know, from before the fire alarm went off. I mean, if you wanted to get lunch or something."

She's asking me out? City girls. He'd never get used to that. Practically married to his job, he didn't mind the company of a beautiful woman, even if she was only going to be here for a couple of weeks. "Sure. Yeah."

"You can just call Orene's or I could give you my number." Her cheeks turned slightly pink.

Tucker pulled his phone from his pocket and brought up the telephone screen. "Here. Call yourself. I'll have yours and you'll have mine."

She typed her phone number in so quickly that her shiny red fingernails were almost a blur, except for the cute little silver bells on her pointer finger.

"I like your fingernails."

She curled her fingers in, laughing. "Kind of fun. I don't usually do decorations like that, but my manicurist wanted to do something special as a holiday gift for me. It's sweet, isn't it?"

"It is. It's my favorite Christmas carol."

"'Silver Bells'? Mine too. When I was in first grade, we did this ice-skating thing on the stage in the cafeteria for the Christmas pageant. I was dressed in this cute little red corduroy dress, white tights, and earmuffs. Like ice-dancing couples, we slid in

our socks around the floor in a big circle and sang 'Silver Bells.'"
She rocked as if recalling the motion of skating across that floor.

"I bet you were adorable." He could almost picture a pint-
sized version of her with a rounder childish face and pink lips.
"You should come with me to the elementary school Christmas
program if you're still in town on the twentieth. There's nothing
cuter."

"You have children?"

"No. I know them all, though. I do safety talks for the school
twice a year."

"I'd like that. You're on. I should be here. I'll put it on my
calendar, which, by the way, is very open except for decorating
that tree, which seems to be getting fancier by the second."

"Don't tell me." He covered his ears. "I'll be accused of
stealing secrets when we win."

"You're going to have to really do something to beat us.
You've never seen competitive until you've seen Natalie in full
action."

"I can almost imagine that." The exhaustion he'd been
feeling seemed to lift. He could spend all day in Sheila's smile—
friendly, compassionate, and full of life.

"Go. You need your rest after last night. I'm going to go up
and check on the Jacob family." She slid back behind the wheel
of the Tesla, and with barely a sound, eased across the lot and
out of sight.

He climbed into his truck, still marveling over how anyone
could change his energy with just a smile.

Chapter Eleven

Following her visit with the Jacobs, Sheila went back to Orene's. Her mind was consumed with figuring out a way to help that family.

She walked into Orene's, surprised to hear Natalie's voice coming from the kitchen. And even more welcoming, the smell of bacon.

"Good morning." Sheila poked her head around the corner. "I didn't see your car, Natalie."

Natalie and Randy were at the table, and Orene was at the stove pushing bacon across the biggest cast-iron skillet Sheila had ever seen.

"We walked over," Randy said.

It was kind of nice how walkable things were here. "Your kitchen always has the best smells," Sheila said, answering a text. "Sorry. The office."

"I thought you left the team in charge," Natalie said.

"I did."

"Then why are they blowing up your phone?"

"It's fine. No biggie," Sheila insisted, tucking her phone in her back pocket.

"Thank you. I hope you're hungry." Orene looked up from the pan. "You slept in late this morning."

"No. Actually, I just got back. I went over to the firehouse to check on the Jacob family."

"That was nice of you. I bet they were surprised."

"I couldn't stop thinking about them. I can't imagine experiencing what they just went through."

"I hope none of us ever has to," Orene said. "Let me get you something to eat."

"I'm not hungry. I'll just have coffee if there's any left."

"Fresh pot just finished brewing." Orene waved her spatula at the end of the counter. "Everyone eats. House rules."

Sheila's phone sounded again. She answered a text and then sat next to Natalie. No words were necessary between them, and the sentiment was crystal clear. Orene had a lot of rules.

Randy said, "I'm personally hoping for your grits and hoop cheese to go with that bacon."

"I've got you covered," said Orene. "Eggs too. Got to have plenty of protein for the first meal of the day."

"She was low-carb before keto was cool," Natalie said.

"Sounds like it." Sheila poured a cup of coffee and sat at the table.

"Don't even know what keto really is, but I know how to keep my family fed." Orene scooped out crispy slices of thick bacon on a paper grocery bag. The grease made Sheila's stomach queasy. She was more of a one-meal-a-day gal most of the time. Even then, she ate mostly salads, and maybe fish or chicken. Never anything fried.

But when Orene set that big plate of crispy bacon on the table, Sheila couldn't keep herself from grabbing a piece, and it was so good she ate a second before Orene got the eggs on the table.

"So I was thinking." Sheila nibbled the bacon. "I know we need to finish planning for the Christmas tree decorating, but do you think once we get that done that we might be able to shop for the Jacob family?"

"Absolutely." Natalie already had a pen and paper in front of her. "Orene was just saying Doris should have a whole punch list made up this morning."

"I got it from her while I was visiting." Sheila spread out the photocopy on the table. "They are going to need a lot of help. Doris is having trouble finding a place that can take in the whole family."

Orene turned her back to the counter. "I've been thinking about that too. I think it would be better if we didn't have to split them up, especially here at Christmas. I could let them take over the living room and two bedrooms, but it'll be tight with the Christmas stuff taking up most of the space already. There's no room for three more adults and four children on top of everything else."

"I could always go back home," Sheila said. "It would give you more room here for them."

"No." It was an emphatic no, and loud, with all three of them shouting at once.

"Okay. I'm not going anywhere," Sheila said, shrinking back. Besides, she was kind of looking forward to having a friendly date with the cute fire chief while she was in town.

"I might have a solution," said Natalie. "They could stay at my cabin."

"No, and being right on the water would be a nightmare for Diane to keep an eye on those kids."

"You're right," Natalie agreed. "Or?"

"What are you thinking?" Sheila glanced over at Randy. "Or, I could take stay there, and maybe you could stay at Randy's. Then the Jacob family could stay at Orene's."

Natalie held up a finger. "I'm going to ask Paul if he'll put them up."

Orene's mouth dropped. "I don't—"

"I know." Natalie closed her eyes. "People think he's a recluse, and because he's never let anyone up on that hillside, they think he's not going to help, but they don't understand why. He's a good man, with a huge heart."

"Yes, he is," Orene said. "It's been very nice getting to know him again since you've come to town, but I don't see him being able to handle those kids rousting about his place."

"I'm not thinking of him putting them up in the castle. The chapel up on the hill is empty. It's got a bathroom and a small kitchen area. We could set up a regular Christmas camp there for them, and there wouldn't be a big hurry to get them moved along. We could decorate it, and it might be a little tight, but that could make it fun if we do it up right. I bet we could put some bunk beds in there. It's got heat and everything they'd need."

"I'll be really surprised if he says yes," Orene said.

"It sounds like a perfect solution to me." Sheila clicked on her phone, scrolled through something, then said, "I can get two sets of kids' bunk beds, that would sleep the three older children and provide room for stuffed toys, for less than six hundred dollars, delivered four days from now. I'll pay for them. And if someone will drive to Richmond to get them, we can have them tomorrow. We'll need a crib as well. I bet someone has a spare or two in this town."

"I'll pick them up," Randy said. "I have a couple of things to drop off for the guys at the police station back in Richmond, anyway. We can put them together when I get back."

"If Paul says no, then my place might just have to do," Natalie said. "We'd have to put some kind of fence up to be sure the kids couldn't get to the water. That really scares me, but it could work in a pinch." She pressed her hand on top of Randy's. "I can stay with this guy through the holidays, or over here with you and Sheila."

"You're going to make us fight over you," Randy said. "Don't hurt my feelings right here at the holidays, babe."

"Stop. You know I love you more than anything." Natalie kissed him on the cheek.

He smiled, blushing slightly. "Yeah."

Sheila shook her head. "I don't think the cabin is an option. Don't share this with anyone, but Diane told me that she and Jack have a twenty-thousand-dollar deductible on their home-owner's. They don't have that kind of money. It could take a long while before they are in a position to get that house into livable shape."

"Oh dear." Orene's face blanched. "That's terrible."

"With the price of homes going up, we're seeing more and more people opting for high deductibles to keep the rates down. It can become a problem, though, like in this situation." Sheila got up and helped Orene with the juice carafe and glasses. They all ate and then Natalie cleared the table.

"I'm going to go talk to Paul. Sheila, do you want to come?"

"Absolutely. I'll drive."

Natalie got up and kissed Randy on the forehead and hugged Orene. "Wish me luck."

"Good luck," they said, but Sheila doubted they'd need it.

An hour later, Sheila and Natalie were walking out of Paul's castle house with the keys to the little chapel on the hill.

"He didn't hesitate one second," Sheila said. "That man would do anything for you. He really is your family."

"I know. He's so good to me. I wish I'd known him when Jeremy was still alive."

"That would have been special. I bet it was hard for Jeremy to have to leave that part of his life behind."

"Had to have been. I can't imagine, but that's the past, and I try not to ponder over things I don't control," Natalie said.

Sheila was pretty sure Natalie wasn't only thinking about Jeremy and Paul, but putting the past behind her after being conned by that louse too. Then again, if that hadn't happened, she might never have met Randy.

"Besides, we have plenty to solve without going down a rabbit hole," Natalie said.

"We do. Let's go to the fire station and talk to Doris. She's going to be so relieved." Sheila headed down the driveway.

"Turn here." Natalie jiggled the church keys. "I'll show you the space. We can take some measurements before we go see Doris."

"Excellent idea. You know, staging is my specialty."

"I'm counting on that," Natalie said. "I want this to be the best Christmas the Jacob family could imagine under the circumstances."

"We can make anything happen together." Sheila gave Natalie's hand a squeeze. "Like Thelma and Louise."

"There will be no darting off cliffs in this car!" She looked over her head. "I doubt it even has a roll bar."

"Even if it does, this thing cost way too much money for that kind of reckless shenanigans."

"Take this path here." Natalie pointed to the gravel road that veered off to the right between two corner fence posts.

Sheila made the turn, and it was only a moment before the little church came into view. It wasn't old, which was what she'd expected. "Why does Paul Grandstaff have a church on his property, anyway?"

"He's a little eccentric. He has a good reason for everything, though. When his wife died, he had this built so he could come out here and be close to her. His daughter is buried in the cemetery. He had Jesse build a resting place for Jeremy's ashes here too. It's really pretty."

"You didn't tell me that. Natalie, that's good." Sheila had worried about Natalie keeping his ashes in her house. It just seemed so depressing. "This place is as charming as can be."

Sheila pulled to a stop. From the outside, the white building with its tall peak looked taller than it was wide. It didn't look much bigger than some of the supersized sheds people had behind their homes for storage, but she'd seen those things turned into tiny houses for families to live in. It could be super cute with some out-of-the-box thinking.

The front doors were a gentle sage green. Tall pencil-point evergreens flanked each side. It was simple, but the elegant detailing, like the wrought-iron shutter dogs and ornate doorknob, probably salvaged from an old building, gave the place character.

A pretty church bell hung in a tower that stretched high above them.

Natalie unlocked the front door, and they stepped inside.

It was chilly. She reached for the thermostat and the mini-split, and the heat started blowing. "We'll get it warmed up in here."

The entry was like a hallway. Sheila, being a real estate agent, out of habit, opened each of the doors. A bathroom on one side, and a kitchenette on the other side. "This will work."

In the main part of the building, only six pews, three on each side, filled the far end near the platform where a wooden bench held a Bible.

"Paul said we can have Jesse get the guys to empty the place and move the pews out to the barn to store them while the family is here."

"I'd suggest we keep two of them. It's a lot bigger inside. It looked tiny from the front, but it's long. We can probably lay our hands on a long table they can use for meals, and put that right over there near the kitchen."

"Great idea. I know the fire station has a ton of eight-foot tables they use for bingo nights. I'm sure they'd lend us one."

"We can throw a heavy tablecloth over it and tack it underneath so the kids can't pull it down, and put something childproof in the center." Sheila twisted, looking left and right. "A Christmas tree in the corner over there?"

"Yeah." Natalie marched to the spot, lifting her hands high in the air. "And it can be tall!"

"I'll find an area rug to anchor a living space. A couch and, ya know, we could use another pew instead of chairs. I think the kids would be fine with a pew to sit on for television, and they can't mess them up since they're wooden."

"True."

"I've got so much stuff at the office for staging. If we struggle to find anything, we could get Randy to stop and pick up some of my inventory."

"We have a great Habitat for Humanity store and a Goodwill not far," Natalie said. "We should be able to dress this up pretty easily. They might even be willing to donate or discount some things for us. You'll be surprised. People will come out of the woodwork to help."

"That's so refreshing." Sheila took a couple of pictures, then used her phone to measure the room dimensions. "We can make this very homey. It'll probably have to take them through at least spring for the insurance company to pay out and come up with a plan. By then, outdoor-living weather will be here, and there's plenty of running space for the little ones."

"I can't wait to tell them." Natalie pulled out her phone and placed the call. "Let's call Doris now."

She punched in the phone number and put it on speaker. "Hey Doris. It's Natalie and Sheila. We've got great news. We've got a place lined up for the Jacobs for the next six months. And it's free."

"What? How did you do that?"

"Paul Grandstaff has generously offered to let us turn the chapel on the hill here on his property into a sanctuary for the family. Sheila and I are going to turn this place into a wonderful temporary home for them."

"They are going to be so relieved." Doris sounded genuinely appreciative. "Please thank Mr. Grandstaff. Not knowing where they'll be sleeping is a huge weight on their shoulders right now. They are so thankful to have a roof over their heads, but they feel like they are in the way here. It's definitely only a temporary solution. They need a place they can consider their home for a spell, and this will do the trick. I'm so grateful."

"That family captured my heart that night. You hear about things like this, but seeing it, being there, I wanted to help. I've been missing that sense of purpose in my life." Sheila remembered the moment she looked into Diane's worried eyes. She'd cleared her schedule for the holidays, but now she had a real purpose. Something she could do that could make a difference. "They are going to be okay. We'll all make sure of it."

"I can't wait for Paul to meet them," said Natalie. "Can you house them at the fire station just through the weekend to give us time to get the place ready? We're going to get bunk beds for the kids and put this place together so they can settle in and feel like they are home through the holidays, or however long it takes."

"We can definitely do that. Thank you, Natalie. This is so generous. I've got a dresser in my garage. It's old, but it'll work. I'll put together a drawerful of necessities for each of the kids. I have them finger-painting little name tags now. I'll use those for them to mark each drawer. It's a mess up here, but they are having fun and the parents are resting."

"A dresser will be great," Sheila leaned in and said into the phone. "If you're taking care of gathering the necessities for the kids, we'll take care of the linens and everything for the bedding for the family while we're putting the place together."

"That's wonderful. I'm marking those off my master list. This will put their minds at ease, although I don't even think the full brunt of what they're facing has really hit them yet."

"I'm sure. I can't even begin to imagine starting over like that."

"I can't thank you enough for jumping into action like this. I just got off the phone with the food pantry. I'll let them know we'll be ready for food on Monday." Doris sniffled between her words, and that made Sheila and Natalie both raise their hands to their hearts.

"Thank you, ladies," Doris said.

"Our pleasure." The joy in Sheila's heart was like nothing she'd experienced before. Giving of yourself, your time, seemed so small, but was so rewarding.

Chapter Twelve

Sheila sat in the passenger seat of Natalie's truck trying not to watch as Natalie tiptoed at the window of Randy's vehicle, kissing him goodbye again. Hopefully, this third kiss would be the last. She was ready to shop.

The weather had warmed up to the forties, so it wasn't nearly as bitter cold as it had been. She closed her eyes, letting the sun warm her face through the windshield, wishing she'd hurry up.

Finally, Natalie hopped into the driver's seat. "Let's do this."

"I'm ready. I was just thinking about what else we might need to get." Sheila picked up a pen from the console and added pillows and a boot tray for next to the door to the list.

And they were off. Thank goodness, at each stop, they were able to strike off something else on the list. At the Habitat Restore they were able to get a huge area rug to create a family living space, and a couch and fun coffee table too. Even a set of nightstands and small lamps for the sleeping area.

As the guys loaded the pickup with the furniture, the owner overheard Natalie talking about the Jacob family's loss and walked over.

"Sounds like you two ladies are doing the work of elves and angels today."

"Labor of love. A generous neighbor donated a building, so we're trying to get it all set up."

"Well, just so happens someone brought in one of those electric fireplaces today. The kind that looks like a mantel. What do you think about me donating that to you? It would make for a homey Christmas with someplace to hang the stockings. My treat."

"You're kidding!" Natalie could barely contain her excitement. "That would be amazing."

"And if they find they don't need it, just bring it on back. No harm, but it sure seems like a fun addition with little ones around, so Santa has a fireplace to come down. Unless you think it might scare those toddlers after seeing their house burn down."

"I hadn't thought about that. Let's see how it goes. I think it's a grand idea. At least through Christmas." Natalie threw her arms around his neck. "Thank you!"

He instructed the guys to load up the fireplace too.

While they waited, Sheila sketched out another floor plan on how they might arrange the furniture, only this time instead of putting the bunk beds in the front corner she put the full-size bed with the nightstands on each side on one wall, and then set up the bunks as sort of a faux wall. It truly would separate the living area from the sleeping quarters.

"That's a great idea," Natalie said, "and it will give them some privacy after the kids go to sleep."

"I'll buy two matching lightweight bedspreads to nail to the back side of the bunk bed frames. What color do you think? Blue maybe?"

"Sure. Everything is pretty much white or wood in the chapel, so anything with a little color would warm it up and make it more inviting. Blue would go nice with the rug and the couch we picked out."

"The truck is full, but if we can stop somewhere on the way back, I can fit that stuff under my feet."

They stopped at the big box store and found the perfect matelassé bedspreads in a cozy winter blue.

"I think that is the fastest shopping trip and most stuff I've ever bought in half of a day."

"Look at all this stuff!" Sheila still couldn't believe how lucky they'd gotten. "This feels like Christmas."

"You're telling me. Better than buying a bunch of gifts that you know are just going to end up in a drawer somewhere. I'd rather help a family every year." Her phone pinged. "Oh wait. It's Randy. He has the bunk beds. He's heading back now."

"We better get a move on then," Sheila said. "I bet we can get this stuff staged before he gets back to Chestnut Ridge. Ask him if he needs us to pick up any tools to put them together."

Natalie texted Randy back. "Nope, he has what he needs in his truck."

"Perfect."

"Oh, and he's bringing coffee and pastries from Giddy-Up and Go," Natalie added. "His sister is sending them for us."

"The one in the horse trailer, right?"

"Yes. She has the best pastries and coffee."

"I know. I'm addicted to her place. I follow her on Facebook so I know where she's parked. In fact, text him and see if he's still there. Is he still there with her? If he could get me ten twenty-dollar gift cards from her, I'll give them to my December clients as New Year's presents. That would be fun and would help her get the word out."

"On it." She typed out the message. "He'll get them while he's there."

"All of my shopping is officially done now." Sheila smacked her hands together and leaned back in the seat, singing to the holiday songs playing on the radio.

It was starting to get dark by the time they drove up to the security gates in front of Paul's property. For the first time since she'd met him, the gates were wide open. She looked over at Sheila. "He never leaves his gate open. I hope everything is all right."

"Let's go check on him first."

Natalie gunned the engine up the steep driveway and followed the road up and around to Paul's house, the one with the faux castle exterior. "Wait here. I'll run and check."

"No way. I'm coming too."

They raced to the front door and Natalie knocked, then opened the door and listened. Hearing nothing, she called his name. "Paul? Are you okay?"

It was quiet.

"He doesn't hear that well," Natalie admitted. "I hate to scare him."

"Paul? Are you here? I noticed the gate was open. I wanted to be sure you're okay." She walked back to his office. The light was on, but the room was empty. As were the kitchen and his bedroom.

"I don't think he's here, Nat."

"That's odd. He doesn't really go anywhere. Did you notice his golf cart out front when we came up?"

"I wasn't really looking for it. I'll go check." Sheila walked outside. The golf cart was parked to the right of the front door.

She went back inside. "Natalie, the cart is here. Someone must have picked him up."

"I'll leave him a note to call me when he gets home. I'd hate to think he might have fallen on the property or something."

"That's a good idea."

Natalie and Sheila got back in the truck and cruised back over to the chapel.

As they turned off the main road, they could see the light from the little church. Light shone from every arch-shaped window, and floodlights lit up about twenty feet all around.

Men were moving about the building.

"He's here," Natalie said with a sigh of relief.

Paul stood outside wearing a wool peacoat directing Jesse and a bunch of young boys moving things on and off of a flatbed trailer.

"Hello, Natalie." His bony wrist twisted in the air. "We've been getting things ready for the Jacobs."

Sheila walked inside to see how much they'd done, while Natalie stopped to talk to Paul.

"Sheila?" It was Nelle, standing to the right of Jesse and helping fold lap quilts on a ladder propped against the wall. "This was such a wonderful idea to help the Jacob family. I hope you don't mind me jumping in. I had a whole cedar chest full of these that I've made over the past few years. This is the perfect time to be sure each family member has something to keep them warm. It's a big space. I hope it gets warm enough for those little babies' feet."

"I bought a couple of area rugs. I think that will help. Once we get furniture in, it'll warm up. Don't you worry," Sheila said.

"I told Jesse I'd like to send a meal to the family at the end of each Monday, Wednesday, and Friday after work. I can always make enough to spare."

"That's so generous. I know they'll appreciate that."

Nelle smiled wide. "I'm like that little drummer boy. My gifts ain't fancy, but they are from the gift God gave me, and I'm pleased as punch to share them."

"Y'all have been busy, Jesse." Sheila noted they'd taken all but three of the pews out, and now in the kitchen space they'd replaced the small dorm-size refrigerator with a full-size one too. "Nelle, did you do all this in the kitchen?"

"I did. Ain't a home without a kitchen ready to fill those little children's bellies. It wasn't anything. I had boxes of mismatched stuff in the back of the kitchen in storage. I'm glad to put it to good use."

"It was meant to be." And just then Sheila watched Paul and Natalie walk in and those boys started hauling in those big heavy rugs. "Excuse me," Sheila said. "Hey boys. Bring that heavy beast over here. Let me show you where to unroll that thing."

She helped them get it in just the right position, and then she showed them where to put the other two. One for under the table with the two pews they'd use for dining, and the other in the center of the bedroom space.

Once the rugs were in place, the chapel looked cozier already.

They had the electric fireplace set up and running, with the couch in front of it.

"You were right about using the third pew in here," said Natalie. "It'll be perfect. Do you think we can sit a television on top of that fireplace? Paul, what do you think? I hate to put holes in your walls."

Paul walked over and took a look. "Jesse can hang a television on the wall. That's no problem. There's nothing that man can't fix back to new. Don't worry about it."

"Are you sure you're feeling okay about this? I was worried when I saw the gate open. I know how finicky you are about it staying closed," Natalie said.

"I know I have been painfully aware of that gate, and honestly, I think that's gone on long enough. If that family is going to be living up here, the last thing we need is to worry about that gate. I think we'll all be just fine without it closed."

"Are you sure?"

"I am. It feels much more welcoming with it open." Paul put his arm around her. "I feel so alive. With you and friends, and now a young family getting on their feet. Helping them feels good. Thank you for inviting me to be a part of this."

She hugged his neck. "You are the best. I know where Jeremy got every single one of his good qualities."

Sheila teared up as she listened to her best friend talk about her late husband. Natalie and Jeremy were so in love. It had been heartbreaking to watch her navigate that loss, but the joy in seeing Natalie learn to trust Paul, Jeremy's grandfather, and accept him as her new family as she built a new life with Randy was heartwarming.

Randy came inside carrying his tools. "I could use some help unloading these bunk beds."

The young guys didn't hesitate. A moment later, they were hoisting mattresses and boxes.

In less than an hour with the extra hands, they had the two

bunk beds put together. Sheila had worked her magic placement and once they were able to explain it to Randy so that he understood, he used a staple gun to affix the bedspreads along the back side, and just like that, it was a separate sleeping space for the family.

"This looks amazing." Paul folded his arms. "I never could have pictured it, but it works."

"Once we get a Christmas tree in the corner and stockings on that mantel, it's going to be perfect."

Paul hugged her. "There is a significant difference between a house and a home, and that difference lies in the feeling of belonging. These things you're doing, they will make them feel like they belong here." He smiled. "I have to wonder if this wasn't the real purpose for this place all along. You make me look at things in a new way."

"Is it too much? Paul, I know you value your privacy."

"*Au contraire,* my dear. I thought I did, but this old heart of mine has never felt more alive since you happened into my life. I'm grateful for these changes, although I do feel quite out of step at times."

"You can lean on me," she said.

"I do. More than you realize, my dear."

Chapter Thirteen

Sunday morning, Sheila and Natalie drove over to Paul's before church to put up signs directing people to the chapel house. Paul's property had been off-limits to this town for so long. Now that it would be opened up, Natalie wanted to be sure people still gave Paul his privacy.

"Paul has been so gracious, but I don't want people to overwhelm him either. He's really used to his solitude," Natalie said.

"I can understand that." Sheila held the sign that read WEL- COME, JACOB FAMILY with an arrow to the turnoff to the gravel road.

They pushed the sign into the hard, dry ground, then rode up the driveway and set out two more. "I think that should do it?" Natalie straightened the sign.

"I'm sure people will respect his privacy," Sheila said. "This should help, though."

Randy arrived with a huge artificial Christmas tree in the back of his truck. "I hope it's okay that I brought this over. It was an old one at the sheriff's office."

"A fake tree? I thought those were taboo in this town," Sheila said.

"They are, sort of, but after what just happened to their house, I'm thinking eliminating any chance of a fire might be comforting," Randy explained.

"That's a really good point," Natalie said. "How tall *is* that tree?"

"Apparently, the old offices had really tall ceilings. They can't get but a six-footer in there now, so this one was in a closet in two pieces collecting dust."

"Doesn't matter. We have plenty of room for any size with the cathedral ceiling," Natalie said.

"It's pre-lit, so it won't take as long to decorate either. Fake trees are my thing," Sheila said. "I'll fluff it out so pretty no one will even be able to tell the difference."

"We can put it up right after church," Natalie said. "We were just on our way to pick up Paul now."

"I didn't want to add more to your plate," Randy said. "A couple of the deputies offered to come help me decorate. Y'all go on to church. We'll be done by the time you get back."

"You sure?" Natalie asked.

"Positive. You're not the only ones that want to help this family," he said.

"You're right, honey." She walked over and kissed him on the cheek. "Thank you, you sweet man."

"I'd do anything for you."

"You're the best." She turned and Sheila walked outside with her to go get Paul. When they drove up, he was already sitting out front on the bench by his front door, dressed in a suit and bright red holiday tie.

"He is *always* early," Natalie said to Sheila.

"No wonder you two get along so well. You're the same person."

"No," Natalie said. "He's even earlier than me. The first week I was driving for him, before I knew he was Jeremy's grandfather, he was waiting on me every time I came. It became like a battle of the wits for me to get here before he was outside waiting on me."

"That's hysterical, and you're so competitive. I bet it drove you nuts."

"It did." Natalie got out of the car to help Paul in.

"Have you been crying?" Paul asked Natalie.

She patted her fingers beneath her eyes. "It's okay. They were thankful tears."

"I suppose those are okay, then." He leaned on his cane and stood, still slightly stooped. They walked toward the Tesla, and Sheila hit the button for the falcon-wing back doors to lift.

"Oh my!" Paul bent forward, peering in the side window at Sheila. "Haven't seen a car with these doors in a while. You might not know, but I represented Clark Gable in Hollywood a lifetime ago. He drove a Mercedes with gull-wings, but I'm sure these have come a long way since then. This car is sexy as all get-out. If I were about forty years younger . . ."

Sheila burst out laughing. There was something about an old man talking about a sexy car that just absolutely tickled her funny bone. "Well, hop on in, superstar. I'm your chauffeur today."

He climbed in and Natalie hopped into the passenger seat. Sheila hit the button and all the doors closed themselves around them.

"Here we go, Pops!" Sheila pressed the accelerator, and they were off.

"Never have been in an electric car. I guess this is the new generation."

"Enjoy it while I'm here. I don't plan to keep it long. I only bought it because it was a good deal and I knew I could turn it into a profit."

"Well, done, Sheila. I respect sharp business minds."

"Thanks, Pops."

His face brightened. She had a feeling he liked the nickname. Which was good because she felt weird calling him Paul, even though that's what Natalie called him.

The church was decorated with fresh garlands on the railings and wreaths on the doors. Inside, each pew was decorated with a sprig of pine with a red poinsettia and bow. Sheila slid into the pew next to Natalie, who was nudging her before they even got seated.

"What?"

Natalie nodded toward the fifth pew from the front.

Sheila followed Natalie's line of sight, and there sat the entire Jacob family. Jack Jacob on the outside, Diane, all those kids, and Betty Jo on the other end. Jack's arms were bandaged, and so was the left side of his neck, but it was so good to see that Jack was recovering well enough to be out and about.

During the service, the pastor included prayers for the Jacob family and their recent loss, and following the offering they passed a coffee can around for extra donations for the family.

"It's the third Sunday of Advent, and we see that despite troubles, God has not deserted us and we are still blessed. I'm going to speak from Matthew 11, verses 2 to 11, today, but we've seen how, despite a terrible catastrophe, the Jacob family losing their home and everything in it, they were blessed. Jack is back on his feet and here with his family, and this community, you've come together to be the feet and hands, helping your neighbor. A blessing indeed."

A Christmas miracle.

After the service, they were getting into the car when Jack Jacob walked over. "Sir," he said to Paul. "I can't thank you enough for opening up your property to accommodate my family."

"Yes, you can. You just did." Paul took a stuttering step turn. "Thank these ladies. It was their idea. A very good one. They've worked tirelessly to make it quite wonderful for you. As have many others in this town. Good folks."

"Yes, sir."

He lifted a knobby finger. "I didn't realize you were the family in need. I've watched your family grow. Child by child. You don't see so many big families these days. I'm glad I could help you."

"I don't know how I'll ever repay you for your generosity, but I will. You can count on it, sir."

"You take care of your family. The rest, well, it has a way of all working out."

"Well, I just wanted to thank you. When they told us . . ." Diane had slipped under his arm, her eyes full of tears, but smiling as her husband spoke. "We couldn't believe it. Thank you."

"Yes, sir," Diane added. "Thank you so very much." She turned to Sheila and smiled.

Sheila felt like a schmuck driving the fancy car, embarrassed by the frivolity of it.

"And you, Sheila, you don't even know us. You have no idea how your support the night of the fire helped me through it all."

"'Tis the season, and treating your neighbor like family—

well, that took on a lot more meaning being there." Sheila felt a lump in her throat. "The news, television, it all desensitizes us to the true impacts the calamity has on people. At the core, we're all people, struggling to do what is right."

"We look forward to welcoming you tomorrow morning," Paul said. "Nelle told me she plans to have a big family breakfast ready for you all."

"I plan to go back to work," Jack said, "but Diane will be sure to save me some."

"You can count on it, honey."

Paul clapped a hand on Jack's back. "It heats up just fine. I know because Nelle seems to always be trying to fatten me up. I always have enough for another meal."

"That's good news." Jack extended his hand. "Well, I don't mean to keep you. I just wanted you to know how grateful we are and we're going to do our part around there. You let me know what I can do for you."

Paul looked a little embarrassed, waving to Diane and Jack as he ducked beneath the falcon-wing door and lowered himself into the back seat.

On the way home, Paul was quiet. Natalie flashed a concerned look, but Sheila wasn't sure it was a bad quiet. She'd been touched by the events since that night, and she sensed Paul was feeling the same way. She couldn't explain it herself, but she felt it to her core. "You're sort of a hero there, Pops."

"Nothing like that."

But she could see his eyes were a little glassy. Then he spoke up. "I was just thinking how profound it is that God can give you a second chance in life to make good on things maybe you didn't do so good the first time. I'm really happy." The pause was long, but finally Paul said, "I'm grateful I have the resources to share."

"I know exactly how you feel." Sheila sighed. There were a lot more important things in life she wasn't giving the appropriate attention to right now.

She felt a New Year's resolution coming on.

Chapter Fourteen

Sheila drove through the open gates of Paul's property. "Home again, home again!"

Natalie twisted around in her seat to talk to Paul. "We're going to check in at the chapel house and see what we need to get done. Would you like to stop in with us?"

"I'd like that very much." Paul looked pleased.

When they pulled up, Randy was walking out to his truck with empty boxes stacked four high.

"Are y'all done?" Natalie said as she got out of the car.

"Everything except for the thumbs-up from you, but I think it looks pretty good. Plus, Daisy had the idea of leaving it a little undone by leaving a box of plastic ornaments for the kids to hang, ya know, at kid height."

"That's a great idea. A way to make it their own."

"That's exactly what she said."

"Missed you at church." Natalie pecked him on the cheek.

"Missed you too. Good morning, Paul, Sheila," said Randy.

"Come on, let's see how they did." Natalie led the way. This once-stark building was now warm and inviting. In the corner, the Christmas tree looked even taller with the big star on top.

Randy said, "The star has colored lights too."

"Wow, over-the-top is perfect for kids."

The tree topper was huge, bedazzled, and a little hideous. Sheila hoped Randy wasn't going to be an awful help on Natalie's decorating team. They might have to vote him off the island to win. "Yeah, I'd pass on that, but you're right, perfect for the kids."

"It'll look pretty at night," Natalie said.

Randy rushed over to the cord. "It looks pretty now." With one touch it lit up. "Look!"

That star cast about a hundred colored dots across the white walls.

Even Sheila had to admit it was fun.

"Doris and her husband brought a dresser full of stuff earlier. I had them put it next to the bed. It fit perfectly." Randy led them over to check it out.

"Oh gosh, it's so cute," Sheila said.

Doris came from around the corner with Tucker on her heels. "I thought I heard voices when we came in," Doris said. "I think it turned out real cute too."

Sheila opened the drawer with the hand-painted sign on which "Annabelle" was surrounded by colorful ladybugs. "Oh my goodness, Doris. Look at these pajamas. They are so cute. I want a pair."

"I had so much fun shopping for each of them. The little ones are my favorite, though." She walked over and opened the blue drawer. "I painted this one myself with the little trucks for little Johnny. That little guy is gonna be all boy."

Little Johnny was the little boy Sheila had held in her arms that night.

"I couldn't resist." Doris held up the cutest blue onesie with THEY CALL ME NO! on the front of it. "I haven't bought baby clothes in way too long. Doesn't look like my son is going to give me any grandchildren, so I went wild. They have the cutest stuff now."

"This is great," Natalie said. "They will be able to settle right in."

"This is amazing. I didn't see it before, but wow. It's a home run." Tucker nodded with approval.

"Here. I have before pictures," Sheila said.

Tucker walked over and leaned over her shoulder to look at the pictures on her phone. Sheila slid through the befores, and then to the afters. "Holy cow. That's a huge transformation. I can't believe you did all this in just two days."

Sheila shrugged, smiling back at him. "It's my superpower. I'm in real estate, remember? Staging houses is what brings in the big bucks."

"Clearly, you're the wizard of them all. Now, if they can figure out how to get the money for their insurance deductible." His arm brushed hers as he turned to join the conversation with the others.

Sheila hitched a breath, touching where his strong hand had just brushed her, and the comment about the insurance deductible registered. "It's heartbreaking."

Doris was rattling on. "As part of my checklist, I also leave a clipboard for the family so they can jot down things they need as they realize it."

"Great idea. You are so organized. Tucker is lucky to have you to handle this stuff."

"Oh, I know how lucky I am," Tucker said.

"Well, you know every great fire chief knows how to pick a diverse team of people to fill all the gaps. As a whole, there's pretty much nothing our firehouse can't handle. It's a team effort."

"Yes, that's for sure," Tucker agreed.

"And humble too." Sheila found herself admiring that about her new friend Tucker.

Color rose in Tucker's cheeks. "I'm going to see if anyone needs some help."

As he walked out, Doris didn't hesitate. "I've never met anyone like him. He really has his stuff together. He's a kind, giving man. Wise beyond his years, or maybe an old soul. I don't know, but this town couldn't do without him."

"That's quite a compliment," Sheila said.

"Call 'em like I see 'em." Doris tucked the little outfit back in the drawer and held up the tiniest little Christmas socks Sheila had ever seen.

"Oh my gosh!" Sheila could feel her biological clock ticking. Too bad she'd never have the chance to have her own family. She'd never go through all that again. She still felt that all the energy she and Dan had put into the temperature-taking and baby-making rituals was part of the downward spiral of their marriage. "Precious. Absolutely precious."

People from the fire station and church were dropping in and out, and everything was coming together quickly.

Someone had completely outfitted the bathroom. They'd added a fun shower curtain, and clearly it was someone with kids because they'd even put down safety strips and added a container that could hold towels. Even a little step stool in front of the sink, painted like a turtle, that had padded steps that lifted for storage without the risk of pinching tiny fingers. *Maybe this is why I'm not a mom. I have no common mom sense. I hadn't even thought of that stuff.*

Nelle had single-handedly taken on getting the kitchen ready, and what she didn't already have, she was able to get people from church to chip in for or donate.

When Sheila walked back into the living room, Randy was telling Natalie that he and Jesse would be hanging the television tonight.

Natalie turned to Doris. "We'll be ready for them tomorrow morning. Whenever you're ready, I think anything else can be a work in progress."

"Not many people had ever been up on this hill, though," Doris said. "I hope that won't scare them a little."

"It turned out the Jacob family goes to the same church as Paul. They came up and spoke to him this morning. It's true he's been a recluse for years, but you know he had his problems too. Living behind those iron gates up in the castle house was his way of protecting his heart, but he's getting out more. I think this will be a really good thing for all of them."

"I'm sure you're right," Doris said. "This is exciting in so many ways. I'll coordinate bringing the whole family over at once. I think Jack is trying to go back to work tomorrow, but we can get the family over and settled and help them put together a nice family meal for when he gets home from work."

"I'll text you." Natalie walked Doris out to her car.

"Sheila, can you come help me with this?" Tucker scooted a big chalkboard to the door.

"Coming!" She ran over and held up the other end.

"It's not heavy, it's just so wide it's awkward to pick up and get through the doorway."

"I see that. I'll get this end and we can come in sideways." Sheila shimmied through the doorway first, and then Tucker took the weight and set it on the ground.

"You're a good partner. Ever consider joining the fire department? I'm always looking for people who think fast on their feet."

"I'll take that as a compliment, but I don't think I'm cut out to be a fireman."

"We call everyone a firefighter these days," he said. "And some of my best are women."

"Really, well alrighty then. I don't like to get dirty."

"I guess I could see that about you." He lifted her hands, turning them over. "Those nails would be history in a hurry, and your hands . . . they are softer than a child's. Very nice."

"Thank you." She retracted her hand, curling her fingers in. "I guess when you were a little boy, you always wanted to be a fireman."

"No. Not at all." Tucker crossed one long, lean leg over the other. "I grew up in a small mountain town, kind of like this one. Pine Creek. Nature and wilderness are what captured my imagination. As a kid, I dreamed of being a lumberjack."

"I can honestly say I've never known anyone who wanted to be a lumberjack."

"What? Not a Paul Bunyan fan?"

"Never yearned for a blue ox either."

He laughed. "I'd roam the woods exploring and climbing trees. Cutting dead limbs. Made my mom a wreck. She just knew

I was going to fall to my death by climbing trees. She kept encouraging me to think of something safer."

"So you chose to be a firefighter."

His laugh came out like a rattle of small stones. "Hardly. I think she was hoping I'd be a doctor or an accountant or something like that."

"Oh yeah, not exactly the outdoorsman type of career."

"Not at all." He crossed his arms, taking in a breath. "A raging fire swept through the area, destroying acres and acres of land near our house. We had to evacuate, and I remember begging my mom to let me stay and help put out that fire. Watching it burn my trees, that forest. It was part of my home. Part of me."

"How old were you?"

"Twelve. I watched the brave firefighters as we left with what we could grab. I remembered being struck by their courage and selflessness. They put their lives on the line to save our house. They didn't even know us. Seeing them so fearless and with no hesitation . . ." He tapped his fist on his chest. "It changed my outlook on life forever. I knew I wanted to be like them and help my community."

"That's an inspiring story."

"I joined the junior firefighters' program, but then we moved. I think my mom hoped I'd forget it about when we moved here and they didn't have a junior program."

"But you didn't?"

"I didn't. I read every book I could get my hands on and as the information became available on the internet, I'd print out reams of paper at school and bring them home to study at night."

"It was burning inside of you."

"I see what you did there. Funny." His eyes twinkled.

She touched her face, self-conscious.

"Yeah, so I convinced the fire chief to let me apprentice, and eventually I spent so much time around there they let me be a part of the team."

"Clearly, this is your calling. Everyone speaks very highly of you."

"Even you?" Tucker narrowed his eyes.

"Me?" Sheila swallowed visibly and shook her head. "No, all I know is you make a great turkey jerky."

"You tried it? My jerky?"

"Of course, it was a Christmas gift," she said.

Tucker lifted his chin. "Technically, it was only a Holiday Warmup gift."

"Oh goody." Sheila clapped her hands. "Am I on the real Christmas list too?"

He looked doubtful. "Have you been good?"

"Very good," she insisted, with wide eyes, and maybe a little bit of a pout.

"You said that with quite a naughty look."

"I'd never." She fluttered her eyelashes. "How dare you?"

That cracked them both up, and they were still laughing when Natalie and Randy walked in.

"Looks like you two are getting along," he said, teasing Tucker.

Natalie looked like she was already planning their wedding.

"We're just talking," Sheila insisted.

"Sure you are," Natalie said.

"I've got to run," Tucker said. Thanks for all y'all have done. The place looks great."

"You're welcome, but we couldn't have done it without Doris," said Sheila.

"I thank my lucky stars she came out of retirement to help me. You don't have to remind me."

Sheila stood there as Tucker walked out. Maybe a moment too long, because Natalie nudged her to get her attention and then gave her a snarky laugh while muttering "We're just talking."

"We were. What?" Sheila grabbed a broom and tidied up the leaves and dirt that had been tracked in, while Natalie put a batch of slice-and-bake cookies in the oven.

An hour later, everything was in place. She had to admit it was one of the best staging jobs she'd been a part of, and it was all childproof. No breakables. Plenty of places to tuck things away.

A play area was created by putting down a whimsical colorful rug with a road and town pattern on it that the kids could congregate on. And to help keep the small place uncluttered, a huge basket in which to hide all the toys away in a hurry.

Randy had come up with the idea of adding hanging rods made out of half-inch metal pipe to the end of the bunk beds for makeshift closet space. It had really turned out cute.

By nine o'clock on Sunday evening, everything was as done as it could be in the temporary housing on Paul Grandstaff's property.

Natalie closed the door behind them and left the single key on a "J" key chain hanging in the door for the family. An extra set was on the kitchen counter with a welcome note and a plate of cookies they'd just taken out of the oven.

With any luck, there'd still be a sweet, welcoming hint of home in the air when they arrived.

Chapter Fifteen

The next morning, Sheila and Natalie caught up on the latest goings-on in Chestnut Ridge over tea with Orene. Orene told them about the upcoming Christmas pageant and all the hullabaloo over the school play. Apparently, the school forbid live sheep in the auditorium. The director was up in arms and threatening to cancel.

"And Mr. Thatcher worked off-off-Broadway for three years. We were so lucky to have him come to direct the Christmas pageant this year. But now, you won't believe it, they are refusing to let them have real sheep on stage. They were going to be in a cute pen, and they promised to clean up, but no. Now Mr. Thatcher is threatening to cancel the whole production."

"That is terrible. After the children have practiced. Why can't they just have some of the kids wear woolly sheep outfits," Sheila said.

Orene shot her a look. "Why? Because that ruins the authenticity."

Sheila shrank back. She clearly did not understand the importance of this play to the community.

Thankfully, Sheila's phone vibrated right then. She snatched her phone off the table. "It's Doris. They are getting ready to take the family to the chapel house."

Natalie called Paul to let him know. "Would you like to come with us to welcome them?" she asked, raising her hand in the air and crossing her fingers. "Wonderful. We'll see you shortly." She hung up with a pleased look. "I can't believe how excited he is."

"That's wonderful," Orene said. "He needs the joy of others around him. You've been so good for him. Now, Chestnut Ridge will do the rest."

"It's one of the best things about living here."

Sheila didn't have to worry about Natalie anymore. It was clear this place was bringing out the best in her.

"You belong here," Orene said to Natalie. "You were born to be a part of this town."

"I believe that."

"You too, Sheila."

Sheila laughed. "You're sweet, but you know I'm a city girl."

"That's what they all say. At first." Orene's grin curled up at the edges.

"Are you coming with us?" Sheila asked her.

"No, thank you. I'm expected at the stadium to help with the final setup of the Christmas Tree Stroll. There's so much to do before teams start checking in. Y'all have everything under control. I'll pay the Jacobs a visit later in the week when they get settled in."

"We'll see you tonight at the stadium then. We've got to lock in our theme early." Natalie gave Orene a wink. "I heard that from someone with years of experience."

"Oh yes. Two trees with the same theme doesn't work. They'll make you go back and tweak it a little if it sounds too much like another, and trust me, there is a list of others who want to enter."

"Why is that? I mean, it's just bragging rights, isn't it?"

"Pretty much," said Orene with a shrug, "but there are some side benefits to winning, like your picture on the front page of the newspaper, free tickets to the Ruritan Club Valentine's Day dinner, and seats at the county fair concert, to name just a few."

"Natalie has been keeping the best part of this stroll from me. I might have to renegotiate. You know, Tucker *was* trying to woo me over to his team."

"See what you've done now, Orene. I'll never get her to concentrate on the project with her head full of possible stardom."

"A girl can dream," said Sheila.

"Are you coming with me or not?" Natalie teased.

"I'm coming, and I'm bringing my coffee."

Orene swooshed them out the door. "Fine. Just bring back my cup."

"Yes ma'am. You know where I'm living." Sheila raced out the door. Staying with Orene was like being back in college, and she was the Sorority House Mom.

Sheila hopped into the passenger seat of Natalie's truck. "I can't wait to see it again this morning. I want to take some more pictures in the daylight before everyone gets there."

"I was just thinking the same thing."

Natalie drove over to Paul's. "It's going to take some getting used to, this gate being opened. My heart kind of jumps every time I see that it's not closed."

"You'll get used to it. Especially when it's raining and you don't have to lean out the window to punch in the code."

"That's true."

Natalie parked next to Jesse's truck at the front of the chapel house.

"Do you smell that?"

"Nelle's got to be in there cooking. It smells like sausage."

"It smells like heaven if you ask me, but I guess any remnants of those chocolate chip cookies we so carefully timed at the end of the night was a waste of time." She pulled the right door open and stepped inside. Christmas music filled the space. She poked her head into the kitchen, where Nelle swayed and hummed along with the music as she stirred.

"Pray tell, Nelle, what are you fixing, and please tell me there's enough for a few extra mouths."

Nelle spun around with a smile. "I never met a bunch I couldn't feed. There's plenty. Hope you like homemade sausage gravy and biscuits."

"I'm sure I do."

"Who doesn't?"

Jesse walked in and pecked Nelle on the cheek. "My gal is the best cook in the county."

"County is all? You better back up on that." She swatted him with the spoon, leaving a mess of gravy on his sleeve.

"She don't fight fair." He swept his finger into the blob on his sleeve and licked it. "I don't care. It tastes like seconds, babe."

"I'll second you, you rascal." Nelle half chased him from the kitchen.

Sheila walked through the chapel. The transformation by the light of day was nothing short of amazing. Like an episode of one of those extreme home redecorating shows.

And although they'd started with a good plan, as different

people added their thoughtful touches, that's when the place really came together.

Sheila had serious doubts Paul Grandstaff would want to subdivide and sell, especially with the family cemetery so close to it, but if he wanted to Airbnb this cute place he could make a bundle.

Clicking off pictures, she hoped she'd recall the feeling of this moment forever.

When she walked back into the kitchen, Nelle was alone and gently lifting hot golden biscuits from a well-worn cookie sheet. She carefully placed two on a piece of wax paper and folded it up.

"Are you making a little snack for Jesse? Y'all are really sweet together."

"He's a good man," Nelle said. "These are for Grandstaff, though. He's a sucker for my biscuits."

"How long have you known Paul, Nelle?"

"Years and years."

"Did you grow up here?"

"No. You know I'm from New Orleans. I grew up in Louisiana. Never thought I'd leave neither, but when Hurricane Katrina came rumbling through back in 2005, I lost everything. My house. My cat. Even my dear husband. We never did find his body. It was tough times."

"Oh my gosh! I didn't know. I'm so sorry."

"Yeah, well, it was bad for lots of folks, not just me. I'd already been through one hurricane and we rebuilt. I couldn't do it again. Not without my sweet husband, so I packed up and headed to North Carolina to live with my cousins."

"You have family in North Carolina?"

"I did at the time. Most of them have passed on now. I never made it there."

"What happened?"

"I was driving an old Chevy sedan." Her laugh was hearty. "Floors rusted out. Sucked gasoline like a kid with a Slurpee on a summer day. I'd about spent all my money on gas by the time I made it to Chestnut Ridge, and darn if my car just decided it wouldn't go one more mile."

"Oh no. On top of losing your home. That's horrible. So you just stayed."

"Well, it was a little more than that. I was stranded in this town, and that was the day I met Jesse and Paul. I cooked for Paul to earn some money to get my car back on the road."

"That worked out for you."

"It did, and before I knew it, Grandstaff offered me a little house on Main Street to live in as part of my pay. Then, he suggested I reopen the lunch counter at the hardware store. With his help, and Jesse's carpentry skills, we did, and the rest is history."

"And you've never regretted staying in Chestnut Ridge?"

"Never. This town might be small, but it's big in heart. You haven't figured that out yet?"

"I kind of *have* noticed that."

"Not like anyplace else I've ever known." Nelle leaned in. "Everyone acts like this is such a big deal for Grandstaff to be offering up this place for that family, but between you and me, he's been helping others for years. People before me too. I'm just saying. He doesn't do it for the recognition. He does it because it's right."

"Really?" Sheila wondered if Natalie knew that about him. "That's interesting."

"He's a very good man."

"Well, I'm glad to hear that, because my best friend needs good people around her."

"Then you should move yourself up here and join in the fun, girl," Nelle said with a lift of her brow.

"I'm not the small-town type."

"You might find that there are opportunities here that you don't have in the city." Nelle went back over to the pot and gave it a big old stir.

Sheila had turned to walk out of the kitchen, her mind still processing everything Nelle had just said, when she heard Tucker come in the through the front door with the Jacob family.

She couldn't wait to see their reaction, but for now just listening was going to have to do. Her heart pounded, excited for them to have some good news.

"We're going to stop right here for a minute," Sheila could hear Tucker say from the hallway outside the kitchen. "We're missing one person."

Natalie scooted into the kitchen and grabbed Sheila's hand. "This is so exciting." She could hear Diane asking her mother, Betty Jo, who was missing.

At that moment, another vehicle pulled up out front. Natalie looked out the kitchen window. "It's a construction company truck," she stage whispered to Nelle and Sheila. They all gathered closer to the window. On the passenger side, Jack stepped out of the car.

Sheila's heart lifted. "I bet Tucker arranged that."

"Be just like him," Nelle said.

Sheila eased over to where she could catch a peek of the doorway just as Jack ran into the house.

"I didn't miss it, did I?" Jack asked.

"We wouldn't have let you," Tucker said.

Diane wrapped her arms around Jack. "Honey, I'm so glad you could be here. I can't even believe all of this."

"Wait until you see what your neighbors have pulled together for you," Tucker said. "As you know, Paul Grandstaff has generously offered this place for your family to use as your home for the next six months."

"It's so peaceful," Jack said.

"It won't be for long." Diane nodded while mouthing a headcount. "Between my littles and Bananas, there's rarely a peaceful moment."

"Maybe it will be different here," Tucker said. "A few days ago this was a chapel. Empty except for a few pews up front, but a swift and adept team made up from members of our community turned this place into one of those 'move that bus' home-improvement moments. I was shocked when I came to see it last night. Welcome to your new temporary home."

Tucker stepped aside.

But no one moved.

Jack lifted little Johnny from Diane's hip and took a tentative step forward. The rest of the children piled close to Diane as she followed, squeezing Jack's biceps, with Bananas looking a little worried and hanging close to their heels.

Nelle must have felt the tension too, because she scooched closer to Sheila.

One more step and Diane and Jack were peering into the kitchen where Nelle, Sheila, and Natalie stood.

"Surprise!" Nelle yelled. "I've got breakfast ready for

everyone! I hope you brought your appetite." She spread her thick arms out, revealing the words HOME SWEET HOME on her red and white apron.

Jack laughed. "You know how to make a man happy, Miss Nelle."

"This is your kitchen," Nelle said. "I won't be in here all the time, but my small gift to you is that every day I'm cookin' at the counter for the next month, Jesse and I will be dropping off the meal of the day, enough for you and your whole family, so you'll come home to a hot meal, and your sweet missus can take a little break from the kitchen."

"Nelle, that's so kind of you." Tears streamed down Diane's cheeks.

Betty Jo hugged her daughter. "Nelle, that is so generous." She sniffled back a tear too.

"Honey, don't be wasting those tears on my food. Wait until you see this place. Show 'em, girls." Nelle pushed Natalie and Sheila forward. "These two have been busy as bees."

"Sure." Sheila hopped into open-house mode. "As Nelle said, this is your kitchen, and Diane, you'll be able to not only fix meals, but see the children right out these two windows while you prepare them. Maybe not a perk right now when it's as cold as all get-out, but this spring, they'll be chasing butterflies and bullfrogs and that'll be heaven. Follow me."

Sheila and Natalie walked out of the kitchen and the Jacob family stepped aside.

"The bathroom is across the hall. It's tiny, but well appointed. I thought that was a great idea. And that stool is adorable! I swear I'd buy a dozen of them if I knew where to find them."

Jack shook his head. "I made that." He swept a finger beneath his nose. "I know exactly who outfitted this bathroom. I made that stool for their baby shower six years ago."

"Well, you and I are going to talk, Jack. I've got a side job for you to make me a few," Sheila said.

"Happy to."

When everyone paraded into the sanctuary, which didn't look like one at all anymore, soft Christmas music was playing. The long table, borrowed from the fire station, had been covered in a red tablecloth and set for breakfast. The mishmash of different-patterned plates looked welcoming. In the center of the table, another plate was filled with red, green, and gold plastic ornaments.

"This is unbelievable," Diane said.

Betty Jo cried out, "Look at the Christmas stockings on the fireplace!"

"Will Santa know where we are?" asked Avery.

"Absolutely. Look, he already put stockings up for each of you."

"Christmas tree!" The children jumped and squealed, then stood in awe of the colorful tree and the lights dancing off the walls, and Bananas raced around the room, finally coming to a stop in front of the bunk beds.

"How are we ever going to thank you?" Diane said.

Then someone spoke as they walked into the building.

"You'll take good care of each other and enjoy the holidays. Interrupt worry with gratitude. Everything is going to be okay." Paul Grandstaff stood in the doorway. "Merry Christmas."

"Mr. Grandstaff, I can't believe . . . This is so generous."

"No, ma'am. I'm grateful to be able to do this small part, but your friends, the community, my granddaughter and her friends, they've given you the real gift of turning it into a home. Well done." Paul Grandstaff clapped his hands. "I look forward to feeling the good energy of your family over here."

"You'll get plenty of that," Diane said with a laugh.

Jack walked over and shook his hand again. "From youngest to oldest, this is Johnny, and we've got Avery, Jimmy, and Annabelle, who is my oldest and best helper."

Paul leveled his gaze on Annabelle. "How old are you?"

"Eight."

"I was the oldest in my family too," Paul said. "That can be a lot of responsibility. You remind me so much of my daughter when she was your age. Have you ever ridden a horse?"

"No sir."

"Ever patted his soft nose?"

"No sir."

"I can't wait to introduce you to my very best friend." He shifted his gaze to Jimmy, the second-oldest child. "You too, young man." Paul straightened. "And I have chickens who lay more eggs than I know what to do with. I bet you all could gather eggs for me once in a while."

"Okay!" the kids said, looking to Jack for approval.

"Sounds like home. These kids know how to collect eggs. We had a few chickens at our house. They flew the coop when the fire started, but I reckon they'll happen back, eventually."

"Yes. I'm sure they will. You all go on with your tour." Paul backed up and took a seat at the long table. "I just wanted to welcome you myself."

"Thank you."

Sheila showed them around the rest of the place, and the older kids all climbed into the bunk beds.

"Mom, look! It's so pretty." Annabelle was delighted when she recognized her own name and the painted ladybugs on the front of the chest Doris had brought over.

"This is amazing. It's too much."

"No, it's barely a start and we realize that," Tucker said. "But it's a soft place to land while you figure everything out."

Nelle banged a metal spoon against a pot. "Y'all come get this breakfast. I'm putting it on the table before my gravy turns to wallpaper paste."

The older kids moved to the table to eat, while Diane moved the baby to a high chair to feed him while the other adults took plates to the couch and pew in the living area.

Just about everyone who had helped set everything up had shown up by now, and there was really no better way to turn this little chapel into a home than to enjoy fellowship with neighbors and friends.

The tentative, nervous air that had filled the place when the family first walked in had quickly lifted. Children chased each other around the Christmas tree, and one of the kids had already crawled into one of the bunk beds to take a nap.

"We're going to be okay," Sheila heard Diane whisper to Jack, which choked her up.

Jack and his coworker ate, and then Jack said his goodbyes. "I've got to get to work. My boss was kind enough to surprise me by letting this guy bring me here for this, but I need to get to work. Kids, I'll see you tonight." The older children ran over and lined up in a row to give kisses. He blew a kiss to Diane as he walked out.

"Oh my gosh, my heart absolutely aches for them. I'm so glad we were able to do this," Natalie said to Sheila.

"I know."

Tucker walked over to Sheila and Natalie. "You ladies have really done something here."

"Happy to do it," Sheila said.

"Not exactly how you planned to spend your Christmas vacation, I guess," he said to Sheila.

"Better than I could have imagined."

"Good. Good to hear." Tucker leaned in. "Jack told me that their insurance deductible is twenty thousand dollars."

"Oh gosh. So many people are doing those high-deductible policies to keep the prices down." She'd promised Diane she wouldn't say anything, so she didn't. Had Jack asked Tucker to keep it quiet too? "Do they have the money?"

"No, not even close." Tucker grimaced. "Who has that kind of cash lying around? Not many folks around here."

"Especially young parents, with so many kids."

"Right."

"Maybe I can help you with some fundraising ideas," Sheila said. "We've participated in so many. There are lots of creative things we could do online to pull money from other areas. It's not likely that it would be easy to get that kind of money donations in this small town."

"I know."

"There are alternatives. Even if they couldn't afford to rebuild, they could sell the land and then reinvest in the purchase of a home." Sheila could probably help them sort through the options.

"Their house was on family land. They've put a lot of time into renovating that place. It's really sad."

"I know it wouldn't be ideal, but there may not be many options. Let me know if they'd like me to brainstorm with them. It's what I do."

"Thanks. Hey, so, I, uh, have to do the preliminary inspection for the Christmas Tree Stroll later today, but if y'all are getting started on your tree tonight, I'd like to buy you a hot chocolate."

Natalie stepped up behind him. "Are you trying to get a peek at our tree plans?"

"No. I was just asking your friend here if I could buy her a hot chocolate tonight."

"Mm-hmm. While we're decorating?" She wagged her finger at him. "I happen to know the hot chocolate is free."

Sheila gasped. "Oh, I see how you are. You're awfully sneaky. I didn't even consider an honorable man like the fire chief might try to steal our winning ideas." She gave him an exaggerated stink eye, trying to hold back a laugh.

"And using the free hot chocolate as bait." Natalie shook her head with a tsk-tsk.

"Well, 'buying' was a loose interpretation of it. I'll tip the guy." Tucker looked at Sheila. "Really. They work for tips."

"I'd take a hot chocolate, but I'll meet you at the hot chocolate stand." Sheila tried to give him a stern look, but she couldn't keep a straight face. "I can't take a chance of you peeking at our top-secret Christmas tree."

"No problem. I'll text you."

"Perfect."

He started to walk away, and then turned. "Umm, seriously, you know we can all see each other's progress every day just by walking around, right?"

"I've heard it can be a fatal flaw, however," Sheila explained. "Orene said folks get in a panic and overdecorate when they think others are better. A sure way to l-o-s-e."

"It happens," Tucker said, seeming to agree. "She's wise, that one."

"We have an excellent plan that we intend to stick to, and I believe we will be a contender for the big win."

"I like confidence in a woman," he said.

"Well, then you're going to fall in love with Sheila," Natalie jumped in. "She has more confidence than anyone I've ever known."

Sheila nudged Natalie and said, grumbling the words through a mortified smile, "Stop. You're embarrassing me."

"You look cute with red cheeks," Tucker said as he walked out.

She felt like jumping into the air the way Rudolph did in the old animated TV special when the pretty doe, Clarice, said he was cute. Waiting until Tucker was clear out of earshot, she turned to Natalie and grabbed her hands. "He thinks I'm cute."

Chapter Sixteen

Sheila's mind was all over the place the rest of the day. When Tucker spoke to her, the way he held her gaze was intoxicating. She yearned for it, and she found herself searching for ways to bump into him. She couldn't remember the last time she was so excited at just the thought of seeing someone again.

Natalie had texted her a list of things to pick up for the tree decorating tonight. She might have been able to find some of the things at the hardware store in town, but while searching online she saw there was a Hobby Lobby in Christiansburg, Virginia, less than an hour away. Chances were better she'd find cute stuff there, plus she might be able to pick up a couple of Christmas presents while she was at it.

And hopefully, some retail therapy would take her mind off of Tucker.

Driving the Tesla through the winding mountain roads was fun. It hugged the turns like a sports car, but she was scared to push it too fast.

It was cold out, but the sun and blue sky made up for it. She put her sunglasses on, and her mind drifted back to Tucker and getting hot chocolate with him tonight.

Why was she allowing herself to get so excited over someone who lived so far from her, and yet, what was the harm in having a little fun? It was just hot chocolate, after all. She daydreamed, thinking about how fun it would be if it ended up snowing. She pictured them making snow angels in a blanketed field of fresh powder.

From the looks of the sky, there was zero chance of that tonight.

Being single at the holidays sucked. Spending Christmas here in Chestnut Ridge with Natalie was already more fun than she could've hoped for. She'd expected Christiansburg to be a small town, but it was actually quite populated. Not only did it have an adorable Main Street, but there was lots of brand-name shopping here, and there were plenty of restaurants.

A sushi restaurant caught her eye, so she swerved into the parking lot and treated herself to a roll and a pot of hot tea before shopping.

The store was just up the street, and luckily, she was able to find everything on the list Natalie had given her. Natalie had texted her pictures of several birdhouses she'd hand-painted for the tree as an example of colors and theme. She was such a talented artist.

Sheila sifted through boxes of wrapping paper to find something just right not only for her gifts to Natalie and Randy, but for the children's gifts she planned to order for the Jacobs.

She couldn't believe her luck when she found a pretty white holiday wrapping paper decorated with snowy trees filled with bright red cardinals, and that gave her an idea. She tossed two rolls of wrapping paper into the buggy and raced off for the floral section.

There are always a few spots in a real tree that are less than perfect. Sometimes even a big gaping hole. It was why she preferred an artificial tree. But rules being what they were, she should be prepared for the imperfection, and she had the perfect idea.

She could fashion an oversize bird's nest and adorn it with a decorative ribbon to correct the problem. It could be a gorgeous solution.

Hadn't she read somewhere that having a bird's nest in your live tree was good luck? She typed it into the search bar on her phone.

Legend has it that prosperity will come to any home that finds a bird's nest nestled among the branches of the family Christmas tree.

"I knew it." She'd thought she'd read that in a magazine once. It made some sense, mostly because it seemed highly unlikely that a bird's nest could make it all the way from the woods to the retailer and through the tree being wrapped in a net and toted home and into someone's house, but either way, there it was in black-and-white.

Maybe it will bring us good luck.

She found some pretty holiday picks while searching the floral section, but she was just about ready to resort to hot glue and pine straw to make a nest when a woman walked over.

"Can I help you find something?" the clerk asked.

"Maybe. I was trying to find a bird's nest, or something to make one. What do you think?"

"We actually have some really cute ones, unless you have your heart set on making one from scratch."

"Take me to the pre-made ones." Sheila followed her over to the table decorations. There were several of the little round ones, even some with eggs in them, but then she saw the perfect one. It was large, probably eight inches across, which could really help fill that space, and it was made with pine straw, twigs, and branches.

"This is perfect," Sheila said. "I want to tuck it into the sparse spot in a Christmas tree to fill it up."

"That's a great idea. You could even maybe set it on some colorful ribbon and insert a few feathers to draw attention to it. Feathers will be over on the craft aisle. Ribbon is over that way."

"You're the best. This is going to be so cute. Thank you," Sheila said.

"You're welcome. Good luck."

"Merry Christmas," Sheila said as she rushed over to the craft aisle with excitement. *Merry Christmas, indeed.*

She walked a little straighter, gathering all the goodies she could find, then stumbled across packages of twelve four-inch birdhouses. Raw wood, they could be painted to balance the colors needed on the tree. They'd be sort of like what Natalie had made, although in miniature and probably not near as pretty; she could do something simple. A must-have.

At the checkout she added a set of paints and paintbrushes, and glitter. *Is there such a thing as too much sparkle at Christmas?*

An hour later, she was back at Orene's house with all the goodies laid out across her bed. She divided everything into piles: "Mine," "Natalie's," and "Projects."

Then she sat down at the table in the corner of her room and started painting the birdhouses, copying the designs on the ones Natalie had sent her the pictures of.

Sheila opted for matching colors and then doing simple holly leaves and red-dot berries, with a little glitter along the edges.

They dried fast over the radiator.

Her phone rang just as she was placing them neatly in a box.

"Hey, Sheila. What are you doing?"

"Can't tell you. It's a surprise."

"For me?" Natalie's voice rose.

"Sort of. I was getting ready to drive over to your place."

"You can*not* drive that car on the dirt road. I'll come get you. I was just heading back from Paul's house anyway. Be there in a minute."

"Perfect timing. I'll be right down." She packed the birdhouses. It took her two trips to get everything downstairs.

Natalie was walking up the steps when Sheila opened the front door.

"Hey, are you ready?" Natalie asked.

"Yep. Here." Natalie shoved huge Hobby Lobby bags toward Natalie. "And there's more." She carried a box and a bag out to the truck.

"This is way more stuff than I had on the list."

"Sure is, but I can't wait for you to see it all. I found some great stuff."

"I picked up barbecue from the Trout and Snout so we could eat before we go over to the high school."

"Good. I had sushi for lunch, and that is gone. I'm starving."

"You are in the best mood." Natalie looked over at her and then giggled. "Is this still because Tucker thinks you're cute?"

"It did perk me up. I'm not gonna lie."

"He's pretty cute too."

"Oh stop. I live in Richmond. He lives here. It's nice, absolutely, but that's all it can ever be." But the excitement couldn't be suppressed, because her heart was already racing. "He is really good-looking, kind, smart. Ugh. I can't stop thinking about him. I have to stop!"

"Whatever."

"Don't whatever me." Sheila refused to have the conversation and was thankful when Natalie turned down the dirt road. The noise under the truck tires made it nearly impossible to have a conversation.

When they turned toward the cabin, Sheila was delighted to see that Natalie had put pine roping along the bridge railing. "It looks so festive."

"Thank you. I've done a few things."

Natalie carried the bag from Trout & Snout over the bridge, and Sheila left everything else in the truck. She'd show Natalie that stuff tonight.

At the edge of the bridge, a garden flag with a wintry scene and Christmas cardinals hung from a fancy black wrought-iron hanger.

"That is so pretty."

"Thank you. I painted it. It's similar to a design in the note cards I just released last month. I'm in a bird phase."

"I see that." She knew Natalie would flip over the wrapping paper she'd just bought. It was so hard for her to keep secrets, though.

"I've got a ton of solar lights, but Randy and Tucker dug a trench and ran electricity to the bridge for me over the summer. I have Christmas lights draped along the pine roping on the bridge. It looks so pretty at night."

"I forgot how long the walk was from the bridge to the cabin."

"It's not so bad once you get used to it." The path they walked along was well worn now. All of a sudden there was a woof, followed by a happy tail-wagging beagle running their way. "Buzz. There's my boy."

"You don't have him in a pen?"

"Why? He won't run off. He knows this is the best place in the world to live."

"Except for the lack of shopping, I'm beginning to agree."

Natalie's head swung around. "I can't believe those words came out of your mouth."

"I happen to have had a wonderful shopping day."

"Where?"

"In Christiansburg. I decided I had time to go a little further than the corner to pick up the goods, and I'm so glad I did. Not only did I need the retail therapy, but you are going to be very happy with some things I found to doll up our birdsy, woodsy Christmas tree."

"You mean our Feathered Friends Home for the Holidays tree?"

"Cute name. It's perfect."

"I think so too." Natalie pushed open the door, and Buzz zipped past both of them and went straight to his water bowl. "I don't know why he won't drink water outside."

"Maybe you're spoiling him a little. He looks pretty comfortable in here." Buzz had already wiped his chin on the carpet and hopped onto the couch, his tail thumping with excitement.

"Guilty." Natalie walked over and dropped a kiss on top of the little beagle's nose. "How can you not? He's adorable."

"He is. I just wish you and Buzz lived closer. I miss you."

"I know, that's the only downside. I promise I'll do better about visiting you next year."

"Good. I'd like that, because I have visited you the last three times." Sheila walked into the kitchen. "This place looks so homey now. You're beginning to make me feel like a slacker. I don't think anything has changed at my house since you left town."

"I'm sure that's not true."

"No. It's the truth. The updated cabinets are nice. Did you replace the flooring in here too?"

"No, those are the original hardwood floors. I did have someone come in and sand them and put a layer of whatever that shiny stuff is on them. They look good, don't they?"

"Yes. Very. It's very comfortable. Doesn't even really look like a hunting cabin anymore. What did you do with all those horrible deer heads that were hanging on the walls?"

Natalie rolled her eyes. "It took some doing, but I got a few of the guys to take them back, to the dismay of their wives. Then Tucker told me about a nature conservation center that would take the rest to display. I felt like I was on some kind of heist driving a truckload of deer heads up there, but they were excited. I was prepared to just donate them, but they insisted on giving me a lifetime membership, a sweatshirt, and two coffee mugs. A win-win."

"You turned this whole little area that was wasted space into a really nice and functional artist's nook. It's so colorful."

"I'm loving working on the note cards. I've done a few full-size paintings. That's one of them." She pointed to a watercolor of the mountains in spring with mountain laurel in bloom and wildflowers in the fields.

"I can almost hear the water in that creek," Sheila said.

"Cherish Creek. The one that runs under my bridge over there. It's the view out that way."

"Natalie, you're just getting better and better. You've really found your gift."

"It feels like I have. Is that weird?"

"No. It's a blessing. I'm happy for you." It brought Sheila joy to see her best friend at peace. "Nelle was telling me that Paul helped her when she first came to town. Did you know that?"

"I've never heard anyone talk about it. Paul's not the sort to brag or take credit, so I'm not surprised I hadn't heard. He's a complex man, but he's fair and kind. If I live to be the kind of person he is, then I can be proud."

"I think you can be proud already, my friend."

"Thank you."

"Yeah, well according to Nelle, Paul giving up the chapel for the Jacobs didn't seem all that out of character to her. He gave her a job and a place to live when she first came to Chestnut Ridge."

"I didn't know that."

"He seemed excited about those children, didn't he?"

"He did. I was surprised he showed up for the reveal. Them being there could bring a lot more to his life."

"For sure. Seeing the world through the innocence of children brings perspective to this crazy, overcomplicated world."

"We all need that."

"We do. Tucker was good with them too."

"Wondered how long it would take you to get the conversation to him."

"Oh stop, Natalie."

"Tucker is very well respected around here. He was the youngest firefighter in Chestnut Ridge. He started as a volunteer. I guess that's why he's not only such an advocate for the volunteer program, but funds the junior firefighters' club himself."

"That's admirable."

"It is. He worked his way up to captain, and he won the attention of the town's authorities, and was one of the first paid firefighters in this town. I think it was his calling. Tucker accepted the offer with gratitude and it wasn't long after that he was appointed as the fire chief. People think the world of him."

"I guess everyone has a story."

"I wish I'd known him when Jeremy was alive," said Natalie. "I feel like I missed out on so much."

"We can't go backward."

They gathered the boxes that Natalie had filled for the Christmas Tree Stroll, and then Natalie took her out back to the porch to see all the birdhouses she'd painted.

Colorful birdhouses in a kaleidoscope of colors hung from the handrail all the way around the back porch.

"Ta-da," Natalie said.

"Wow, it looks like a lot more when they are all hanging like that." Sheila stopped to count them. "Is the tree big enough for all of these?"

"I may have gone overboard, but figured I'd err on the side of too many. We can give the extras away as gifts."

"Good idea. Every single one is different. I'm having trouble picking my favorite." Sheila took a moment to really look closely at each one. "I can't believe the detail. I think I like the ones where you painted the lifelike birds on them the best, but the ones with the jingle bells are cute too. I want to live in one."

"I know. I think the green one is my favorite."

Sheila liked the way Natalie had glued tiny battery-operated lights around the front, and the little stockings with Wynken, Blynken, and Nod on them. "We're totally going to win. They are all fabulous." She turned and hugged Natalie. "You are so talented."

"Thank you."

"I have a surprise for you later, but it's not much compared to these."

"I'm sure whatever you did is wonderful. Randy made a tree topper. He wants to surprise me too."

"So, I guess we should head over to the high school now."

"Let's go." Sheila helped Natalie collect all the birdhouses, placing them in a big red plastic tub so they could put them in the back of the truck.

"One of these days I might have to put in a bigger bridge so I don't have to hike everything over to the truck," Natalie said as she and Sheila each carried one end of the big tub.

"That would be a priority for me, but you've never minded walking."

Natalie reached down and patted Buzz on the head. He knew to stop and sit when she hit the bridge. He shifted from paw to paw, hoping for an invitation, but when one didn't come, he lay down.

They loaded everything in the truck and headed to town. It was already getting dark, and every light post along Main was lit up with a giant set of silver bells that blinked, making them look like they were ringing.

"It looks so festive." Sheila peered out the window. "Look at all the pretty window decorations too. I didn't notice them in the daylight."

"The Christmas spirit is alive and well in Chestnut Ridge," Natalie said. "I told you this is a magical place."

"It certainly is." Sheila's mind wandered back to when she was just a kid and Dad would ride them around to look at all the lights in the neighborhoods. Something so simple had felt as if her parents had stopped the world and transported them into their own private snow globe.

"If only it would snow while I'm here, it would be perfect," said Sheila.

Chapter Seventeen

Natalie and Sheila met up with the rest of their team at the high school stadium for check-in at the Christmas Tree Stroll. Randy and the couple who lived next door to him, Eli and Amanda, were waiting for them at the Chestnut Ridge High School football stadium gate with a wagon full of decorations in tow. They got in line behind several other teams awaiting their turn to be admitted and given their location assignment.

"The first night of the week-long decorating window is always the busiest," Amanda said. "Don't let it freak you out."

"Natalie said that you've done this competition before," Sheila said.

"In the past I've always helped the library decorate their tree, but who can say no to Randy and Natalie?"

"No one." Sheila knew Natalie's enthusiasm was contagious. That girl could talk a complete curmudgeon into volunteering.

During Sheila's divorce, she'd been that cranky party pooper, but Natalie always pulled her into something to get her mind off the bad stuff and invested in the good.

The line was moving along, and finally they were inside the

stadium. They were watching the other competitors, and Amanda knew most of the people in line around them.

Finally, the lady with the clipboard walked over to them. "You're in aisle two, slot fifteen."

"How many slots and aisles are there?" Sheila rose to her tiptoes to see out across the field as the woman started running down the rules with Natalie. "It looks like they go on forever," Sheila whispered over her shoulder to Amanda.

"A hundred and twenty trees," Amanda said. "I'm going to warn you. It's addictive. You may as well mark your calendar right now for next year."

"I don't know about that."

"You'll see. They create a town walk using the Christmas trees to create the lanes, and holiday-themed street signs the school workshop classes make. They also make all the benches so folks can stop to rest and enjoy the hot chocolate. The benches are sold and the proceeds added to the scholarship fund for kids entering community college. One year, one of the teams made it snow on the hour every hour on judging night. It's hard to explain, but once you experience Christmas in Chestnut Ridge, you'll never forget it."

Sheila marveled at how Amanda's eyes danced as she spoke. She had the beauty and grace of a princess, and when she reached for her husband's arm, Eli looked at her with adoration that made Sheila's heart pound. *How special it must be to have someone look at you like that.*

"You can set up your theme sign on the ground or in your tree, but it must not sit out farther than a foot from the tree, to be sure we allow the zoning department's minimum aisle clearance for compliance. It's all on this sheet. Good luck."

Natalie turned to them. "We're ready! This is going to be so much fun."

"And a lot of work," Sheila said as she tugged on the wagon. "You lead the way."

Amanda swept around to the front. "I know exactly where we are. Come on. Follow me." She skipped through the trees like a fairy flitting through a familiar cozy forest.

Several groups were already decorating their trees, and the smell of the trees was so inviting that it did seem like Christmas.

Some trees had short needles, some long; some trees were skinny, and some so rotund that they had to be placed on the outer edges. It had to have taken a creative bunch to figure out how to set up the placement chart for all of these trees to fit into the space.

Across the way, in one corner of the field, the tallest tree rose above them all. The fire truck had its ladder extended high in the air. Two men hung over the rungs, dropping decorations along the top section.

I wonder if one of them is Tucker.

"Here we are!" Amanda stretched her arms above her head, the tree still towering a good foot above that. "She's a beauty!"

"It's just how I'd pictured it." Natalie admired the height and fullness of the tree. "Exactly what I requested. Six foot, since that's the size most people can fit in their home and this tree will be delivered to a family, and I went with the Fraser fir."

Sheila walked around the tree, pulling some of the tangled branches and fluffing it as she went. "We've got one big naked spot on this side."

"No worries," Natalie said. "I read a whole article about tree fillers. We'll work with it. There's no such thing as a perfect tree. Even the fake ones have some open spots."

"You're right, we'll fill the gap with something adorable. A statement piece." Sheila pushed her hand in the awkwardly empty hole in the tree, trying to get an idea of the size they'd be working with, and hoping the cool bird's nest would work.

Natalie had been carrying a big flat Christmas package in gold foil with a red velvet ribbon. "I brought this to kick everything off. Are you all ready?"

"What is it?" Amanda clapped her hands. "What do we do?"

"This is our theme sign. I've been working all week on it," Natalie said.

"She's telling the truth." Randy playfully pouted. "I got stood up for our Tuesday *and* Thursday dates this week."

"I did not stand you up," Natalie defended herself. "You knew good and well where I was, and what I was working on."

"I'm still pouting."

"Anyway." She shot him a playful glance. "Are y'all ready?"

"Yes!"

"Each of you get over here and grab hold of one of the wrapping-paper tails," said Natalie.

"Oh goodness gracious. You've been on Pinterest again, haven't you?" Randy shook his head.

Sheila noticed that Natalie had wrapped the flattish box as pretty as a picture, but she'd left six three-inch tabs around the edges that she'd doctored up with extra tape. "I see what you mean. These paper tails." Sheila pointed them out.

Each of them grabbed a tab, and then Natalie said, "Three, two, one . . . *pull!*"

They pulled their tabs, and the paper pulled away. Natalie dragged the rest away to hold up the theme sign for their team Christmas tree.

"It's perfect!" Amanda danced, and Eli reached up and took her hand and gave her a twirl.

The sign was painted on canvas, and unlike most holiday decor in bright reds and greens, this one was a soft, glittery neutral background that made the tree branch and berries stand out like they were three-dimensional. Brightly colored birds dipped their beaks in the snow, and one flew toward a birdhouse in the background carrying a ribbon in its beak, trailing like a jet stream behind it, that read HOME FOR THE HOLIDAYS.

"Really well done," Eli said.

Sheila said, "To further excite this little party, I made something, and I was worried it might not work on the tree, but now that I know we have that big gaping hole over there, I think it's going to be perfect." She dug through all her bags and then handed the box to Natalie. "Open this one."

"What is it?" Natalie opened the box and pulled a bird's nest out. "This is great. How did you even know?"

"When you texted me the pictures of your birdhouses before I went shopping, I remembered hearing somewhere that having a live Christmas tree with a bird's nest in it is good luck. What do you think?"

"Did you make this?" Natalie asked.

"Well, I bought the bird's nest, but I added the birds and feathers," Sheila admitted. "Isn't it charming?"

"It couldn't be more perfect. Yes! Tuck it into that spot right now. We'll work everything else around it to set it off."

Sheila carefully settled the nest right into the branches. It fit snugly and was just cozy enough that the soft red and white feathers set it off.

"I hope the nest brings us good luck."

"We don't need luck." Amanda started taking birdhouses out of the big red tub. "Look at these. You hand-painted every single one?"

"I did."

"Here's the sketch of the whole idea, but we need to let creativity pave the way."

Everyone leaned in like a team huddle with Natalie as the quarterback. "Thank you all for being on my team. There are so many ideas to choose from, but in the information Orene had in her notebook the past five years I didn't see anything like this." Natalie set the sign aside.

"I've never seen anyone use birdhouses like this. I'm so glad you included me."

"I thought we'd divvy up the jobs."

Sheila raised her hand. "Can I show you my other surprise?"

"Another one? Yes! Bring it on." Natalie followed Sheila over to the cart.

"I know I'm not an artist like you," Sheila prefaced. "But I saw these teensy birdhouses, so I tried painting them in the colors that were in the pictures you showed me. You can doctor them up. Do you think they're cute?"

Amanda was the first to react. "I want to hang those. They are perfect for the top part of the tree and little fillers. I feel like I didn't bring anything to the table."

"Don't be silly," Natalie said. "We're all in this together."

They spent the next hour spreading everything out on the ground to be sure they could space everything out just so and not overdo it.

"I just had the best idea," Amanda said. "Eli, can you go home and cut off a couple of fresh holly boughs and bring them back? We can tuck them in here and there. The fresh greenery will give us another dimension of color, and the berries will tie in with the cardinals."

"I'm on it," Eli said.

"Before you go, Eli, can I get a vote of hands?" Randy looked across at them. "Topper first, like the firemen are doing, or last? I'll be honest. I've always been a last-thing-is-the-topper kind of guy, but I get it that when the trees are out here in the open like this, it might be easier to do it first."

"I never thought of that. And no wall to lean against when you're up on the ladder to stretch over." Eli made a face as if he was leaning toward putting it on first.

"I'm good either way," Sheila said.

"Who's in favor of putting the topper on first?" Randy counted hands."

Randy, Eli, and Natalie raised their hands. "We'll do it now, before you leave," Randy said. "Majority rules."

The team next to them was already decorating their snowman tree. They'd brought a nifty ladder that had handrails at the top so you could really lean in. "Couldn't help but overhear," one of them said as he stepped closer. "I'm Bubba. We had a bit of a challenge with the topper this year too. We're already put ours up. You can use our ladder. My brother welded it for us, just for tonight."

"Awesome!" Randy high-fived Bubba. The two teams introduced themselves, and then Randy ran out to his truck to fetch the surprise tree topper.

"You don't have any idea what he made?" Sheila asked Natalie, who looked to Amanda.

Amanda shook her head. "No, but he used Eli's brad nailer on it."

"Guess we're about to find out," Natalie said with an edge of nervousness in her voice.

For Natalie's sake, Sheila hoped that Randy read her mind and got it right, because Natalie did not like to lose and the tree topper was a key element. She crossed her fingers, hoping it all worked out.

Randy came back carrying a tall box.

"That looks incredibly tall," Natalie said.

Sheila could have sworn she saw her visibly swallow just then.

"Let's see it!" Sheila was determined to make it seem great, but as Randy lifted the brown bags from the top of his creation, she didn't have to fake it.

It was a double-decker bird condo painted in Christmas red, with shimmery white beads around the edges of the black tin roof like faux snow, and he'd drilled holes into little snowflake patterns in the side panels. A Christmas tree shape was cut out of the front window.

"It's perfect! Even the red is exactly the right shade," Natalie said.

"I might have peeked at your colors when I was over there the other day. Just to be sure."

This was a man who knew his woman, Sheila thought.

"I have these metal prongs like they use on the yard signs so that we can push it down from the top and then wire-tie it in a few places so it sits steady."

"What a great idea."

"Natalie, I thought you could make those big airy bows like you do so well, to kind of make it look like it's in a blanket of snow or clouds. I brought ribbon."

"Definitely. This is amazing. Okay, guys, let's get this tree topper up and get these nice folks their ladder back."

They went straight to work, and it took some time, but finally, twenty minutes later, they had the birdhouse perfectly attached to the top of their tree. The height of the topper made for a dramatic and eye-catching display.

While they fussed with that, Natalie and Amanda worked on the ribbons that would tuck in from the four sides, overlapping them just so.

Even the snowman team was cheering. It looked so good.

"Okay. Guys, you have outdone yourself. Eli and Randy, you are excused for holly duty. But before you go, we have all week to get this done. We can do it all tonight, or work on it a little each day," Natalie said.

Amanda said, "I'm just going to tell you from experience that it's sometimes best to stick to the plan and get in and out, otherwise you'll keep tweaking as you see all the other amazing trees come together, and sometimes less is more. You can really get twisted up and make it a chore instead of a joy." She shrugged. "We have a really awesome idea. I think we will give them a run for their money if we don't get sidetracked."

"Great advice," Sheila said. "I'm with her. I'm fine with getting it done as quickly as possible. I have some other things I'd like to get done this week too. Like help the Jacob family."

They all nodded in agreement.

"It'll be an all-nighter then. Here we go." Natalie turned and hugged Randy.

"I'll bring snacks," he said.

Amanda spread out a blanket by the tree, and all three gals sat cross-legged to work on the rest of the ornaments.

"I figured we could start assembling the aromatherapy portion of our tree, and each take turns hanging the birdhouses to get up and stretch."

"Sounds good. So what do we do?"

Natalie opened a large plastic container. Zesty orange filled the air.

"That smells so good. It makes me want a mimosa," Sheila teased.

Next, Natalie opened a clear jug of cinnamon sticks and cut lengths of gold cording. "We'll thread the gold cord through the center of the round orange slice, gently tie it on the cinnamon stick, and then do a simple overhand loop knot." She demonstrated as she walked through the steps again. "I spray-painted a bunch of green pine needle bunches gold. I figured we could bind them with a cinnamon stick and the gold cording too. Like this." She laid the natural tassel next to the orange ornament. "Cute, right?"

"It is, and they smell amazing." Amanda picked up a dried orange slice and completed an ornament, laying it next to Natalie's. "Identical twins. Very cute, and easy." Amanda picked up the ornament and reached behind her to hang it on the tree. "Look how pretty the orange looks against the tree."

"I'll hang my third of the birdhouses first. You girls go ahead." Sheila got up and nudged the heavy red tub closer to the tree, then started hanging the colorful birdhouses around the tree—scattering them and making sure they were perfectly not perfect, with just enough asymmetry to make it interesting.

After stepping back, she repositioned two of them, knowing they still had a bunch more to hang. "Thoughts?"

"Incredible," someone from the snowman team exclaimed.

"Where did you buy those birdhouses? I have to get one for my grandmother."

Sheila pointed toward Natalie. "Talk to that gal. Natalie hand-painted them."

"You're kidding. Can I get you to paint one for me?"

"I'll do you one better. You pick out the one you want and you can take it after the judging is complete."

"You've got a deal." The woman stepped closer. "This is really innovative. Look at all this stuff you've made."

Amanda and Natalie kept creating the orange ornaments while Sheila pulled the bag of feathers from their heap of supplies and tucked them into the tree one at a time, then paired a gold tassel with each feather. "Okay, I'm done here. Your turn, Amanda."

Sheila took Amanda's spot on the blanket and worked on putting the final touches on the gold pine needle bundles. She'd just finished the last one when her phone rang out. Her heart leapt. She reached for it in her back pocket and looked at the message, hitching a breath as she read it again.

"Is it Tucker?" Natalie asked. "I see that look in your eye. It is, isn't it?"

Sheila's stomach swirled. "It is. I've been summoned to the hot chocolate kiosk."

"That's so sweet," Amanda squealed. "Have fun. He's such a great guy. Do you know where the kiosk is?"

"No idea." Sheila was already on her feet, though. "Point me in the right direction."

"Head up this aisle, then turn left. You're going to head all the way to the end. The kiosk is on the other side of the goalpost. You can't miss it."

"Sure can't, because the tall good-looking fire chief will be standing there next to it." Natalie jumped between them and threw her hands in the air. "And then score!"

"Funny," Sheila said. "Y'all need to stop. It's *just* hot chocolate."

"It's never *just* hot chocolate," said Natalie.

Sheila took off, but she could hear Amanda and Natalie still egging her on from a distance. But as much as she denied it, she couldn't quit grinning. She took in a big breath, trying to steady her nerves. She was more nervous than the first time she slow-danced with John Rimarski in the eighth grade, and she could feel her knees knocking that night.

Chapter Eighteen

Tucker stood next to the hot chocolate kiosk, wishing he'd never acted on his impulse to ask Sheila to meet for hot chocolate. She was a looker, no doubt about it, and her quick wit and confidence showed by the way she picked on him even though they didn't know each other that well yet. The simple gesture seemed nice enough at the time, but now that he was standing here waiting on her, it felt pretty lame. It was also a giant waste of time, since she didn't live around here.

The whole firehouse probably knew by now, since they'd heard him talking to Tommy about it. Was this some kind of subliminal desperate move for company over the holidays?

It wasn't.

He liked being married to his job. Didn't have a problem with it at all. It was rewarding keeping the people of Chestnut Ridge safe. He was never lonely. There was always something good cooking at the station house, and when he wasn't with others, he enjoyed his own company just fine.

Why he opened this can of worms just to spend a minute with

a woman who'd be gone in a couple of weeks, he couldn't say. Just as he was regretting it and considering leaving, she stepped out from around the last aisle of trees and walked his way.

Her smile made him pause.

Her arms swung gracefully as she made her way to him in a deep forest-green top that hugged her shapely form. She was wearing her hair down, and he liked how it swept over her shoulders as she walked. She raised her arm and waved.

He acknowledged it with a lift of his chin. *Stunning.*

"How are you?" She walked over and gave him a quick hug. "I am having such a fun night."

"Good. And the real festivities won't even start for a week. This is just the pre-work."

"I can't wait to see the transformation as all the teams start decorating their trees. I've never heard of anything like this before."

"I'm not sure why no one has stolen the idea for the Christmas Stroll. We've been doing it for as long as I can remember. It was one of the tree farmers who originally came up with the idea."

"That makes sense. A way to get people excited about the trees." She looked around. "It's really clever."

"Wait until all the trees are decorated, and everything is in full swing." He pointed to the stands. "People fill the stadium. The view from up there is very different from when you're walking among the trees."

"I didn't even think of that. I've always thought it was touching when they carol with everyone holding colored lights in the outline of a tree," Sheila said. "Our band did that in high school. I haven't thought of that in years."

"From the stands the sound of the people caroling as they stroll through the trees rises like a fancy orchestral performance. Seriously, it's like being in a holiday movie."

She rubbed her hands up her arms. "I just got a chill. I can't wait. It's sort of romantic."

"Very romantic," he assured her. "There've been a few proposals during the event."

"That's so sweet."

"It is. I think a Christmas proposal would be pretty special anyway, but here, oh yeah, it would be kind of magical." All his anticipatory anxiety fell away. "What kind of hot chocolate can I tempt you with?"

"You mean I have choices?"

"Absolutely."

She licked her lips. "I do like mint."

"We've got good old-fashioned kids'-style hot chocolate with or without marshmallows. We've got your peppermint. Gingerbread. Pumpkin white hot chocolate, and there's a version with Kahlua available too. Then we've got the Mexican hot chocolate with the cayenne kick, and don't you worry, we also have mulled-wine hot chocolate, and if you're super daring, there's a limited-edition moonshine hot chocolate with a one-cup limit and the required snickerdoodle cookie to go with it, because it's a given that you can't drink moonshine without the evening involving a little snickering." He leaned over and whispered, "It might really have more to do with soaking up some of the alcohol in it, but whatever."

"Moonshine hot chocolate with a side of snickering? Sounds dangerous."

"Most definitely." He shook his head. "I personally don't

recommend that one." *Especially on a first date,* he thought, but withheld that comment. It wasn't really a date, after all.

"Well, in that case . . ." She tapped her Christmas-red fingernail with the tiny silver bells on it against her glossy lips. "I think I'm going to stick with the kids' hot chocolate *with* marshmallows."

"What? Not even the peppermint?" He kicked his foot in the grass. "I had you all figured wrong."

"Disappointed?"

"Hardly. I want you to have exactly what you want."

"Thanks. What're you having?" she asked, and the way she pushed her hair over her shoulder made him swallow twice before he could answer. Was she flirting? Or was it his imagination?

"I'll be having the pumpkin white hot chocolate."

Her jaw dropped. "I totally had you pegged for the spicy Mexican."

"I'm glad I surprised you." He turned to the couple tending the hot chocolate bar. "I'm going to have my usual, and my friend here is going to have regular hot chocolate with marshmallows."

They started whirring, pouring, and decorating, and then handed two red cups his way. "Enjoy!"

He dropped a twenty-dollar bill in the glass pickle jar for tips.

"You are an excellent tipper. Thank you."

"You're welcome." He took a sip of his drink. "You're really going to have to try this before the event is over. I've had every flavor, and this is by far the best."

She took a slug of hers, marshmallow sticky on her lips. "Mmm. This is really good too. This isn't one of those little packets you mix with water."

"No it is *not.* Here. You have to try mine."

She shrank back, her face twisting in disgust. "I'm sorry, but pumpkin and hot chocolate, even with white chocolate, somehow just doesn't go together."

"I get it. I do. I was hesitant for a few years, but when I worked my way through the whole list, I had no choice but to finally try it for myself. I'm telling you, it's surprisingly rich and delicious."

"I'm pretty happy with this—"

"Come on." He held out the cup.

She sighed. "Don't let it be said that I won't try new things." *If only . . .*

She took the cup and hesitated, before lifting it to her lips.

"Trust me," he said.

"Famous last words." She rolled her eyes and took a teensy sip.

"Well?"

Her eyes narrowed, then she took another sip.

"Good?"

She nodded slowly. "This is so good. Thank you." She looked into his eyes.

"Thank you." He cocked his head. "For trusting me."

A quiet moment hung between them, and he wondered if she was feeling the same vibe he was.

She handed him his cup back. "Well, you prove to be trustworthy. Yeah, I'm definitely getting that next time."

"I can get you one now."

She bit her lower lip. "I think I'd kind of like to look forward to a next time."

He smiled. She did feel it. It wasn't his imagination. "Yes. I'd like that too." He took a step and waved her to follow. "How 'bout you let me take you on a little walk through the stadium and give you the lay of the land."

"Excellent." She followed comfortably at his side.

"Right now it's pretty stark. Just the trees, and only a smattering of folks get started as early as us . . . ya know, the overachievers."

"The best!"

"Without question, but later this week, all of the street signs will mark the rows and aisles, only a few of them are in place now." They walked along and he explained the different types of trees.

"How do you know so much about Christmas trees?"

"Not just Christmas trees, all trees really. We have several tree farms in the area and I did seasonal work for most of them over the years. I also worked as a forester and did some wildland firefighting when they needed extra hands over the years."

"Like those smoke jumpers?"

"No, more like ground work with fire suppression and management. It was a great experience and I make sure all of my volunteers get that education as well. We need to protect our natural resources."

"Isn't that dangerous?"

"Yes, but the proper training and teamwork make it less so. But yes, it's dangerous. I wouldn't mislead you on that."

"You know what you were meant to do with your life." She seemed impressed.

"I do." It was nice to see her positive reaction. Lots of women thought being a fireman was a childish hero dream. There was so much more to it. "Here we go. Look." He pointed to the pole that rose from the intersection. "See, right now we're at the corner of Candy Cane Lane and Winter Wonderland Way."

"That's cute."

"There will be signs throughout and you can chart your walk on the maps they'll be handing out. Some people download them early and they'll break up the Christmas Tree Stroll into a few nights. While it's open to the public, a different restaurant hosts each night. Folks can come and have dinner, stroll, watch from the stands, and the schools and churches have time slots where they sing from up in the bleachers. It's pretty cool."

"The whole town gets involved."

"Yes, and every year it's tweaked a little based on the previous year, so we continue to build engagement and it works."

"That's fun. I saw your tree when we came in," Sheila said. "The biggest one here."

"Oh yeah. I always call dibs on the biggest tree they can lay their hands on."

"Bigger is better?" she asked.

"No. Size doesn't make it a sure winner, but I have a lot of volunteers, so the bigger tree gives more people a chance to participate. It seems only fair."

"Of course." They continued to walk through the trees. "Look at these little trees. That's pitiful."

"People fight over who gets those little things. You couldn't pay me to try to make one of those look festive."

"The Charlie Brown tree will forever be a favorite."

"With the one heavy ornament bending the top all the way over," he teased.

"Yep. I once put one ornament on a peace lily in my office. I guess that was pretty much the same idea."

"I don't think I want to know that about you. That seems borderline grinchy," he said.

"Me? No way."

"Have you ever participated in a Christmas festival back in Richmond?"

She shook her head. "Well, not exactly, but that doesn't make me a grinch."

"Scrooge?" He raised his shoulders and gave her one of those are-you-sure looks.

"No. I'm not," she tried to convince him. "In Richmond, we have a grand holiday light display at the gardens. Christmas lights never get old. I go every year. I usually get invited to join friends to see their kids in the Christmas pageant. The singing is horrible, and the instrument-playing even worse, but seeing the kids up there giving it their all . . . It's so cute. I cry. Every single time, I cry. They are so precious."

"You like kids?" he asked.

"I do." The thought of not having children still made her stomach sink. She eyed him as if wondering if that was the answer he was looking for.

"Never had any?"

"No," she said, avoiding the why. "How about you?"

"I've never been married. I'm old-fashioned. I want to get married first, then start a family. I like having a plan. So, the short answer is no. I've never had any children. Not yet."

"But you want them?"

"Definitely," he said, but he must've sensed the shift in her mood, because he leaned in, and for some reason she felt like she could share this with him. Something she never spoke about, but . . .

"It's funny how people who don't want children get pregnant

all the time. And then those of us who want them . . . we're not always blessed."

"That's true."

"I was married. My husband and I both wanted children, but we never could get pregnant. We divorced, and less than a year later he remarried, to a woman he'd gotten pregnant." She shrugged. "I'm happy for him. He'll be a wonderful father."

"That stings."

"He swore us not having children had nothing to do with him leaving, but I'm not so sure. I don't know why we couldn't get pregnant. Everything medically seemed fine. Anyway, that's too much information. I'm sorry." She wrung her hands. *What am I doing?* "I'm sorry. I never talk about this."

He touched her arm. "No. It's fine. I'm glad you felt like you could share that."

"So, I do what I can for the kids my friends have. If that's all I'm ever meant to have, then I'll be the best bonus aunt I can be. I get a lot of satisfaction in knowing I help parents find the perfect home in the good school districts for their families. It's not the same, but it helps."

"Natalie had told me about your success in real estate. That's really cool. She said you're married to your work."

Sheila laughed. "Yeah, pretty much. Only better than my marriage experience."

"I hear ya. People say I'm a workaholic, but it's not the work, it's the people involved and my little piece of the bigger community picture that makes it so special."

"I get it."

"We're a lot alike in that respect it seems. I satisfy that missing piece of not having a wife and kids . . . yet . . . with my work with the junior firefighters. I offer safety discussions at the schools. They always invite me to the plays and Christmas pageant. I get it about the crying. It's hard not to get emotional about the performance of a child. So unfiltered. Usually something funny happens."

"Right?"

"Last year, the third graders were doing their little songs and the first few were carols. I don't remember what they were, but then the music went up-tempo and this little girl who'd been standing there looking angelic through the first two songs suddenly starts shoulder popping and bebopping through 'Jingle Bell Rock.' I was laughing so hard I couldn't see."

"I can just imagine. We'd be a pair at that." She could picture them practically in tears, trying to hold it together but the more she laughed the more he would. They'd be a hot mess together.

He smiled wide. "I hope you weren't just being polite before when I mentioned going to the school pageant night with me. I would really like it if you'd come with me. If you're not doing anything, assuming you'll still be in town . . . I'm rambling. I'm a little out of practice here. I like your company. I hope you'll come."

Tucker wasn't like any man she knew. He was virile, manly, and yet so tenderhearted. The tickling threat of tears made her blink. *I can't believe I met you, and that you live so far away. Why is it that the perfect ones are never within reach? But you're here now. Just enjoy it while you can, Sheila. No harm in that.*

"It sounds like a lot of fun," Sheila said. "I'd like to attend with you."

He took her hand. "Thanks. I'm looking forward to that." He swung her arm, and then spun her around.

She giggled and stumbled over her own feet. "I wasn't expecting that."

He caught her, steadying her. "Sorry. I won't do that again. Come on, I want to show you the fire department tree."

She cocked her head to the side. "I don't know. Will I get accused of stealing ideas from you?"

"Well, our theme is transportation, and we're filling the tree with all kinds of trucks, cars, horses, skates, you name it. We're calling it Ninety-nine Ways to Get Home for Christmas and at the end of it all, we're donating every toy on the tree to kids around town."

"Oh my gosh. That's the best idea." She bit down on her lip. "Is it horrible that I'm just now thinking I should suggest to Natalie that we donate our birdhouses to the senior center?" Her brows drew in tighter. "I'm sorry. It's just such a good idea."

"No harm. I think that you cheating off my paper is for the better good. We can call it a coincidence." He playfully nudged her shoulder. "Are you gonna tell me about these amazing birdhouses of yours?"

She slapped her hand over her mouth. "Espionage! You just tricked me into telling you my idea."

"No, I'm pretty sure you just stole the best part of mine."

"We're in cahoots now," she said. "Might as well tell all."

"Yep."

"Birds. Feathers. Birdhouses and natural things like pine cones, gold pine needle tassels, dried orange and cinnamon ornaments. It's going to be so gorgeous. Did you know Natalie is an artist?"

"I do know that."

"She hand-painted the birdhouses. Randy built a whopper of one for the tree topper."

"Sounds interesting. I guess we don't have to worry about stealing ideas from each other's teams. The ideas are very different, and both are very well thought-out. It can be our little secret."

"To being in the top five." She lifted her cup to his.

"May the best team win." He sipped. "Hoping it's us."

She almost spit out her hot chocolate. "I can't believe you said that."

"Got to be honest."

"Well, Natalie does not like to lose, so don't think she's going to go down without a fight."

"Right this way." They strolled on and stopped at a festive kiosk in the center. "There are three of these. Two at the entrances and this one, where volunteers will hand out the maps of the stadium. Trees are sort of in categories, which is why mine is way over there and yours will be over here, with the trees that are nature-related, outdoorsy, and animal-related."

"Reindeer Run Way." She pointed to the street sign the men were straightening as they walked by. "And does that say Hunters and Habitat Highway?"

"Clever, right?"

"Yes."

"Then, over there are the ones that are traditional in style. Retro, to current, to like space exploration, sci-fi, or the stars and planets. You'll be surprised at all the different ideas. I never tire of the Christmas Tree Stroll."

"It *is* sort of wonderlandish. I'm enjoying this."

"One year we got blanketed in six inches of snow."

"Did they have to cancel everything?"

"No. We go on rain or shine. Or sleet and snowflakes? What-ever. We never cancel. Everyone just puts on their snow boots and weathers it. It changed the way everything looked, all coated in ice and snow."

"I hope it snows."

"You'd like that?"

"I'd borrow some warmer clothes and march right down every one of these lanes."

"I'd treat you to hot chocolate."

"That's sweet."

"Tell you what. If it snows, you promise me I can walk you through here." He stopped and faced her. "Deal?"

"Absolutely."

"I'm gonna hold your hand and we're going to have red noses and hot chocolate and mittens with icy fingers."

"It sounds like the most perfect Christmas I could imagine."

He walked, imagining with each step what it would be like to be hand-in-gloved-hand with Sheila. He liked the way her delicate hand felt in his. Tiny and soft.

He hadn't pictured himself walking with anyone in a long time. At least six years.

His job and women, they just didn't go together, and he wasn't willing to compromise his dedication to his calling. Fire-fighting brought him joy. Not just the act of putting out fires, but everything that went along with it.

"Let's walk over to the professional path." He air-quoted "professional."

"I see why you air-quoted the word now. Dentist, lawyer, bondsman, police, doctor, the bank, the pharmacy, and look, the biggest tree in the place. Yours."

"Not mine, the Chestnut Ridge Fire Department."

"Well, the way I see it you're the heart and soul of that operation."

"That might be the nicest thing anyone has ever said to me."

"It's well deserved." Her tone was sincere. "You should be very proud of what you do."

"I am."

"Hey, I see Doris over there. I recognize a few of the others from Orene's party too."

"They were all there. No one misses Orene's parties."

"I can't blame them. She's a natural-born hostess."

"Will you come back for them occasionally?"

"Her parties?" Sheila's eyebrows shot up. "I wouldn't miss them. I just hope I'm invited."

"You know Orene will invite you."

"Probably. She did threaten to put my name on my bedroom door since I stay there every time I come to visit Natalie."

"Not the cabin type?"

"Not at all," she admitted.

"Too bad. It's nice up there." He could imagine a very nice weekend with her in that cabin.

"I'm going to take your word on that, and reserve my right to my own opinion."

"I do admire an opinionated woman."

"That makes me sound a little bossy or something. I'm not sure that was a compliment."

He raised his hand. "Nothing but compliments from me, my friend."

"Oh, well in that case, I might have to come back more often."

"I hope you will." He stopped short of inviting her to stay with him if Orene didn't invite her. "Orene must think you're a pretty terrific guest. I mean, to offer to name a room after you and all."

"I think I get extra points for being friends with Natalie. You know, because Jeremy was from here and all."

"You both get extra points from me for that too."

"Even me?" She looked surprised.

"Especially you."

She blushed, and he resisted reaching for her hand. "There are so many different kinds of Christmas trees. I mean, not just short and tall, fat and skinny, but the species, colors, and everything."

"Yes, and they all come from tree farms within a hundred miles of here. We like to help our neighbors. Some are donated. Some are purchased from county funds. We splurge with putting money back into our businesses' pockets and skimp in other areas like concessions, but folks around here like doing all of that. It works."

"What's your favorite kind of tree?"

"The Norway spruce can handle heavy ornaments and are really aromatic."

"That scores big with me."

"Except their needles are sharp, and they drop their needles fast. So some of them will look a little Charlie Brown–ish by the time the judges come around."

"Oh, is that experience talking?"

"It is. The Fraser and Canaan firs are really nice, and we almost always pick a big fir for our competition tree, but I get a white pine from Jesse's brother's farm for my house. It backs right up to Natalie's cabin. I'm not sure if they are my favorite, or if it's the tradition I like, but that's what I do."

"Have you already decorated your tree at home?"

"No. I do it a couple of nights before Christmas, sometimes even Christmas Eve."

"I usually put my artificial tree up the day after Thanksgiving, but since I was coming here, I didn't put one up this year."

"My tree is your tree. Orene's tree is your tree. Natalie's tree—"

"I get it. I get it." She dropped her empty cup in the trash can at the corner of Holy Night Circle and Mistletoe Lane.

He stopped and looked straight up. Above them, a mistletoe ball hung from the crossbar of the football goalpost.

She followed his gaze, and then her eyes darted toward him. He felt her arm tense.

"It's tradition. I didn't make the rules, but. . . ."

She took in a breath. Wanting a kiss, but also not wanting one. "I . . ." She wrinkled her nose, not wanting to say no, but knowing it wasn't the time.

"Yeah. It's just a thing. Silly. Come on." He grabbed her hand and tugged her out from under the mistletoe. "But no sense taking a chance on ticking off the Mistletoe Adherence Committee."

"We don't have one of those where I come from."

"You better stick close to me then."

"You're going to keep me safe?"

"Only if you stay very close." He watched her swallow back whatever it was she was thinking. He hoped maybe she was thinking exactly what he was. That maybe it wouldn't be so bad.

Not moving a muscle, he waited until she finally looked down at her watch. "I better get back to Natalie and Amanda. We intend to pull an all-nighter and get our tree done so we can free up our schedules for the rest of the week."

"All night?"

"That's allowed, isn't it?"

"Sure. The night shifts from the plant and the hospital will be here. There won't be too many people overnight, but sure it can be done." He liked the way her lips curved up at the corners. "Mind if I check in on you before I leave for the night?"

She paused, and for a moment, he regretted asking. "I think I'd like that."

Sheila turned and walked away.

He inhaled deeply and, just before his fist pumped in celebration, she turned and smiled, waving to him. Almost busted.

He jogged over toward the fire department tree and saved his celebration for when he was out of view.

His heart pounded as hard as that day he made the sixty-yard run to the winning touchdown. A rush like no other that left him a little lightheaded.

You couldn't put this feeling on a Christmas list.

This might be the best Christmas ever, and the big day is still a week away.

Chapter Nineteen

Sheila could barely keep from running back to Natalie and Amanda. *Was there something in that hot chocolate, or was Tucker really that easy to be with?* Feeling giddy over it, she took an extra loop through another path of trees, trying to calm herself down before she reached Natalie, else they'd be teasing her like no tomorrow about him.

Walking through the maze of Fraser and Canaan firs, and white balsam, not to be confused with the eastern white pine, which had the long soft needles, as Tucker had explained, she smiled so wide her cheeks ached. She spotted a huge Norway spruce with the giant pine cones. Feeling like a winner on *Jeopardy!*, she twirled in appreciative satisfaction for identifying each of the species now that Tucker had explained each of them.

I'm practically a Christmas tree aficionado now.

Most of the trees were still bare except for a paper sign with the sponsor's name on it, but the ones that the teams were busy at work on were all pretty amazing. This event was a lot more impressive than she'd expected.

She finally came to the aisle where she'd left her friends, and when she got to their tree, she stopped. Completely unbiased, she could say the Feathered Friends Home for the Holidays tree had an enchanting way about it. The natural elements, birdhouses, and pine cones were dusted with the lightest strokes of sparkly iridescent paint, as if Jack Frost had just kissed them, which brought it all together in a resplendent way.

"Impressive!" It was honestly the best word to describe their tree. She clapped her hands together in a slow, methodical bravo. "Maybe I should let y'all finish without me."

"She's back!" Amanda set down the pot of glittery paint and her brush and rushed to Sheila's side. "I was beginning to wonder if you ran off with Tucker."

"Or ditched us," teased Natalie. She walked straight up to Sheila. "Yep. I sense a certain sparkle in those eyes. One that's been missing for way too long."

Sheila squeezed her eyes shut and turned away from Natalie, pretending to fix an ornament on a tree. "Stop. It was just hot chocolate."

"Oh, that is not a hot-chocolate-sugar-high smile," Natalie said with a smirk. "And hot chocolate doesn't take that long."

"I took a couple calls from the office too."

"At night? Over the holidays? You have got to cut those apron strings, Sheila. I thought you said they are capable."

"They are."

"Then why are you micromanaging?"

"I . . ." Sheila looked confused. "Oh my gosh. I am. Aren't I? I suppose I have nothing better to do."

"You have lots of better things to do. Haven't you figured that out?" Natalie looked like she couldn't believe Sheila hadn't seen it before now.

"You're right. I'm the most awful boss in the world. I do have time to do things. I just need to trust them to do what they're being paid to do."

"And when it's not perfectly the way you'd do it, it's a training opportunity. That's all. It's how the best leaders operate."

"Thank you, Natalie. I know better. I guess knowing and doing don't always correlate."

"Well, I want you to enjoy your time here, and the rest of your life. Expanding was a smart thing, now put it on autopilot like that Tesla."

"Point taken."

"Enough stalling. Spill everything about Tucker," Natalie said. "Now."

Sheila felt ridiculous for feeling this way. It really was just hot chocolate. "It must be the sugar."

Natalie slid her hand to her hip. "Hello? It's me you're talking to."

Amanda shook her head. "Who could blame you? Own it, girl. Tucker is the most sought-after bachelor around. He's successful, sexy, and I don't think I've ever heard anyone say anything bad about him. Not even ex-girlfriends."

Sheila didn't mind hearing that. "Okay, fine. It was nice. We walked through the stadium. It's really fun with all the holiday-themed street names, and the hot chocolate is no joke. They have a bunch of different flavors."

Amanda clapped her hands. "Please tell me you got the pumpkin white chocolate. I always get it with the splash of Kahlua in it. It's so good."

"You too? That's what Tucker had. It sounded horrible to me."

Natalie's nose wrinkled. "Chocolate and pumpkin?"

Sheila pulled her hands to her hips. "I know. I thought the same thing, but Tucker coerced me into trying it, and I can promise you it's the best hot chocolate around."

"Well, we have to give him points for having good taste," Amanda said.

"Because of his hot chocolate choice?" Natalie asked.

"No, because he's apparently taken a liking to your best friend here." Amanda laughed, nudging Natalie at the same time.

"Y'all stop. What? Did we go back in time to seventh grade while I was away?"

"If we were still in seventh grade, we'd be fighting over him," Amanda said.

"Truly," Natalie said. "Enjoy it. No one is asking you to get all serious or married or anything. Just have an awesome holiday while you're here in Chestnut Ridge."

Amanda added, "Maybe he'll kiss you under the bleachers next time."

Maybe he'll kiss me under the mistletoe. But there was no way she was saying that out loud. They'd never let her live that down.

"Let's talk about something that matters. This tree and winning this Christmas Stroll," Sheila insisted. "I honestly don't know how this could be any prettier. You even hung my little birdhouses while I was gone. They look pretty."

"You were gone a long time," Natalie said.

"Randy and Eli came back, helped, and took off again," Amanda said. "They are back at my house shooting pool."

"They did not." Sheila wasn't buying it for a second.

"Did. Look, they left snacks for us," Amanda said.

She looked at her watch. *I was gone a long time.* "I'm sorry. I only meant to be gone like ten minutes. Are they coming back?"

"I don't think they need to," Natalie said. "There's really only one more thing I'm considering doing once we finish tucking all the holly sprigs into place, which you are now in charge of."

"That adds so much." She repositioned one sprig and picked up a handful to get to work. "That was a great idea, Amanda." Sheila leaned in, looking for a wire or hook. "How are they staying in place?" One of the spiny leaves stuck her as she investigated. "Ouch, that's sharp."

"Be careful." Amanda winced. "Glue dots." She handed over a box of them to Sheila. "It's simple to just press them in place that way, and easier to avoid the pointy edges, which are a bit unforgiving, as you can see."

"It's like a paper cut. Invisible, but it smarts." Sheila wiggled the branch, and the holly bunch sat steady. "Perfect. I like the glue-dot idea."

"Yep. Amanda fits right in with us," Natalie said.

"I'm a glue-dot expert," Amanda said with no apology. "The permanent ones work almost as good as hot glue, if you ask me."

"And you can't see them." Sheila watched Natalie fuss with a box. "Need help?"

"That depends. I collected these from around the cabin." She unfolded the top of the box.

"What are they?" Sheila lifted a strange, woodsy, bark-like thing from the box. "A flower?"

"It is now. I made it out of natural things on my property."

"That's a sweet-gum ball in the middle. Those hurt like you-know-what when you step on them barefoot." Sheila cocked her head. "But I've never seen those other things."

"You're such a city girl," Natalie teased, fully aware that just a short year ago she had considered herself one. "Look, I glued milkweed pods in a circle to make a star-shaped flower. Then, I glued a sweet-gum ball in the middle. If you don't like them, I might just make a wreath out of them, but I thought they were kind of fun."

"I like them. I think we have enough ornaments, though, don't you?" Amanda cocked her head as she eyed the tree, as if trying to decide.

"What I was thinking was to use either white ribbon or natural jute to create a garland out of them. Maybe one every two feet or even three feet apart. Either that or lay out the garland on top of the tree skirt to make it look like a flowery serpentine design."

"I vote for the tree skirt. I think it would add a lot of interest without taking away from the tree."

"I have to agree," Sheila said. "I think anything else we do will only take away from it."

"Then that's exactly what we'll do." Natalie held up a spool of white ribbon and a wheel of jute. "Which do you like?"

"White," they both answered.

"Me too." She unraveled a long length of the white ribbon and started twirling it around on the tree skirt. They played with it until they came up with just the right number of graceful curves, then started attaching the pod flowers to it and glue-dotting everything in place.

From the wide, gauzy red and white sheer ribbons generously woven in and out of the branches from top to bottom, to the lights dancing off of every sparkly accoutrement, the tree dazzled without question.

Each birdhouse had its own personality, and Natalie had jazzed them up with so many tiny details that they earned a deserving pause.

"Who is ready to turn on the tree topper?" Sheila asked.

"I've been dying to see what it looks like lit up. I hope it's bright enough," Natalie said.

Sheila plugged the topper into the power strip.

"Look!" Sheila pointed to the back of the two-story birdhouse. In tiny drilled-out holes, the letters spelled HOME TWEET HOME.

The girls gathered around, and as if rehearsed, they all let out a simultaneous "Awww."

Natalie's eyes glossed over. "He didn't even know the name of our tree. I swear that man can read my mind. It's perfect!"

"It is," Sheila agreed. A tiny green 3D Christmas tree with fairy lights rose from inside the front window of the tall birdhouse topper. "How'd he do that?"

"I have no idea, but it's pretty awesome." Natalie couldn't take her eyes off of it.

A male voice broke their collective fixation on the tree. "I know I'm treading on my competitors' playing field here," said Tucker. "But I wanted to stop by and say good night before I headed out."

Tucker admired their tree appreciatively. "Very well done." With a lazy smile and the lift of his eyebrow, he eyed Natalie. "Even better than I imagined."

Natalie's head swung toward Sheila. "You told him our theme?" Then she playfully added, "You tree traitor."

"He showed me his first," Sheila defended herself.

"Mm-hmm." Amanda and Natalie nudged elbows.

She glared at them and grunted out a quiet "Stop." *How embarrassing.* Mortified, she avoided making eye contact with Tucker. Trying to keep the conversation on the tree, she smiled in his direction. "It truly is a beauty of a tree, isn't it?"

His scan started on Natalie, then went to Amanda, and stopped on Sheila. "It looks like it was taken straight from the heart of a fairy-tale winter forest. I'd say it would be considered a very desirable neighborhood in a really good part of town if we asked a real estate expert."

Oh my gosh, he's trying to speak my language. "An affluent enclave, for certain." Sheila spoke in her most convincing Realtor tone. The one that people seemed to react to the most. "And in the very best school district."

"Of course," Tucker agreed. "We might even say 'top*flight*,' right?"

"Ha, see what you did there." Sheila laughed a little too heartily. "Yes. Top*flight*." She pushed her fingers through her hair, and the glance that just passed between Amanda and Natalie didn't go unnoticed. *Oh gosh. I'm flirting?*

"Seriously, though," Tucker said, "this is a very nice tribute to the area. The craftwork from the natural materials ties in really well."

Sheila watched the sense of accomplishment wash over her friend. Their tree was a testament to Natalie's creativity.

"Doesn't look like y'all will be pulling an all-nighter after all," Tucker said.

Natalie agreed. "Good teamwork like ours is hard to find, but we nailed it."

"You did." Tucker shoved his hands in his pockets. "My team is slower going, but then it's not easy balancing heavy construction trucks and roller skates on a tree, and putting hangers on tiny Matchbox cars is sort of work for daintier dexterity than I have." He lifted his large hands, splaying his fingers. "And our tree is more than twice the size of this one."

"Are you asking for our help?" Sheila asked.

"No, we've got plenty of help. But I *am* offering to drive *you* back to Orene's if you're done," he said to Sheila. "I have to go right by her house on my way home."

A wave of panic slid through Sheila, but before she could politely decline his offer, Natalie answered for her.

"That would be great, Tucker," Natalie said. "I'm staying with Randy tonight and Amanda is riding with me, so if you give Sheila a lift I wouldn't have to backtrack."

"Oh?" Sheila was caught off guard by Natalie's comment, but there were worse things that could happen. She turned back to Tucker. "If you don't mind. Sure. It would be great if you could give me a lift."

"Done," he said. "We should take Miss Orene a snickerdoodle back, don't you think?"

"That would be great," said Sheila. "She'll be asleep, but she'll enjoy it with her tea in the morning."

"You drink tea too, don't you?"

"I do."

"Well, then we'll get plenty for you both." Tucker looked at the stacks of boxes and supplies lying around the tree. "How about we help pack up, and I'll put the cart in the back of your truck?"

Natalie started putting empty boxes one inside another to get it down to a manageable move. "There's nothing heavy left. Amanda and I can manage the wagon."

"Are you sure? I don't mind."

"I know you don't. Y'all go get your cookies before they sell out." Natalie already had the boxes in the wagon. "See. We're done."

"Are you ready then?" he asked Sheila.

"No. Not until we get pictures with our tree. Will you take them for us?" Sheila handed Tucker her phone.

The girls squeezed together tightly in front of the tree and smiled. Tucker took the pictures as they repositioned to one side of the tree and then behind the canvas sign Natalie had painted.

"Thanks." She took her phone and swept through them. "Good. Yes. I can't wait to send these to my office. They won't believe it." She bent down and picked up her tote bag. "I'm ready now. You two are sure you don't need our help?"

Natalie and Amanda both shook their heads. "We've got it. Good night. We'll talk to you tomorrow."

Just out of earshot of Tucker, Amanda said, "Sheila, Eli and I are going to smoke a turkey tomorrow. I hope you'll join us. Bring Tucker too if you want. It's been so fun working together."

She hated being the fifth wheel. "No. Why don't y'all two couples have a date night? I'll do something with Orene."

"Every night is date night for us. You're invited. If you change your mind, please come. Bring Orene if you don't want to invite Tucker."

"I'll think about it." But Sheila knew she wouldn't go. It was just too awkward being the only one without a significant other. It left her feeling a little lonely, and she'd rather avoid that. She waved to the girls and walked over to Tucker. At least she wasn't lonely tonight.

They walked over to the snack stand.

"You were holding out on me earlier," Sheila said. "There were cookies the whole time?"

"I can't play my whole deck of cards on our first date. It's a small town. Choices are limited."

Date? "Was that a date?"

"Wasn't it?"

"Is this our second one?"

"Of course. Aren't you keeping count?"

"I may be in over my head."

"Somehow I doubt that." The wink was playful, not flirty, and she appreciated that. "I'm glad you're in town. Online dating is so impersonal that it feels wrong at the holidays."

"I know! I feel the same way. Plus, it's weird dating someone new with gift-giving at the holidays and all. I'd just rather not."

"That's always interesting. So you've done some online dating?"

"It's the way these days, but I feel like I can date someone for weeks before the true person is revealed. Like there's this whole dating façade you have to break through."

"Glad it's not just me. You're a breath of fresh air," he said.

She knew what he meant, and his honesty was refreshing too. She relaxed and let him lead the way to the snack shack.

"Six snickerdoodles," he told the young woman wearing a Santa hat.

She turned to bag them.

Tucker said, "The mayor's wife makes these. Her mom used to make them before her. They're a seasonal tradition around here."

"Merry Christmas." The girl handed the wax-paper bag to Tucker, who handed it off to Sheila.

"We don't need all six of these." Sheila turned back to the counter. "Could I get an extra bag to split these up?"

"Sure thing."

"Thanks." Sheila took only two and gave the rest back to Tucker. "You'll enjoy these tomorrow morning too."

The stadium had quieted now that most of the teams had called it quits for the night. They walked toward the wide exit tunnel, but then Tucker tugged her toward the stadium stairs.

"Come on. I want you to see this so you can see the difference once all the decorating is done." Before she could even consider what could be worth climbing a bunch of bleacher stairs for, he was laughing and shouting, "Race you!"

"Wait. You're cheating." She balled up her fists and started running up the stairs. "No fair. You jumped the starting line." It had been a long, long time since she'd run stairs in high school, but she charged up despite the fact that his stride was twice as long as hers.

"Fine." He stopped. "I'll take a penalty stop. Get going, slowpoke. Counting down three seconds. Three-Mississippi, two-Mississippi, one-Mississippi."

"Not cool!" She gave it her all and was one step behind where he stood challenging her.

He slammed his sneaker against the next seating plank and they were neck and neck, all the way to the top.

She squealed as she touched the back wall just a nanosecond before he did.

They burst out laughing.

"That was unexpected," she said.

"You're fast. That's what was unexpected." He laughed. "I had to really hustle." He lifted his hand in a high five.

She clapped his hand. "Well done."

The air up here was so cold that they could see their breath, the condensation lifting in puffs as they panted.

She put her hands on her knees. "If I'm sore tomorrow, it's your fault."

"You look like you're in good shape. I think you'll be just fine."

"I'm no firefighter, but I do try to stay in shape." She turned to the field, quickly realizing why he'd raced her to the top. "This view, it's phenomenal."

"Yeah. It is. It's fun to walk the field, but it's a whole other experience up here. Isn't it great?"

"It is." She lowered herself to the seat, retracing the paths they'd walked earlier. "Candy Cane Lane. I didn't even realize there were color changes in the aisle lighting. You can see how it's mapped out way better from up here."

"You can. The kids over at the community college came up with that idea when they were creating the new maps for the event. It's the first time we've done it. I think it really adds to the experience. They were hoping it would drive more people up into the stands to kind of even out the traffic. This place is filled with people during the judging."

"Smart marketing."

"There's a people's-choice award too. And this year, not only will the team win the award and a free dinner for the whole team at Trout and Snout, but also everyone who voted is entered into a drawing for a free dinner for two as well."

"I hope I win. I'm not a picky eater, but I haven't had one bad meal down at the Trout and Snout. I love that place."

"Who doesn't? What's your favorite food?"

"My favorite Italian restaurant closed last year, so I haven't had much Italian lately. I miss that."

"You're in luck." He snapped his fingers. "It just so happens I make the best lasagna around."

"I believe you are bragging." She leaned her shoulder into his.

"Maybe a little." His neck reddened. "Can I make some for you one night?"

"That's a lot of work. You don't have to go to all that trouble."

"I'd like to. Come on. It'll be fun."

She hesitated. *Why not?* "I think I'd enjoy that." She lifted her chin. *Enjoy the moment.* She plopped down onto the bleacher. "When would you like to cook for me?"

"I'm off Wednesday through Friday morning, so let's do Thursday. Unless something catastrophic happens, there won't be any interruptions."

"Okay."

"It's a date, then." He looked pleased with himself.

"Yes, but who's counting?" She caught herself looking into his eyes, her shoulders slightly hiked. *Oh my gosh. I'm flirting with this man. And it's nice.*

She grinned through the nervous set of her teeth, smiling but trying not to make too big a deal about it, although she knew Natalie would.

Chapter Twenty

Sheila stuck to yoga these days, and her lungs were reminding her that she might need to add a little aerobic activity to her days too. Almost afraid to ask, she said, "Are we going to race all the way down too? I feel like I need fair warning, or at least a head start."

"No racing down." He stretched out his hand and helped her to her feet.

She was thankful they took the easy way down by way of the stairs and handrail at a reasonable pace, instead of bouncing off each bleacher from seat to seat.

It was hard to imagine this stadium without the field full of trees. From here she could smell the mix of sweet hot chocolate and cookies with the sticky pine sap. It smelled of Christmas joy.

A flicker of light caught her eye. At first, she thought it was a bug catching a glow from the stadium lights, but it wasn't. Not a hundred of them.

She lifted her hands out in front of her. "Do you see that?" They were tiny flakes of snow floating to the ground. "It's snowing!" She grabbed the back of Tucker's jacket. "Look! It's so pretty." Her hands splayed wide, as if she might actually catch one of the tiny flakes, so light that they were drifting like bubbles. "Were they calling for snow?"

"No." He brushed a tiny white pellet from the shoulder of her coat. "How about that? I guess we just got lucky."

She couldn't agree more. "Very lucky."

He seemed amused by her excitement.

With nothing but the twinkling lights and the warmth of their shared company, they walked down the bleachers, then out into the parking lot to his truck.

He opened the passenger door for her, and waited until she climbed up into the passenger seat to go around to the other side.

Tucker got in and started the truck. In the stream of light from the headlights, the snowflakes seemed to fall faster.

"I wanted to see snow so badly," she admitted. "You have no idea. I hope it snows a foot!"

"Careful what you wish for." He drove the short distance to Orene's house and parked out front.

"You made tonight so much fun. Thank you." Christmas seemed more Christmassy this year. Orene had left the front porch light on, but the rest of the house was dark.

"Looks like Miss Orene already called it a night," Tucker said.

"Probably. She was up at the crack of dawn helping get everything set up and ready for the Christmas Tree Stroll to begin."

He shook his head. "I hope I'm half as active as she is when I'm her age."

"Me too," Sheila mused. "I've always thought of myself as a real go-getter. I work long hours, and never take much of a break, but when I'm around her, I feel like she's running circles around me."

"I'm glad you're staying with her for the holidays. I worry about her being in this big old house alone. She says she doesn't get lonely, but it just doesn't seem right."

"People are coming and going like it's the bus station, and no matter what the hour, she's always so welcoming."

"Orene is the heartbeat of this town. Sort of everyone's bonus grandmother. Her family has been a huge part of this town for generations. They were very prominent at one time."

"I can see that from the history just around the house. Letters from presidents. Pictures from fancy parties. So impressive for that time period."

"It was."

"She insists she plans to live to a hundred," Sheila said.

"I have no doubt she will," Tucker said. "And her reputation will live on way longer than that in Chestnut Ridge."

Sheila wasn't ready for the evening to end. "Would you like to sit on the front porch? Maybe have some cocoa or coffee?"

"I could do a cup of chamomile with you."

Her insides danced. "Tea? Really? That is not what I expected from a big, strong fireman."

"Well, when you grow up with Orene influencing you, it's hard to resist a good cup of tea."

"I'll get us some." They climbed out of his truck and walked to the porch.

"I'll be out here counting snowflakes." Tucker sat in one of the rockers.

"Better yet, catch one for me." Sheila went inside and put the teakettle on the stove. As the water heated, she looked through the cute teapots and matching cups Orene had displayed in the glass-front cabinets in the kitchen.

She wouldn't dare help herself to any of the ones in Orene's treasured displays in the other room, but Orene used these all the time.

Behind a red teapot, she spotted a fun set with snowball-fighting reindeer wearing Santa hats. *Perfect.* She set it on the counter and then found the tea tray she'd seen Orene use for front-porch serving.

It seemed to take forever for the water to come to a boil. She looked through the cabinet for chamomile. Turned out Orene had four flavors of chamomile. Who knew there were that many?

She filled a tea ball, placed it in the pot, and waited for the water to boil.

Worried that Tucker might wonder what was taking so long, she went out to the porch. "It'll be just a minute. If you're chilly, you can wait inside with me."

"No. It's nice. Take your time. I'll be here when you get back."

It was as if he'd read her mind. "Okay, I'll be right back."

The kettle was just beginning to whistle when she walked back into the kitchen. She swept it off the stove so as not to awaken Orene.

Tucker had his feet up on the railing, and hands behind his neck, rocking under the twinkle lights of the porch.

He sat forward as she walked up and handed him a cup of tea. "Thank you." He closed his eyes and inhaled. "Nice."

She sat in the chair next to him. "This probably won't surprise you, but she had four kinds of chamomile tea." She counted them off on her fingers. "Chamomile Mango, Honey Vanilla Chamomile, Cinnamon Apple Chamomile, and Chamomile Lavender. I don't know about you, but spraying lavender on my sheets helps me sleep, and I even like it in my bath salt, but in a drink it tastes like soap. So I picked the mango."

"Good choice. It's been a long time since I've had to have my mouth washed out with soap."

"My mom used to always threaten me with that too."

"I never tempted mine. I think she might've really done it." He sipped the tea. "This is nice."

"It is. The snowflakes are almost gone."

He pointed toward the light. "There are still a few. I caught you a couple, but they melted."

"I'm hoping for a white Christmas."

"I hope you get your wish. What's on your Santa list this year? Assuming you've been good, of course."

"I'm quite certain I made the nice list, but since I'm not home, he won't know where to deliver anything."

"Santa knows where all the good kids are."

"Too bad I'm not a kid anymore." She imagined what it might be like waking up on Christmas morning with children tearing through wrapping paper. Something she'd dreamed of for so long. She pushed the feeling aside, not wanting to lose the joy she was feeling at the moment.

"Will you be here on Christmas Day?"

"Yes." Sheila felt compelled to explain, though. "I'm driving to Virginia Beach to visit my mother. She's in a full-care facility there. That's where my sister lives, but I'm coming right back for a few more days."

"I'm sorry to hear about your mom. Has she been there long?"

"A long while." She wasn't even sure why she'd mentioned the specifics; she rarely spoke about Mom to others. But for some reason she felt comfortable with Tucker. It seemed okay. "She's been battling Alzheimer's for years. She had early onset that we'd all joked about as forgetfulness for years. Then it got to the point, well . . . she doesn't know me or my sister most days."

"That's got to be hard."

She nodded. "It's a devastating disease. Mom used to have a bubbly personality. The disease has stripped so much from her. Some days it's as if she's not even in there."

"It's hard on the family."

"I never miss the family days, even though Mom might not know the difference. If for no other reason, I get the chance to thank those that are there for the day-to-day. They are truly angels, and they take such good care of her."

"It takes a special person to provide that kind of care," he said. "It's nice you can get away from work so long. I guess this would be a slower time for real estate."

"Mm-hmm. It can be seasonal for sure. I own my own real estate firm. I'm a broker, have a team of agents working out of my office now. Things are good."

"Do you like living in the city?"

"It's all I know. I've never lived anywhere else."

"I can't imagine living where I don't know everyone. I wouldn't trade the quiet for all the hustle and noise of the city."

"Have you ever spent time in a city?"

"Sure. I've been to Chicago, Vegas, D.C., for training and conventions. Spent a vacation in New York City once. I was supposed to be there a week, but I was ready to come home after three days."

"I've often wondered what makes people change their mind

about where they live. In my business, I see it all the time. City folks wanting to move to quieter areas and vice versa. It's awful when couples have different mindsets. It's nearly impossible to find a place that meets both needs. That makes me nuts."

"Yeah, you can't fake the closeness of a small community."

"It's like one big family here. I only know a couple of my neighbors, and that's only because I sold them their houses. It's nice feeling like a part of the community here."

"Folks seem to like you being a part of it. They aren't always so welcoming to outsiders."

"Really? Well, then I'm flattered."

"You should be." He set his nearly empty teacup on the table. "I'm looking forward to cooking for you on Thursday."

"What can I bring?" she asked.

"How about salad?"

She liked that he didn't tell her to come empty-handed. It wasn't her style. "I can handle that. What time should I come over?"

"I'll pick you up," he said. "I'm kind of old-fashioned that way."

"I'll drive. I'm kind of not-so-old-fashioned. I like to be in control of my entrance and exits."

"I understand, but you could walk home if you wanted to leave. My house is just around the block from Orene's."

Suddenly, the Christmas lights along the porch and in the trees all went dark.

Sheila gasped. "I think our quarter ran out."

Laughing, he said, "They're on a timer."

"Oh. Right. It *is* getting late." She hated for the evening to end.

"Yes, and I should leave." He stood. "I'll see you on Thursday, and since it's just around the block, would you let me pick you up? A lady deserves to be treated like one." He took both of her hands in his and gave them a simple squeeze that sent an epic zing through her.

"Yes. I'm comfortable with that. I'll be waiting on the porch."

"Thanks. I appreciate that." He walked from the porch to his truck in a confident stride that struck her. He was self-assured, and assertive, in a very pleasant way.

She whispered into the night, "I can't wait."

When she crawled beneath the cool cotton sheets that night, she was still smiling. As she lay there, reliving the evening, the moonlight flickered between the tree branches like a good-night wink.

Chapter Twenty-one

Thursday afternoon, Tucker walked through his house one more time, fussing over stupid things like the angle of his recliner in front of the television.

Just stop.

We're not even going to be watching television.

You've got this.

But for all the self-talk, he still found himself going to a lot of trouble for a woman who would be leaving town soon. And not only going home, but to Richmond, which was nowhere he had any desire to spend time.

It's fun. She's nice. What's the harm?

She and Natalie were best friends, and Natalie was the widow of his best friend. They *should* be friends.

Between making sauce and chopping fresh herbs for the lasagna, he rolled over the same thoughts in an internal battle most of the day. He hadn't met anyone quite as smart and entertaining as Sheila in a long time. She was easy to be around, and he liked that.

The savory aromas from the kitchen filled the house, and

he'd even made dessert, although it wasn't often anyone had room for it after eating his lasagna.

All that was left was to pick up Sheila.

But it was way too early for that.

He pulled on his jacket and headed over to GG's Mountainside Garden & Gifts on Main Street.

It was chilly, but it would be colder soon with the sun beginning to dip behind the mountains. Walking up the hill to Main Street from his house was always a welcome workout. He made the new recruits do it ten times a day while they were in training.

At the top of the ridge, he turned and walked up Main Street.

"Hey, Chief," Tommy called out from the gas pumps across the street.

Tucker waved and crossed the street toward him. The little store next to the gas station had been an empty eyesore until Greta and Gary, a couple from Norfolk, decided to retire to Chestnut Ridge. They bought the dilapidated concrete block building from the city for next to nothing and poured in a pile of money to get it up to code and turn it into the welcoming retailer it was today.

Locals were hesitant about them coming in and setting up shop on Main Street, but the sweet elderly couple had captured their hearts. Gary was one of those guys who could engineer anything and always volunteered to help with projects, and Greta could work miracles with plants and flowers. The building was now painted a sunny orange, and they'd allowed the senior art students of Chestnut Ridge High to paint a mural on the side of it representing the history of the town, with a horse and carriage as it might have been back in the 1900s, huge chestnut trees, and mountain laurel in full bloom.

Tucker pulled the creaking wooden door open and walked inside. The peppery scent of evergreens mixed with the fragrance of paperwhites and amaryllis in funky colored wax balls that lined the counter. Foil-wrapped potted plants and shiny pottery with extravagant ribbon bows filled a rack, ready for gift-giving.

Greta rounded the corner wearing a bright red apron decorated like a Santa suit with white trim, a shiny black belt, and a gold buckle. "Tucker? Merry Christmas." She swept her hands together. "What do I owe the pleasure?"

"Looks pretty in here, all decorated for the holidays."

"Thank you." She looked around. "It does, doesn't it? Gary was moaning and groaning about how much time I spent decorating the tree in the front window since I'm doing one for the Christmas Tree Stroll too, but I told him . . . every person in this town will enjoy it at some point. Can't go anywhere if you don't stop next door for gas, right?"

"That is true."

"I saw your team at the high school last night. They were working like acrobats trying to decorate that huge thing. They had one gal up on Homer's shoulders, putting a bulldozer between the top branches. He's lucky she didn't drop that metal monster right on top of Homer's head!"

"You're right. As hardheaded as Homer is, he might have dented it, and that's going to be some kid's Christmas present this year."

"What a great idea."

"I thought so. I can't wait to see what the tree topper looks like. I'm trying to stay out of it and let them run with it this year, which isn't easy for me."

"I know. You're so competitive. If you don't win a trophy, you'll be kicking yourself, though. But don't worry. I'm rooting for you." She giggled until she snorted. "Get it. Rooted. Plants?"

He grimaced. "I got it." She was known for her silly puns and that laugh. The unapologetic snort could be incredibly annoying on someone else, but it was entertaining coming from her. "You're right, but if we don't win I guess it'll just be because it's someone else's turn to take home the prize. I'm practicing being a good sport." He thought about Natalie, Amanda, and Sheila's tree. It would be nice for them to win. Sheila would really get a kick out of that.

"I know you dig hanging out with me and my buds," she said, with a wink and a nod to a bucket of rosebuds, "but what did you really stop in for?"

He shook his head at the second gardening pun.

"Oh, I have to ask about you and that woman you were with last night. Let's be mistletoe-tally honest here, Tucker. Y'all looked like you were more than just friends racing up the bleachers."

"You saw that?"

"I did. Oh, quit your blushing. You deserve some fun. All you do is work. You're going to waste the best years of your life alone. You should share them with someone."

Tucker bristled, unprepared for the teasing. "How much do I owe you for the therapy session?"

"On the *green*house. So can I sell you some mistletoe? Seriously, that was a hint. I have some."

"No. I don't need mistletoe to get a kiss. Do you ever run out of those jokes?"

"Never. Ask Gary. He's heard them all." Her graying hair bounced across her shoulder as she shifted her weight. "At least twice."

"I'm just looking for something kind of simple. Nice, but not overly romantic. You know, more like for friends."

"All you want is friendship with that pretty woman?" She folded her arms. "Seriously, Tucker. Get with the program here."

"She goes back to the city after the holidays. It's just dinner between friends, and I want it to be special, but not assuming. No pressure. You know what I mean."

"Whatever you say." She raised her hand in a wave as she turned and led him to the back of the store. "I'm not here to judge."

That's not stopping you from preaching on about it. But he really didn't mind.

"I've got all kinds of great holiday live plants. It makes it nice because they last. Amaryllis, poinsettia—"

"Everyone does that. I wanted something kind of different."

"The paperwhites are gorgeous. They can be a little fragile, but if you mix a one-to-seven vodka-water drink to give it a little nip each day, those things will stand up nice and straight. Probably do the same to that gal too." She ran her hand across her nose, laughing. "Or, I've got these bundles of Fa La La La Lavender. Grew them myself. And check out this Christmas ribbon. Is it not absolutely gorgeous?"

He thought about Sheila's reference to lavender in her sheets.

"I think I'll steer clear of the vodka tip and take the Fa La La La Lavender." Then he pointed to the ribbon. "Not the fancy ribbon, though. I like the one with the hand-drawn snowmen and snowflakes on it."

"Excellent choice. Fun and not too fancy." She shuffled through the bound lavender until she was satisfied with one and then took it to the counter.

Greta pulled a shiny pair of scissors from her apron pocket and snipped the edges of each stem of lavender. The aroma lifted into the air as she pulled a green rubber band around the bunch, and then in one fluid movement, as graceful as a bird, she tugged a length of ribbon across a yardstick screwed to the table and cut it to length. In just a moment, she'd tied a flowing bow with long sweeping tails, each one with a V as sharp and slender as the tail of a barn swallow.

"What do you think?" She eyed it carefully, then turned and smiled. "I like it."

"I do too. Thank you."

She walked him over to the register and rang it up for him. "Need a bag to skulk back to your house covertly? Wouldn't want people thinking you might be interested in someone. Like we aren't already."

"That would be nice."

She pulled out a plastic bag, then tucked it back in the drawer in favor of a paper bag with handles. "This will do better. You don't want to crush my pretty bow."

"That *is* the best part," he said.

"Thank you, Tucker." She tucked the flowers into the bag. "You might share with her that she can grow some of her own lavender by gently shaking the seeds from the dried flowers and planting them."

"Merry Christmas, Greta." He walked out of GG's with the bag. Every few steps, the fragrance from the lavender would waft up around him. *Thank goodness I didn't drive. My truck would smell like this for a week.*

Five minutes before he was supposed to leave to get Sheila, he still hadn't decided which shirt to wear. *Don't look too dressed up. Don't look like I don't care.* Finally, he opted for the Christmas sweater that the team gave him a couple of years ago. It was definitely a winning ugly-Christmas-sweater candidate, but it seemed playful and fun, and that was really all he wanted to convey.

He looked at himself in the mirror. *It's too horrible to be misconstrued as trying too hard. This will work.*

Walking to his truck with the bag from GG's, he wondered why he was making this so difficult. It took literally three minutes to drive around the corner to the Mountain Creek Inn to pick up Sheila.

As promised, she was sitting on the front porch waiting for him.

He wondered if she'd struggled over what to wear.

She stood and waved. In a bright red sweater to the hips and black leggings, she looked ready for anything.

He met her halfway up the sidewalk and handed her the bag. "Thought you might want to put these inside."

She cocked her head. "What'd you bring me?" She took the bag and looked inside. "Lavender. Thank you, that was so sweet."

"And better than in tea."

"Don't you worry. I'm going to go put these in my room. I'll sleep like a baby tonight." She pulled the bunch all the way out of the bag and gave it a big sniff before rushing inside.

As soon as she hit the stairs to her room, Orene walked outside. "Brownie points." She gave Tucker a slow nod. "Very nice touch."

He looked away.

Sheila came back carrying a covered dish, and Orene scooted back inside.

"Ready?" Sheila asked.

"Definitely," Tucker said, hoping to get out of there before Orene grilled him.

"Y'all have fun," Orene called after them with an impish grin.

"I'm so glad you brought me the lavender. I was focused on being on the porch waiting for you and almost totally forgot to bring the salad."

"Oh, well, everything happens for a reason, I suppose." He took the covered dish from her. "You look very nice."

"I'd like to say the same thing." She started laughing. "But I don't think I can. That sweater is horrible. Can I borrow it for my office party next year?"

"What would I wear?" He acted hurt. "You mean you weren't going to invite me?"

"Good point." She headed to the truck, but he beat her to the door and held it while she got in.

"You're guaranteed to win if you wear that," she said.

"I do like to win." He tugged on the fake tie that was knitted into the neckline. "Shall we?"

She was still shaking her head when he got behind the wheel.

Two turns and then into the driveway. She turned and looked at him blankly. "Seriously? I could have walked here in the time it took you to drive to get me and bring me here."

"I told you. See. Win-win. You're still in complete control of when you leave."

"I definitely am." She got out. "This is not the kind of house I expected you to live in. Was it in your family?"

"No. Mom and Dad lived high up on the mountain in Pine Creek. No one in my family ever lived in a house like this. Growing up, we lived in a modest ranch with a view that went on for

miles. It was really quiet, which was nice, but it was kind of shel-
tering too. Maybe that's why Chestnut Ridge was so appealing,
because of the close-knit community."

"Maybe?"

"I wanted to live close to the firehouse too. When this old
beauty came on the market, I pounced on it."

"When was she built?"

"Nineteen ten."

She took in the well-preserved Georgian home, reflective of
that era. "You give Orene's porch a run for its money."

"Yeah, her porch is great. When I was a little boy, my uncle
would take me to visit Orene. I used to dream about her house. I
thought it was the prettiest house in the world."

"Probably why this one caught your attention. Similar in
style. Probably built about the same time."

"Yeah, only hers has always been well kept. By the time I
got my hands on this one, it had been empty for years. It lacked
attention, and sort of fell apart."

"I know how that is," she mumbled.

He heard her, but he didn't acknowledge the remark.

"The epitome of Southern refinement. I feel underdressed,"
she said, as he ushered her in through the antique seeded-glass-
paned front door and into the grand foyer. She looked up. "Even
the fixtures are in period. Well done, Tucker."

"Thank you. I take that as quite a compliment from someone
who sells homes for a living."

"This is outstanding. The way you furnished it minimally,
leaving the grandeur of the intricate moldings and textures of
the natural marble, granite, wood, and fabrics to shine through,
is really well done."

"Not sure that was my intention, but now that you say it, I guess it does. The kitchen is my favorite." He led her that way.

"I can smell that lasagna." She moaned. "If it's half as good as it smells, I am in for a treat."

He went through the tall doorway with the transom window above it. "Prepare to be treated."

She could see why the kitchen was his favorite room in the house. A kitchen should be the heart of the home, and you could feel the beat in this one. "This is like something out of *Southern Living*." She stopped and turned to him. "You are a complex character, Tucker."

Filled with pride that she liked it so much, he smiled. The kitchen was all his favorite things from those *Southern Living* magazines his mother had pored over through the years. From the Sub-Zero fridge, and the old-style gas range with the pot filler and double ovens, to the two-drawer dishwasher, which was perfect for a guy who didn't dirty many dishes each week.

Sheila set the salad dish on the counter, next to where he'd set out plates and silverware.

He pulled the huge pan of lasagna out of the oven. "Sorry, but everything I cook is enough for everyone at the firehouse."

"Don't apologize to me, but I'd be willing to bet you had two pieces in your freezer you could've thawed rather than make a whole new one for me."

"That would be true, but I wouldn't have impressed you."

"I don't know. That's the good thing about Italian food," she said. "It's always even better reheated."

"I'll be sure to send you home with a doggy bag." He pulled a bottle of red wine from the wine rack. "Care for wine with dinner?"

"Yes, please."

"This is from a local vineyard. I like it. Not sure what you'll think."

"I'm sure it will be fine."

He uncorked the bottle, poured two glasses, and then lifted his glass to her. "I'm glad you came to Chestnut Ridge for Christmas."

"Me too." Sheila took a sip from her glass. "This is very good."

"I'm glad you like it. Maybe sometime when you come to visit Natalie, we can all go to the vineyard. They have a nice wine tasting and tours in the spring. In the summer it's too muggy to enjoy. The owners are friends of mine. Shyam and Sarah. They just got married. They're terrific. I'll introduce you."

"They sound great, and I'll add touring the vineyard this spring to my list. That sounds like fun."

"Are you ready to eat?"

"I am."

They served themselves and took their plates over to the large table. They ate dinner, sharing stories about their pasts between cheesy bites of lasagna.

"I'm so glad you already promised me a doggy bag, because I want to eat this every day for a week. It's so good."

Tucker craved more of her easy enthusiasm and confidence. *I could picture myself eating these leftovers with this woman every day in every week.*

Chapter Twenty-two

Sheila set her napkin down and took another sip of wine. "That was the best lasagna I've ever had, and I've been to the best Italian restaurants in the country. Promise me that you won't make that for me for at least a year."

"Why?"

"Because it's so good. I just ate my weight in it. It'll take me three weeks to work those calories off."

He laughed. "I think you'll be fine."

She moaned. "I don't know about that."

"Too full to get up and move around?"

She cut her eyes at him. "What do you have in mind?"

"Well, I was thinking that if you were up to it, we could run over to Joe's tree farm and you could help me pick out my Christmas tree."

"Do I have to walk there?"

"It's not far, but somehow I don't picture you carrying your half of a sappy fresh Christmas tree with those fancy fingernails and pretty outfit."

"You've got that right. I can point and pick, but you're on

your own lugging a tree around like a lumberjack and getting all sticky."

"Have you ever been to a Christmas tree farm?"

"I've always been more the artificial tree kind of girl, and I'm not embarrassed to admit it."

"Shameful." He got up and walked around to pull out her chair. "Come on. I want to treat you to the real experience."

She got up and they cleared the table together, making quick work of it, and then they bundled up in their coats. Tucker wrapped a scarf around his neck and pulled a camel-colored one from the coatrack next to the door and spun it around hers. "You'll need to keep your neck warm. The wind is cold up there." His warm hand grazed her cheek.

"Thank you."

They walked outside and got in the truck. He turned the radio to an all-Christmas-song station. They hummed and sang as they drove to the other side of the mountain.

Tucker turned down the radio and pointed out a big Christmassy barn quilt with the words JOE'S CHRISTMAS TREE FARM arched above it in pretty scrolling white letters that covered the entire side of an old red barn. "This tree farm actually backs up to Natalie's property."

"I never saw anything next to her." That didn't make sense to her. "She's out in the wilderness."

"Well, yeah, the tree farm is beyond a pretty deep area of trees, like a hundred acres, but their land connects. The Christmas tree farm has been in Joe's family for six generations. They even had a Norway spruce go to the White House for the Blue Room back in 1923. It was a pretty big deal."

"Those are the kind with the big pine cones. Your favorite."

"Yes. That kind. It's Joe's specialty, although over the years they expanded. Now they grow several types of trees."

The temperature display on the dashboard read thirty-eight degrees, and the heavy cloud cover made the night sky look inky black.

Along the winding mountain road, red flags with bright green Christmas trees on them confirmed they were still on the right path, but she was beginning to wonder if they would ever get there.

Finally, right after an S curve that scared the bejeebies out of her, lights lit up the sky. There had to be a hundred vehicles parked in the lot in front of the biggest red barn she'd ever seen. Horses hitched to wagons full of people clip-clopped by the truck, headed for the hill.

"Are we going for a wagon ride?" She couldn't hide her delight.

"Unless you'd rather walk up the mountain."

"I'm all for horsepower."

"I've noticed," he said as he got out of the truck. "You're really going to have to tell me how you like that Tesla sometime."

She met him at the tailgate, kind of wishing she'd never driven the Tesla to Chestnut Ridge. "Owning one of those was never on my radar, but it was just too good a deal to pass up." She told him the story while they waited their turn for the next wagon up the mountain.

"I would have had to make that investment too. You'll make a bundle on the resale."

She nodded. "Without question."

The team hitch pulled up, and a guy dressed as an elf helped them climb up the podium to board. They nestled side by side on the straw bales, and as soon as the wagon was full, the cowboy holding the reins gave a command and they lurched forward. A moment later, they were on their way up the hill.

"This is fun!" She looked around at all the smiling faces. The paths were lit, and Christmas music filled the mountainside. She giggled, nudging Tucker at how cute the little boy and girl were seated across from them. "There are so many trees. They seem to go on forever."

"It's a big tree farm. They supply one of the biggest grocery-store chains too. This is just a side hustle for the locals, although it's not a very well-kept secret, as you can tell by the number of cars in the lot."

"It looks like people are coming from miles away."

"They are. You'll see when we check out. They have a big map on the wall where people can mark where they came from. It's surprising."

The two draft horses came to a stop at the cowboy's command, and the elf hopped down and began setting up for their disembarkment.

Tucker steadied her from behind as the elf took her hand to help her descend from the wagon.

As they walked, people kept stopping to say hello to Tucker. It was a little like being with a rock star.

Crisscrossed wooden signs with colorfully painted road names not so different from the ones at the Christmas Tree Stroll pointed the way to trees by type and size.

"They ought to do the Christmas Tree Stroll here," she said.

"We used to, but it actually complicated business for Joe, and then when we had more and more tree farms popping up, the town felt like they needed to give them all fair support. Joe is still everyone's favorite, though. At least to the locals."

"Sounds smart." She eyed the signs. "So, which way should we go? How tall of a tree do you need?" He could definitely do a tall one with the high ceilings, but what a bear to decorate. *Who'd want to do that?*

"I was thinking about a twelve-footer. This way."

Of course he was. "You're going to need a tall ladder to top that thing." She took long steps trying to keep up with him, since he was a good foot taller than she was.

"I'm going to put the tree where the room opens up below the upstairs. We can just reach over the railing."

"We?" She shook her head. "I'm not dangling by my ankles over your railing. That is not going to happen."

"Where's your sense of adventure?"

"It got up and left."

"I've done it before," he said, with confidence. "You'll see it actually works out quite well, and the chandelier adds another dimension of lighting that is really amazing."

"I can't wait to see that."

By the end of the evening, they'd ridden on the wagon, picked out a tree, chopped it down, because of course why would he let them just take the easy route with a chain saw, and watched the tree get dragged down the hill behind a horse on a sled.

Then they met Santa in the big barn and watched kids whisper their hopes and dreams for Christmas morning into his ear. He was a good Santa. Real beard and the jolliest ho-ho-ho she'd ever heard.

While the team prepared their tree for transport, she and

Tucker huddled around one of the big block fire rings to make s'mores.

They took turns roasting the marshmallows and assembling the treats.

"S'mores and hot chocolate is my new favorite way to stay warm in the winter," she said.

"They are yummy." He reached forward to sweep a bit of marshmallow from her cheek. "There."

She moistened her lips, the touch of his hand still catching her breath. "Thank you."

"Sure." Someone called out his name from across the way. "Looks like the tree is ready. Let's go."

Tucker paid the bill at the checkout while she perused the gift shop. When he went to pull the truck around, she bought a cute Christmas ornament with the tree farm name on it as a souvenir. *I hope I never forget this night.*

When Tucker pulled up, he got out and helped the guys load the tree, and then they headed back down the mountain.

"That was so much fun. Thank you for letting me help you pick out your tree," she said. "And those campfire s'mores are sinfully good. I swear I'm going to have one of those built in my backyard."

"S'mores anywhere are the best, but would a firepit really fit in at your house?"

"There is probably an HOA rule against them," she said. "Who knew I'd like them so much?"

"Umm. Sometimes we don't know what we don't know until we do."

She pretended to count off the words. "Easy for you to say."

"You do know," he said, "if you help pick out the Christmas

tree, you are officially obligated to assist in decorating it, don't you?"

"Tonight? I'm beat. Really? Do you have the energy for all of those shenanigans tonight?"

"No. Besides, I have to put the tree in a bucket of water and let it hydrate before the sap gets all sticky where they cut it."

"But we just cut it down. Do you really have to do that? I thought that only applied to the ones that had been sitting on concrete for a few weeks after being cut months ago and shipped down."

"Not true. A tree will take on water for about six to eight hours even if we just cut it down, and you always want to be sure your tree is well hydrated and always has an adequate supply of water."

"This sounds like fire-chief talk."

"It's safetyspeak."

"Whew, so, I'm off the hook for decorating your tree tonight." She swept the back of her hand across her brow. "That was a close call."

"You are off the hook, but I do have another idea." He pulled up and parked right next to her Tesla in Orene's driveway.

"What's that?"

"Let me take you for a ride up on the parkway tonight where you can look down over the entire county. It looks so pretty with all the houses lit up. It won't take thirty minutes, tops."

"That sounds great. Want to drive the Tesla?"

His eyes widened. "Oh, I do. I happen to be a big fan of horsepower too."

"I thought so." She bent down and grabbed the key fob from her purse. "Here you go. Good luck."

"Good luck? I don't need luck. You're coming with me."

"Oh, I'm definitely coming, but that car has a lot of buttons, bells, and whistles. It's like playing a video game for the first time."

"I always was pretty good at video games."

"We'll see."

Sheila was in a fit of giggles by the time Tucker accidentally mashed the button to unlock her car. All at once, all the doors on the vehicle opened up.

"Whoa." Tucker sounded like a twelve-year-old at his first tractor pull. "Okay, I knew they did that, but that is really awesome." He ran his hand over the back falcon wings, then slid into the front seat. "It's like a cockpit in here."

"Sure is." She gave him a quick rundown, not wanting to torture him further, although it was kind of fun watching him try to figure it all out.

He slowly pulled out onto Main Street and then rolled up onto the Blue Ridge Parkway. "This thing is wild. The ride is so smooth. Of course, I am used to diesel-powered heavy machines." He went the speed limit, but seemed completely impressed with the car.

She looked at him with surprise. "You're not going to gun it?"

"Can I?"

"Go for it." She shook her fist toward the windshield. "Let's do this."

"I know the road really well. There's a good long straight stretch coming up. Hang on."

They came out of a tight curve and then he pressed the accelerator, and she could've sworn she could see his heart pounding.

His grin was so wide that all she saw in the dim colored lights from the dash was his teeth.

It was a smooth and exhilarating ride, and she was so glad he'd done that, because she'd been sort of dreaming about it, but was too chicken to try it herself.

"That's incredible. Did you see how fast we were going?"

"I felt the centrifugal force!"

"You did not. But it was cool. Should we try the hands-free?"

"I wouldn't dare. You do it, but not fast."

He let off the gas and rolled back down to a legal forty-five miles per hour. "Here we go."

Sure enough the Tesla kept them right between the lines.

"That's freaky."

He put his hands back on the wheel and took over control. "That was amazing. Thank you. *Merry Christmas to me*." But now he swerved off the side of the road. "Now it's your turn to be amazed." He put the car in park and sat there a second. Then he looked at her. "Can you get us out of this tin can?"

She pressed a button, and the doors opened.

"Thank you. That was much faster. It might have taken me all night, and you've got to see this." He jogged around to her side of the car and gave her a hand. She stood, and he grabbed her hand and walked over to the wall at the edge of the overlook.

"Oh my gosh!" Sheila pulled her arm up against his body. The cold air nipped at her nose, but the view . . . it was breathtaking. He was right about the colored holiday lights across the valley. They seemed to twinkle as far as the universe. "This must be how it looks to Santa as he's looking for those of us on the nice list."

"Definitely." He stood behind her and wrapped his arms around her. "Warmer?"

"Yes. Very nice."

They stood there looking out over so many miles of tiny light dots. Homes where people were celebrating with their own special traditions. It was a powerful reminder of the importance of the season.

The thought made her shiver.

"You're cold." He pulled off his coat and draped it around her shoulders, then ran his hands up and down her arms. "Better?"

"Thank you" came out in just a whisper. "Thank you for bringing me up here. I could look at this every night."

"We can. It's always changing. The seasons, the temperature, the wildlife. You never know what you'll see."

"There's a lot more to life up here than I ever realized. I guess I can understand Natalie's decision a little better now."

"I'll bring you back tomorrow in the daytime."

"Are you trying to get me to agree to *another* date?"

"Would it be so awful if I was?"

She pondered the question.

"Would you say yes?" he pressed.

"Yes," she said. "I think I would."

"Then, I'm asking, but not just any date. My team puts together all the holiday food boxes for the families in our county who are in need. A few years ago, I realized I could make it a bigger opportunity by spending my time prepping everything for them. So I assemble all the boxes, marking them with the name/ address and putting them out on the tables in our community center. That way when the team comes in the next morning, it's a pretty streamlined process."

"So what exactly are you asking me to do?"

"Help me do the prep work on Monday night. I'll put the boxes together, and I have a feeling your handwriting is much prettier than mine. You can write on the boxes."

"That sounds easy enough."

"You're hired, but I have to warn you, the hours are awful and there's no pay. Just the feel-goods of knowing you've helped a neighbor."

"That's what makes it a date, and not a job. Count me in. No matter what."

"Well, then pack your pj's, and a toothbrush, because it'll take all night. We'll work overnight Monday night, and my team will take over in the morning to put everything together on Tuesday for delivery Christmas Eve. Overnight, like all night. You good with that?"

"Are you worried that I might be afraid of the dark?"

"No. I just wanted to be clear that it was an overnight date, but you know, not for sleeping. Wait, that didn't come out right. No funny business either."

Her lips curved at the outer edges. "Oh darn, there really is no pay? There better at least be mistletoe."

"Didn't I tell you to be careful what you wish for?"

She jumped around, trying to get warm. "Yes. Several times now." But she seemed to be wishing for the same things over and over.

He tugged her in under his arm. "Come on. Let's get you back home. It's too cold out here."

"One second." She pulled her phone up and tucked in close to him. "A selfie to remember this moment."

He bent down, the whiskers on his cheek scraping her neck lightly and his breath warm against her cheek.

The flash went off, and she turned in to him, unsure if it was his or her own heart she felt beating. "We better go."

Back in the Tesla, Tucker drove back to Chestnut Ridge. The streets were empty, the town as quiet as if no one lived there.

"I'm sorry for the night to end. It was really fun," she said.

"It's been really nice." He patted her leg. "Thanks for a terrific night. I hope we can do it again?"

"Then we will."

"How about tomorrow after we go to the elementary school pageant?"

"I forgot about that. I'm leaving tomorrow night to head down to see my mother at the assisted living home. The party at the Hilltop starts at noon and it's a five-hour drive. I'm going to drive home, then I'll just be two hours from there on Saturday morning."

"That makes sense." They got out of her car and he tossed her the keys. "It was a real treat to drive this thing. Thanks for that. Best Christmas gift ever."

"You're welcome."

He turned toward his truck, and then turned back. "I just had a thought. What if you drove straight to Virginia Beach on Saturday morning?"

"That's a long ride to get there before noon. I hate driving in the dark."

"What if I drove?"

"You mean . . . come with me? To Virginia Beach?"

"Yeah. I've never been there. It's a party, and I'm great with people. Especially old people. Besides, it's a long ride. Wouldn't it be more fun together?"

"I don't know." She wasn't sure what to think. "This is a little strange, don't you think?"

"Not really. It's Christmas. Who wants to be alone on Christmas? I'll be a complete gentleman." He held up a three-fingered salute. "Scout's honor."

She wasn't entirely sure that's what she wanted either, but why not? He was a nice guy. And having company would make it a much easier trip, since she had to come all the way back to the mountains afterward.

"The Hilltop party starts with a talent show. The staff, and some of the patients, entertain. Last year one of the ladies sang, and I swear you'd be hard to convince me that she wasn't Carol Channing herself. She was adorable. She sang 'Diamonds Are a Girl's Best Friend' and she wore this big boa and one of the nurses handed out these blinking fake diamond rings the size of Ping-Pong balls. It was funny."

"That sounds like a complete hoot. I'm ready. Let me squire you to the event."

"Oh, that sounds a little hoity-toitier than the level of this celebration. It's not that fancy, but that being said, *if* you come with me, there's a condition."

"What's that?"

"You have to give Mom a pretty Christmas corsage. She adores flowers."

"I'll pin it to her robe myself."

That was fun to imagine. Wouldn't Mom just adore getting flowers from a man as handsome as Tucker. "You drive a hard bargain. Some people dance when the talent is a musical number, not to Christmas carols, of course, but you know real songs," she explained. "Will you dance with me?" She really thought he'd balk, and she was really just trying to push his buttons, but to her surprise, he looked completely delighted by the idea.

"Sure," he said. "I'll even dance with your mom."

Stunned, but completely enamored by the sweet thought, she barely knew how to respond. "Okay, now that I've got to see. I'm gonna warn you . . . she will probably lead."

"That doesn't surprise me at all." His eyebrow lifted slightly.

"Are you saying I'm bossy?" She held up her hand, stopping him from answering. "Scratch that. I don't even want to know. It is going to be funny, though, because Mom is about four foot something these days. She'll come up to your belly button." Just picturing her petite mom dancing with this tall, rugged fireman was enough to crack her up, but at the same time, it was sweet.

"I'll let her dance on top of my feet, like my nieces do. No problem. You are a little controlling. Anyone ever tell you that?"

"That's just a nice way of saying bossy." She looked toward the North Pole. "Did you hear that, Santa? He's not being nice to me." She crossed her arms and gave him that "so there" look.

"No fair. If there's coal in my stocking, I'm holding you personally accountable," he said.

"You had better neaten up, then. Haven't you heard? Santa knows when you've been bad or good."

"I plan to be very good."

She could tell by the look in his eyes that him being very good could be very bad for her. *Dear Santa, I've been very good all year long, and I'm trying to keep it that way, but this is very tempting. Please don't let me get my heart broken.*

Chapter Twenty-three

Sheila paced her room, thinking about Tucker and her change in plans. They'd be leaving Saturday morning together. Natalie was never going to believe this.

Things are moving so fast. Too fast?

Don't read too much into it.

He's another man who wants children. Why set myself up for a replay of what happened with Dan? But there are other ways to have children in your life. Is it really a deal breaker? Was it even the reason Dan left? He said it wasn't. Oh, Mom, how I wish you were still yourself. I need you so much right now. My life is just not what I thought it would be by now.

She needed to talk to Natalie about this.

She swept the tears from her face and pulled herself together. She grabbed her coat and raced outside before Orene could catch her and see that she'd been crying, and drove toward Natalie's cabin. The roads were so dark, and she remembered Natalie telling her not to drive up the mountain in the Tesla, but this was an emergency.

This wasn't something she could text or tell her on the phone, though. Butterflies batted around in her belly, making her drive a little too fast, but the Tesla hugged the curves as she headed out past town to the mountain.

All of a sudden, she wondered if Natalie was even at the cabin, or if she was at Randy's house.

Sheila pulled over and texted Natalie.

SHEILA: Are you home?

NATALIE: At Randy's. Come over.

Sheila turned the car around to head back to Randy's, hoping she wouldn't pass Tucker on the way. If there was one thing about a bright red Tesla, it didn't fade into the background. There'd be no mistaking it was her.

She held her breath all the way to Randy's driveway.

Natalie stood at the door waiting. "What's up?" she asked. "Is everything okay?"

"I don't know. My plans changed."

"Is something wrong? Is your mom okay?"

"She's never fine anymore, and that makes me sad. But I'm overwhelmed. Tucker wants to go with me. I said yes. I think things might be really good." She blushed, trying to contain her excitement. "I don't know. Is this a bad idea?"

"What?" Natalie's eyes danced. "And that's why you're frantic? Get in here." She waved Sheila inside. "Oh gosh. You are in a state." She hugged her, and Sheila cried again.

"Are all these tears about Tucker?" Natalie asked.

Sheila looked around for Randy. "Is Randy here?" she whispered.

"No. He's next door helping them with something."

Sheila sat down and lowered her face into her hands. "I think I really like Tucker."

"You think?" Natalie scooted closer. "That's great."

"I don't know. He lives here."

Natalie grinned. "But so do I. It could be perfect."

"Let's not get ahead of ourselves. It's still early and we're getting to know each other . . ."

"Y'all kissed. I can see it all over your face!" Natalie danced in her chair.

"I did not say that. Besides, isn't it too soon for him to be coming to Virginia Beach with me?"

Natalie's eyes widened. "To visit your mother, *and* your sister? Who is to say what's too soon. I mean, better for him to know everything out of the gate, right? It's your life. Oh, Sheila, I know how much it hurts to see your mother like that. It's not an easy situation. It'll be nice to have company."

"He'll probably never want to see me again after that."

"He's interested. That says something, and men process differently than we do. This is Christmas magic. Did you wish on a snow globe or something?" Natalie teased.

"No, but we bought his Christmas tree together last night, and I did some wishing on the hayride, and over s'mores at Joe's tree farm."

"Isn't that romantic? I know you enjoyed that. Sheila, you can trust him."

"Can I trust *me*?" Because right now that was her bigger problem. What seemed like a fun way to spend the holiday was beginning to feel like a very big hope for something more, and that was scary. "I don't even know what I really want. I thought I did, but now I don't."

"Yes. You can trust your heart. I'm happy for you. It's okay to not put all your eggs in your career basket. You work too much. You need to live."

"Work is safe. I'm in control of that. I'm scared."

"Being scared means you care." Natalie got up and came back with a glass of water. "Here. Take a sip and settle down. This is all wonderful. You do not need to worry."

Sheila took in a breath.

"So, you're leaving tomorrow night?"

"No, we're going to drive early Saturday morning, but we might stop in Richmond at my house on the way back."

"That's good. It means he wants to understand where you live too."

"You think?"

"Absolutely. Or that might be the point where you can't trust yourself. He *is* super hot."

"I know! Oh gosh, but it's not the superficial stuff. It's him. All of him that is so amazing. I mean, he's coming with me to see Mom, and you know how depressing that is."

"I know. I'm so sorry you're going through all of that, and it's been such a long struggle for her. Do you want to stay here tonight? We have an extra bedroom here at Randy's. You know that."

"No. I'm more comfortable in my room at Orene's."

"I thought you and Tucker were getting close. I could see it in his demeanor, but I just wasn't sure what was in your head."

"Too many things, apparently," Sheila said. "Hopefully, I can clear it a little on my way back. Wish me luck."

"You don't need it," Natalie said.

*   *   *

On Saturday morning, Tucker drove over to Orene's.

"You're right on time."

"You ready?"

"I am." She tossed him her keys. "You're driving so I can sleep, right?" She was only teasing, but he caught the keys mid-air.

"My pleasure."

She hadn't really expected that response. Dan had always complained about early morning driving, so she'd always been the one to drive on family trips.

Tucker took the wheel, and they headed east.

He was a good driver and she had no problem drifting off to sleep. By by the time she woke up, they were already halfway there. "You're making good time," she said, looking at the navigation panel. "Need me to drive some?"

"Not unless you want to. I'm fine," he said.

She opened her bag and handed him a protein bar. "Hungry?"

"Thanks." He opened it and took a bite.

"I appreciate you driving. The worst thing about visiting Mom is the long drive."

"Driving is relaxing for me," he said.

"What *is* your schedule for work? I can't seem to figure it out."

"That's probably partly because I hang out around the fire station when I'm not on duty, and when I'm on duty, I'm still out and about town keeping tabs on things. We work one day on, day off, second day on, day off, third day on, then four days off before starting the whole cycle all over again."

"What if they need you? You couldn't exactly race back to the scene of a fire five hours away."

"One thing I learned early on was that a good fire chief always builds a team of people who can operate successfully without him. I'm there for my team, but I also know that those times when I'm away and they step in, they are prepared."

"As should any good leader in any industry, but I'm going to say that it's always hard for me to let go of the reins. I do try," Sheila admitted.

"You've got to do it for your people. They need to know they've earned your trust and let them prove you can count on them."

It was good advice and something she readily agreed she needed to work on.

"I'm going to call in an order for a corsage so we can pick it up on the way in." She pulled out her phone and started searching for florists.

"No need. A deal is a deal. I got one yesterday. It's in my bag."

"You did?"

"I did. My friend whipped up a pretty wrist corsage. It has a red and white rose and a fancy ribbon. I think she'll like it. It's very Christmassy."

"That is too sweet." She'd only been joking that he had to get one. She always bought one special for Mom for the day. No matter how good or bad the day was, Mom always perked up with the flower corsage. "Thank you."

Thirty minutes later, they turned in to the parking lot of the Hilltop. "This really isn't much of a hill."

"You're right. Not compared to Chestnut Ridge. But it's high to the flatlanders here at sea level."

"Seems like a popular place today."

"It's always well attended."

He parked and then turned and looked at her without a word, making her nervous. She almost wondered if he was going to say he wasn't coming in. That would've been such a Dan thing. Her ex pulled those shenanigans all the time.

He leaned over and kissed her softly on the cheek. "Sheila, I really am glad to be here with you today. I haven't enjoyed some-one's company like this in a long time."

She knew how he felt, but if she uttered even a single word, she was afraid she'd cry. Happy tears, but tears nonetheless, and she had no intention of doing that. She simply nodded and smiled. "Let's do this." She got out of the car and took in a deep breath.

He took her hand as they walked inside.

"A lot of these people don't visit except Christmas and birth-days," she explained. "I understand. It's so hard on the days they don't even recognize you, but if there's any teensy chance of her understanding she is loved, or reliving a special memory, I want to be there to help make that happen."

"How often do you come?"

"It's been less often the last few months. But I try to get there every other week. It's only a two-hour drive from my house, but she sleeps a lot. I found I was only spending any real time with her less than half the times I went. My sister lives right there. She keeps me posted, and I call often."

"That's got to be hard." He pushed the button to open the doors, but she didn't move. "Are you okay?"

"Yeah." But even she knew it didn't sound convincing.

"If you'd feel better if I didn't come in, it won't hurt my feel-ings. It's okay. I know I kind of filibustered you into letting me come. If you're uncomfortable . . ." He paused. "I was kind of looking forward to giving my new friend that pretty corsage."

She cocked her head, unable to hold back her grin.

"And see that show. I do a pretty good Carol Channing too." He raised a hand in the air as if he might even demonstrate.

"Oh no. Please don't. Let's go inside. I'm fine. Really."

He laughed all the way in the door, where they were checked in by one of the nurses and given lanyards with their names in big, bold letters.

Sheila scanned the room for her mother, but didn't see her right away.

"They may not have brought Mom out yet. I usually help her down. Let's go check."

"I'm right on your heels."

He smiled and said hello to everyone they passed.

A couple of the nurses she'd known for a long time gave her that "aha" eyebrow raise, and that felt pretty good. Tucker was a good-looking man, and dressed in khakis and a button-down shirt as blue as his eyes and a fun Santa tie he was hunkier than Mr. December on the fireman calendar.

"Nice facility," he commented.

"One of the best in the area."

When they got to her mother's room, MS. CYNTHIA ALDRIDGE was printed on the placard outside the door.

Sheila tapped twice on the door, which was partially closed. "Knock, knock." Sheila stepped through the door. "Mom? Hello?"

The nurse's face lit up. "Miss Aldridge. Look who's here to go to the party with you," she said to Sheila's mom, who was sitting in a wheelchair with her hands clenched in her lap. "Look who just walked in."

Her mother wouldn't turn her head.

The nurse tried to be encouraging. "She's not really in the mood for a party today, but I promised her she'd have fun. Do you remember how much she enjoyed it last year?"

"I do," Sheila said. "Mom? It's me, Sheila." She placed her hand on her mother's shoulder. "I'm here to go to the party with you."

The nurse looked apologetic.

"You look very pretty. Is that a new outfit?" She knew it was, because she'd mailed it especially for this a couple of weeks ago.

Cynthia turned, her green eyes searching Sheila's for a long moment. "You look like my daughter. I have two daughters."

"I'm sure they love you very much."

"Yes." But her mother's attention had moved on. A playful smile made her lips tremble slightly. "Do I know you?"

"No ma'am," Tucker said. "Not yet. I'm Tucker. It's almost Christmas. My favorite time of the year and I was excited to come to the party. I brought you something to wear. May I?"

Her mouth formed an O and her eyes danced. She shot an excited glance at the nurse and then to Sheila. "I love presents."

Sheila nodded. "Me too."

Tucker didn't miss a beat. He swept the clear box from behind his back and presented it to Mom. Then he took a knee and slipped the wrist corsage on her slight arm. "It looks very pretty. Merry Christmas, Ms. Aldridge."

"Thank you, Tucker. That's such a fun name." She repeated it in a little song. "Tucker, tuck, tuck, tucker, tuck."

Sheila's heart jumped. It was a big deal for Mom to remember a name, even just a moment later.

Mom plucked at one of the petals of the flower. "What kind of flowers are these?"

Tucker said, "The kind to guarantee a smile."

She lifted her fingers to cover her lips as she tittered. "You're a very nice man." Her tiny shoulders folded in as she enjoyed the attention. "And very handsome."

His cheeks colored. "Thank you, ma'am. Coming from a striking woman like yourself, that makes my day."

"Shall we go show him off?" the nurse said hopefully.

Mom nodded. "Most definitely. The others will be so jealous."

Joy rose in Sheila's heart. It was good to see Mom this happy.

"Wheelchair or the rollator?" the nurse asked, although she was already sitting in the wheelchair.

"I can walk," she insisted. "But wheel me down, please." The nurse stepped behind the wheelchair and navigated the old woman through the doorway.

They shuffled along until they got caught behind a crowd of nurses and patients.

Tucker stepped next to the nurse. "I'd be happy to wheel her down. Looks like you have your hands full today."

"That would be great. Yes. Thank you." The nurse turned to Sheila and hugged her. "It's so good to see you. I was really doubtful she'd give in today. I was so worried you'd be disappointed, but we just never know."

"Please don't ever feel bad about that. I understand and I appreciate you being here with her all the time. Thank you so much."

"Your family is very special to me."

"We love you like family. Cassie will be here on Christmas Day, but I brought you a little something. I know they say we can't do this, but if you don't take it, I'm putting it in your car, so just tuck it in your bra and say thank you, okay?" She slipped a tiny envelope into the nurse's hand.

"Merry Christmas. So nice to meet you, Tucker."

Sheila looked at her mother, sitting demurely with her hands in her lap. And although that lost look was still there in her gaze, she looked happy at the moment.

Tucker pushed the wheelchair toward the activities, again greeting people in the kindest way as they wove between workers, a Santa in full getup, and other patients heading to the large community room where piano music was already filtering out into the hall. Tucker commandeered a spot for the three of them near the makeshift stage.

Sheila sat in the chair next to Mom's wheelchair. Mom reached for her hand and gave it a squeeze. A treasured moment.

The show began, and Sheila was sniffling back tears as nonchalantly as possible as an elderly man played "O Christmas Tree" on a lap steel guitar. At the end of the instrumental, someone flipped the switch on the Christmas tree and it lit up.

Mom's eyes lit up too, and she clapped and clapped, as did many of the others as if it were the first time they'd ever experienced a tree lighting.

One of the doctors pointed to the man with the lap steel, and he started playing again, the doctor leading them all, belting out three verses of "O Christmas Tree."

Tucker, seated on the other side of Mom, reached behind Mom's wheelchair and passed Sheila his handkerchief.

She took it with a smile, dabbing at her eye makeup, and

feeling her heart rise into her throat as he rested his gentle hand on her shoulder.

For the next thirty minutes the staff led the entire group in the most popular carols. There was pitiful participation at first, but by the third song it was loud and quite fun.

The Carol Channing look-alike repeated her number from last year, and Tucker even wolf-whistled following her performance, which garnered a long gloved hand draped in his direction for a kiss, which he happily obliged.

"You are too much," Sheila said.

"It's joyful," he insisted. "Where's your Christmas spirit?"

"Alive and well, thanks to you," she said.

An eighty-five-year-old man stepped to the piano. Although they'd announced that he'd be playing "Let It Snow," he began playing "Raindrops Keep Falling on My Head." People didn't seem to notice, though, and since others were dancing, Tucker asked Mom to dance.

Her eyes lit up, but she looked at Sheila for approval.

"It's fine. Go on. He won't let you get off-balance," Sheila assured her.

Tucker took Mom's frail hand and danced right there in front of her wheelchair. Mom beamed. Before the song was over, he bent down and whispered something in her ear. She nodded, and he gracefully spun her. The others clapped and cheered.

Sheila's heart never felt so full.

The old man at the piano moved into a brilliant rendition of "Silent Night" with extra runs. He must've been an accomplished musician in his younger years.

Mom fell asleep in the wheelchair, so Sheila and Tucker wheeled her back to her room to tuck her back into bed.

They wrote on her whiteboard and left a piece of cake on her nightstand.

They shut the door behind them to leave, and Tucker stopped her to give her a hug. "I know this must be so difficult."

"It is, but you made it really special. Thank you."

"I'm glad I got to be here." They left the Hilltop and stopped in at Cassie's house, where she was hosting her annual holiday party for the entire neighborhood.

People were coming and going, and it took Sheila a few minutes squeezing between people to track down her sister in the throng of people.

"There you are. Sis?" Sheila carried a bag of small gifts for her sister and family. "Merry Christmas."

"Sheila? I was hoping you'd have time to stop in. I'm so glad you're here." Cassie hugged her, then looked at Tucker. "Who is this?" Cassie gave her a curious and suspicious look.

"This is Tucker. He's a really good *friend* of Natalie's, and mine now." Sheila emphasized "friend," but she could already see Cassie's wheels turning.

"Yes, we are." Tucker smiled easily toward Sheila, then turned to Cassie. "Really nice to meet you. I see the resemblance between the two of you."

Sheila sucked in a breath, satisfied with the day. "We just spent time with Mom. It went better than I could have hoped."

"I'm so glad." Cassie shook her head. "You just never know, I think that's the hardest part. It's been a tough week."

"I don't know how you deal with it every week." Sheila hugged her sister. "This is so hard."

"I know, but I'm glad you're here, and even if Mom didn't know it was you, I think in her heart she feels the connection."

"She looked so happy." Sheila was so thankful for the way things had turned out.

Cassie whispered into Sheila's ear. "He's so, so, so handsome. That probably made Mom happy too."

Sheila swatted her away. "Not funny. We're friends."

"Seriously? Get that." Cassie's eyes widened. "I'm not joking."

Thankfully Sheila's nephew raced into the room right at that moment, and she didn't have to comment.

"Aunt Sheila!" He wrapped himself around her in a big hug. "Merry Christmas."

"You too, Kyle." She handed him the bag she'd been carrying. "One present is for your mom and dad. Everything else is for you."

Kyle leapt in the air, landed, and pumped his fist into the air. "No way!" His smile spread across his face when he took the bag and realized how heavy it was. "Thank you! I can't wait to open them."

"Hon, come meet Sheila's friend Tucker," Cassie said. Her husband, Bert, walked over and shook Tucker's hand. It took only a sentence or two for them to fall into deep conversation, and they walked off talking.

Sheila took a moment to soak it all in, finally sharing everything from these last few days with her sister over a cup of eggnog.

Cassie said, "I don't even care if this is forever, it's just nice to see you dating someone. And he's nice."

"He is."

"Can you help me refresh the dessert trays?" Cassie asked.

Sheila was already carrying a dish to refill the sausage balls, eating a couple on the way. "I'm on it."

She heard Bert call over to Kyle. "Son, I have someone for

you to meet. This is Aunt Sheila's friend, Tucker. You won't believe what he does for a living."

"What?"

"He's the fire chief."

"No way. You're a real live hero." The little boy danced with excitement. "I want to be a fireman someday too."

"Jackpot." Cassie leaned in to Sheila. "Y'all just made his day. And you didn't think to call me and tell me you're dating a fireman?"

"I don't even know if it's anything. It's very new," Sheila whispered, but definitely feeling something as she watched Tucker so at ease with everyone. "He's pretty great."

"This is going to be Kyle's best Christmas present, meeting a real fireman." They watched as Tucker bent to get eye-to-eye with Kyle.

"I wish I'd known," Tucker said. "I'd have brought you a hat. You get your Aunt Sheila to bring y'all to Chestnut Ridge someday. I'll show you around the firehouse."

"Can I slide down the pole?"

Sheila was glad to see that Tucker avoided ruining the little boy's dream by admitting they didn't have a sliding pole at their firehouse. It had been kind of a big disappointment for her too. Instead, he promised a ride in the fire truck and the chance to be the one to make the siren and lights come on.

"That child will never be the same," Cassie said to Tucker. "You're more important than Santa at this moment."

"That should secure my spot on the nice list." He gave Sheila an exaggerated glance. "She keeps trying to get me on the naughty list."

"I do not. You just keep misbehaving."

They noshed on the heavy hors d'oeuvres. Cassie always threw an amazing party, and this was the most fun Sheila had ever had at one. Dan had always bellyached his way through it, holing up in front of the television in the den. But this was different.

"We've got to hit the road," Sheila finally said. "We haven't decided for sure, but we were talking about possibly driving straight back tonight."

"I'll go get the car," Tucker said. "I'll pick you up out front."

"Thanks, Tucker."

Cassie said, "I'd *move* to the mountains for that guy too."

"You would not, but he does seem too good to be true, doesn't he?"

"Or just good. Don't dismiss something wonderful when it lands in your lap."

"It's nuts. I know. Why are all the good ones already taken, or live in some horrible place?" Sheila shrugged. "If only he lived in Richmond."

"Is Chestnut Ridge really so awful?" Cassie asked. "You said Natalie is happy there."

"It's not really that bad. It's sort of charming. Just small."

"And what's more important? Population or the perfect relationship?"

Her sister always had a way of getting to the nitty-gritty, pushing personal agendas and noise out of the way to get to the real point. "I do also have a business to consider."

"But do you really? You could sell houses anywhere, and this guy would make pretty babies with you. He's hot!" She fanned herself. "I mean like fireman-calendar hot."

"Babe. Standing right here," Bert said.

"Sorry, honey. You're super hot too." Cassie patted his cheek, then turned to Sheila and rolled her eyes. "Don't discount this," she said. "You are wonderful. I want you to have everything I have in a relationship. Just keep your options open."

"Okay, okay." Sheila stepped back. "Don't push. Like, seriously, we had our first date a week ago."

"Well, you wouldn't know it. It's like y'all have known each other for years."

"You should've seen him with Mom," Sheila said. "She was smitten, and he was so patient and kind."

"We both know that's a lot easier when you're not having to do it twenty-four/seven. She's in a good place there."

"I know. I'm sorry I gave you such a hard time about it. I understand now. I do. I promise. Can we put all of those bad scenes behind us?"

"Already behind us, Sheila. I love you. Sisters fight. Families suffer. It's part of the ride. It's really good to see you looking so happy."

"It feels good."

"Merry Christmas, and good luck with Tucker." Cassie handed her a small box. "This is just a little something from us. Merry Christmas."

"You didn't have to do that." Sheila hugged Cassie, Kyle, and Bert and then headed outside, where Tucker was waiting in the car.

She waved as she walked down the sidewalk, so thankful for this new friendship, and filled with hopes and dreams she thought might never be possible for her.

"Want to go to the mountains or your house?" he asked.

"Let's go back to Chestnut Ridge," Sheila said, "where it feels like Christmas."

Chapter Twenty-four

Tucker merged the Tesla into traffic on the highway. "You know," he said, "they're having a cookie sale in front of GG's Mountain-side Gardens & Gifts tomorrow on Main Street to raise money for the Jacob family. Can I talk you into helping me bake cookies first thing in the morning?"

"I can help. What kind are you baking?"

"My tradition." He glanced over and caught the look in her eye. "Honestly, I buy the slice-and-bake rolls, but I press red and green chocolate covered candies into them. People think they're great. Don't you tell anyone they aren't made from scratch."

She zipped her lips, and pretended to toss the key over her shoulder. "I'd never, but I make really good pecan snowball cook-ies. I know the recipe by heart. It was Mom's favorite."

"Those sound great. Can we do both? I mean people are expecting my traditional cookies."

"Sounds like a plan."

"Well, little miss I-know-my-recipe-by-heart, can you make a shopping list? We'll stop and pick up everything we need on the way back. It'll give us a chance to stretch our legs too."

"Absolutely." She pulled a small notepad from her purse and started the list. "If I triple the recipe how many would that be?" She pressed the pen to her lips as she calculated. "Let's see, each batch makes about three dozen, so that's about a hundred cookies."

"Minus the ones we eat?"

"Oh no, sir. There'll be none of that. This is a fundraiser." She playfully smacked his arm.

"I can promise you there *will* be," he said unapologetically.

"You'll pay double for each one you eat then," she said matter-of-factly, and moved on. "Do you have cookie sheets, or should I pick up some tinfoil ones at the store?"

"I have some and double ovens, so we should be able to make short work of it," Tucker said. "Maybe we should quadruple your recipe. You know, so we have plenty for us too."

"We can do that, but you're not getting free cookies." She wagged her pen in his direction. "You have to buy every one you eat."

"You are a serious fundraiser."

"It's for the Jacobs, Cookie Monster." She swatted his arm playfully. "What's wrong with you?"

"Fine. Definitely quadruple or quintuple it. I'll buy all you can bake."

"You're helping me. That's a lot of little balls to roll out."

"I'm not afraid of spending time in the kitchen with you." In fact, he was looking forward to it.

They stopped in the last large town on the way home and got everything on the shopping list. She was a good sport when he made her toss things in the cart as he whizzed by. He liked that about her.

And when he grabbed extra paper towels and hurled them in

her direction following a quick spin shouting, "Heads up!," she actually caught them like a wide receiver.

Back in the car, with everything they'd need to bake cookies in the morning, she fell asleep, and didn't wake up until he pulled up in front of Orene's house.

Tucker touched her shoulder softly. "Hey, sleepyhead. We're back."

Her lashes batted as she awoke and sat up in the seat. "I'm sorry. I didn't even realize I'd fallen asleep."

"Well, not everyone can keep up with my grocery-store aerobics program."

She laughed. "That was fun."

He handed her the keys to her car. "Call me when you get up so we can get going on the cookies early. I'm sure I'll already be up."

"Okay. I'll call you." She opened the car door. "Thanks for a really perfect day."

"I thought so too. Sweet dreams." They both got out of the car.

He walked over to his truck and waited until she went inside and her bedroom light came on before getting in his truck to leave.

Sunday morning, the sun was shining, and the temperature was forecast to be in the fifties later in the day. It would be a great day for last-minute shopping, and he had no doubt the cookie sale would be a big hit.

He'd already set out all the baking ingredients and baggies for the cookies. If he'd only thought to ask Sheila for the recipe, he could have gotten started without her. He went to work on his slice-and-bakes, though, and was putting the first ones in the oven when she called.

He answered with a hearty hello.

"Good morning to you, too," she said. "I slept like a rock. Did you sleep well?"

"I did," he said, although the truth was he'd woken up several times with her on his mind. "Are you on your way over?"

"Yes. I'm already walking. I'll be there in a couple of minutes. Can you take the butter out? We'll need it softened to get started."

"Already done."

"You really are a mind-reader. See you in a minute."

He found himself pacing and peeking out the window, waiting for her. *Why am I this excited? I just spent the whole day with her.*

He looked out the window again and saw her coming up the sidewalk, huddled in a navy-blue peacoat and white toboggan like the ones Orene knitted with the big pom-pom on top.

He hung in the kitchen trying to act nonchalant so she wouldn't think he was anxious, but he abandoned that plan before she even got to the porch.

"Welcome, cookie-recipe princess." He motioned her inside. "Ready to commence baking?"

"Sure." She unwrapped herself from the hat, coat, and gloves. "It's supposed to be nice this afternoon, but it's still cold this morning."

Her nose was pink. Tucker stepped up and wrapped her in his arms. "I'll warm you up."

She giggled, and that warmed him up too.

They got straight to work. The recipe wasn't complicated,

and she was right: rolling all those little balls out of the thick shortbread-like dough was the biggest job of all.

It only took a half hour for them to get the first sheets in the oven, and then it was a constant flurry of action. Putting them in, taking them out, the sugar dip, cool, dip them again, and set aside.

Between each batch of her recipe, he sliced and baked the sugar cookies with the candies in them, which actually looked pretty all piled up on his counter.

That wasn't the only flurry in that kitchen that morning.

Along about the sixth baking sheet full of cookies, they were rushing trying to keep up, and during the dip-into-confectioners'-sugar phase, he dabbed a smudge of it on her nose.

She retaliated by tossing some in the air, which dotted the front of his red long-sleeved T-shirt. And then it was on.

They were both wearing copious amounts of the white powder on their clothes, hair, and faces when the oven timer buzzed and they finally called a truce.

"Last batch," Sheila announced.

"Thank goodness. That's a lot of cookies."

"And I've got a bill for you for all the ones you ate."

He dipped his hand into his pocket and took out a twenty. "Here, let's just call it even."

"Excellent. That and twenty-five baggies of cookies at two dollars a pop will put another fifty dollars plus this twenty into the fundraising pot. Not bad." Sheila took another twenty out of her purse. "Let's call this the corporate-match program."

"I like the way you think." He plopped down in a kitchen chair.

She joined him at the table. "I don't think I've done that much baking ever."

"We didn't even burn a batch," he said. "I call that a good day."

"A victory, for sure."

"You know, it's been really nice getting to know so many sides of you this week."

"You too." She leaned forward playfully. "I only hope we can still be friends after our Christmas tree wins."

"It's anybody's game. We'll have to wait until they announce the winners tonight to find out, but I'll be dressed for success." He picked up a box from the kitchen table and started setting the bagged cookies into it.

"Oh, really?"

"Yeah, can't claim the big trophy in confectioners'-sugar-and-butter-stained clothes. There will be pictures in the paper."

She started stacking cookies in the box too. "Don't be so cocky. I think our tree has a very good chance of winning."

"We'll see."

"And if you lose, am I still invited tomorrow night for our all-nighter putting together the food boxes at the fire station?"

"I already locked in your offer to help. There are no backouts."

"I wouldn't dream of it."

He picked up one of the boxes of cookies. "What do you say we walk these down to the bake sale, and then I'll see you tonight at the Christmas Tree Stroll?"

"That sounds good, because I'm definitely going to take a nap."

"I may be doing the same. I had no idea baking that many cookies would be so tiring."

They dropped off the cookies and Greta set them out on a

pretty tray. "These will go in a flash. It's a good thing you showed up when you did. We were running so low I thought we were about done," Greta said. "We've brought in some good money. This was a great idea."

"Can't go wrong with cookies," Tucker said.

"Maybe I should've gone into cookies instead of flowers." Greta wrinkled her nose. "No. I like my plants."

"You're in the right business," Tucker said. "The flowers you put together for me were a big hit. Thanks for making me look so good."

Sheila raised her hand. "My mother adored that corsage."

"I'm so glad. It's nice to meet you. I'd heard from Orene that you were going to be in town."

Tucker hoped that was all Greta was going to say, but Gary gave him a look that told him that he'd heard a thing or too as well. Acting fast, before Gary and Greta could embarrass him in front of Sheila, he ushered her toward the door. "Well, we're going to get out of here. Have a good day, and thank you."

"I'm going to walk back to Orene's. I really enjoyed today," Sheila said. "I'll see you tonight?"

"Definitely."

At four o'clock, Tucker walked up to the high school football stadium, looking forward to seeing Sheila again.

He'd tried to take a nap, but ended up daydreaming about how nice it might've been had Sheila come to his place for that nap she'd mentioned, and that ended up keeping him awake.

Across the way, he saw Sheila walking with the rest of her team. "Hey," he shouted, and broke out into a jog to catch up to them.

Natalie was the first to turn around. "Hey, Tucker!"

The cute swivel of Sheila's hips as she turned to wave wasn't lost on him, and left him a little breathless.

"It's the big day." Tucker stopped between Sheila and Natalie. "Mind if I join you?"

He was talking directly to Sheila, but Natalie answered. "The more the merrier. We're going to do a quick walk-through to see all the competition now that everything is set up."

No one said much of anything as they walked through admiring the competition.

"There are so many trees, and they're all so different," Sheila said. "It would be hard to pick even ten favorites out of all these."

"It's like comparing apples to oranges." They stopped at the last aisle. "I'd hate to be a judge," Natalie admitted.

"You and me both." Sheila paused. "I do think we have a shot. Our tree holds up, but the competition is stiff. One of my favorites was the snowflake-themed tree with the white fur tree skirt. All the silver, white, and mirrored snowflake ornaments were simple, but I just couldn't take my eyes off of it."

"Yeah, I'm not even sure what kind of lights they were using. They were tiny like fairy lights but they were more twinkly. That one is definitely a front-runner," Amanda agreed.

"And the Woods Brothers racing team tree with the checkered flags and how they have those cars racing on those tracks all up that tree and not going off the track is a mystery," Tucker said. "It defies gravity. And their tree skirt with the drivers' names lit up was pretty cool."

"I was here when the judges came by this morning," Natalie told them. "They had clipboards and looked all serious, making notes the whole time."

"Did they seem to like what we've done?" Sheila asked.

"It was hard to tell. They seemed to spend more time at our tree than the others, but I don't know if that's good or bad. That could have totally been my imagination. I heard one of them say something about the handmade ornaments, and touching the golden tassels to see if they were real pine needles. I hope we didn't break a rule or something."

"I don't think so," Amanda said. "We should be proud of it no matter what."

Tucker squeezed Natalie's arm and pointed toward a judge walking down the aisle. "Look, they are starting to hand out the envelopes." The judge stopped at each tree, talking to the team and handing each an envelope.

"My hands are sweating." Natalie wiped them on her pants. "I'm so nervous."

"Don't freak out," Tucker said. "They personally thank every team when they provide the scores. They'll announce the winners from the stage after everyone has their individual results. Good luck. I'm going to go over with my team."

"See you later. Good luck," Sheila called after him.

"I see that look in your eye. You really like him," Natalie said. "I've been poking fun, but there really could be something here, couldn't it?"

"I don't know. I think I'm just super emotional. It's Christmas."

"I know this is a hard time of year for you. Ever since your mom's diagnosis and the big falling-out with Cassie over it."

"Cassie and I are in a better place now," Sheila admitted. "The visit with her was nice. I feel horrible for giving her such a hard time."

"Sheila, you were just trying to do what you thought was best. It's not an easy situation."

"I made it worse for all of us." A tear slipped down her cheek. "I regret that."

"No regrets. No, ma'am. Apologize, put it behind you, and make every next day the best you can."

"I've done a lot of wrong things."

"Like what?" Natalie looked confused.

"Like trying to hold you back in Richmond with me when you needed to move on," Sheila admitted.

"You didn't hold me back. You comforted me when I was suffering. You're the best friend I could ever ask for. Don't ever doubt that."

Sheila hugged her. "You're the best. I'm just going to try to be as good as you are."

Amanda walked over, breaking up the moment. "There's still some time before they announce the winners. Relax," she said, and blew out a long slow breath. She looked like she might need the reminder to relax more than any of them. "Are y'all okay? Sheila, are you crying?"

"I'm just excited. Aren't we all?"

Natalie hugged her from the side. "We are!"

A tall woman in all red walked up to Natalie. "Well done. We are excited to have new teams this year. Thank you for joining us. Here is your scorecard. You're welcome to open it, but please do not discuss your results with anyone until after the announcements." The judge handed Natalie the envelope and moved to the next tree.

"Yes, ma'am." Natalie stood there clinging to that envelope with the name of their tree written on the front.

As soon as the judge was out of sight, the team gathered around Natalie, who opened the envelope in hushed squeals of anticipation.

"We put our heart and soul into every detail of this tree," Natalie said. "I wouldn't change a thing." Natalie wiggled in excitement. "Let's hope it was enough to win."

"What's it say?" Sheila peered over her shoulder.

"Do we even know what a winning score is?" Randy asked.

Amanda shook her head. "Not really. The highest score possible is one hundred. So you know, it depends on how the judges score, but if you think of it like getting an A plus, then that's a pretty good chance."

Natalie closed her eyes, then opened the card and read the score. Her eyes flashed up.

"What? Is it good?"

"Very." She turned the card around. "Shhh."

"Oh my gosh. We've got a great chance of winning."

"I think so too."

"I'm dying to find out." Natalie nudged Sheila when she noticed the people across the way watching them. "We better be quiet about this. No sharing. You heard what she said. I'd hate to lose from a forfeit for breaking the rules."

"No kidding." Sheila turned and looked toward the top of the stadium as jingle bells sounded. "What is that?"

"Look!" Amanda pointed to a section of the bleachers on the far right. One at a time, colored lights began to come on between the jingle of sleigh bells, and then all at once it was the outline of a Christmas tree, and then like a choir of angels the children holding the lights began to sing, and the lights in their hands swayed with the melody.

With the final note from that song, across on the visitors' side, another group formed the shape of a bell out of white lights as they began singing "Silver Bells."

And one right after the other, they volleyed carol after carol from side to side. Ten songs in all.

"That was fantastic." Natalie clapped, and Randy stood behind her with his arms around her, clapping too. "But I'm going to die of anticipation if they don't announce the winners soon."

The stadium lights came back on, and the kids filed out of the stands like little soldiers marching through the Christmas Tree Stroll lanes singing "A Holly Jolly Christmas."

Everyone joined in the festive moment.

Bringing up the rear, none other than Santa himself, with a procession of elves handing out candy canes.

"This is an amazing night." Sheila turned, expecting to see Natalie, but instead Tucker was there. "Oops. When did you get back?"

He claimed her arms and squeezed her shoulders sweetly. "I didn't want to miss you seeing all of this for the first time. I see it every year, but to see it all through your eyes for the first time is really exciting."

"No one could have prepared me for this. I can't even explain it after seeing it myself." She turned back. "And I think you make it even more special."

"I think you're pretty special."

Santa's voice rose from the PA speakers throughout the stadium. "Ho-ho-ho. Merry Christmas! The time has come for us to announce the Annual Christmas Tree Stroll winners."

The entire place roused into a roaring cheer.

"Is that all the noise you can make? Give me one big 'Merry Christmas.'"

"Merry Christmas!"

"Ah, yes, we could blow fog across the nation with all that hot air. I wouldn't even need Rudolph's shiny nose with your help. Now, are you ready to hear the official Christmas Tree Stroll winning entries?"

The mayor took the mic. "I've been announcing the winners of this event for the last four years, and I came to every stroll for at least twenty years before I ever became mayor. I have to say, this year y'all brought amazing innovation, beauty, and generosity to the mix. It's the best year, but then maybe I say that every year."

Tucker reached for Sheila's hand and gave it a squeeze.

Sheila looked over at Randy and Natalie, and Eli and Amanda. The other two couples stood arm-to-arm too. Everyone was on pins and needles waiting for the big announcement, and at that moment she knew she'd already gained the best prize. She leaned into Tucker, placing her other hand on his biceps.

The mayor paused until the crowd settled down. "The categories of winners this year, in no particular order, are: Storyline or Theme; Unique Design and Creative Use of Lights and Decorations; and Display and Placement of Decorations. We have such great representation in all of them. Of those three winners, the grand prize of bragging rights for the year and this eye-catching banner with their name on it hung in the school will be presented for the best overall presentation. Is everyone ready for this?"

A resounding "Yes" lifted from the stands.

"Here we go." The mayor shuffled big red-and-green Christmas envelopes, and then opened the first one. "This year's winner in the Unique Design and Creative Use of Lights and Decorations category, cited for its use of alternative energy and all-upcycled ornaments, is Solar Spruce, designed and decorated by the senior class of Chestnut Ridge High, for their six-foot Norway spruce. A hidden solar-energy panel on the top of the tree is providing the energy for all the lighting and the colorful spinning Moravian star on top. Ornaments are made from aluminum cans, paper plates, and old magazines. Now, that's innovation."

The team, wearing matching high school jerseys, bounced arm in arm in celebration. Their excitement was contagious.

"Next, the winner of the Display and Placement of Decorations category." The mayor chuckled. "They seem to make it into the top every year."

Tucker looked at Natalie. "That's got to be my guys."

"The Chestnut Ridge Fire Department for their Ninety-Nine Ways to Get Home for Christmas. They have generously decorated this twenty-two-footer full of bikes, trucks, skateboards, skates, horses, you name it, and every decoration is a toy that will be distributed in our county. I, the mayor of Chestnut Ridge, can speak for Santa when we give this team a hearty thank-you for their generosity."

Santa danced across the stage, ho-ho-ho'ing. "And I didn't even have to ask. Thank you. You are truly ho-ho-ho-heroes in every way! I believe there are enough shiny handlebar bells on that tree to put one on every bicycle in the county. Maybe in every car! Well done."

Sheila threw her arms around Tucker's neck. "Congratulations! That's wonderful. *You're* wonderful."

He looked down into her eyes, her face just inches from his. "You make me want to be."

The mayor took the mic from Santa and shuffled him off the stage. "You'd think that guy got enough attention this time of year. This is my minute in the spotlight, Santa." The mayor summed up the winners of all of the categories and special mentions, and then it was time for the big announcement of the evening.

Sheila and Tucker pulled themselves together and focused their attention back on the mayor and the final envelope. "And now the winner of the Christmas Tree Stroll. Drumroll, please."

Everyone in the place slapped their hands to their legs, and in the stands the kids were pounding their feet until the whole place rocked like a concert. "Our winner of the Storyline or Theme category is Feathered Friends Home for the Holidays."

Natalie and Sheila both leapt so high that Sheila bumped Tucker right in the nose.

"I'm sorry," Sheila squealed the apology, but then bounced toward Amanda and Natalie.

Tucker rubbed his nose.

"I can't believe it. I'm so proud of us!" Natalie hugged Randy. "Thank you for your help, babe. Y'all are all amazing. I can't believe it!"

"This team decorated a six-foot Fraser fir and somehow they hand-painted the tips of every branch with iridescent paint, making them appear as if ice has crystallized on them. The use of real pine needles painted to appear like golden tassels was ingenious, and the birdhouses on this tree are nothing short of artworthy. And I've been informed that some of the birdhouses will go to the senior center. Be sure to head over and congratulate them on a job well done."

Tucker turned to Sheila. "I'd like to be the first. Job well done." He dropped a kiss on her forehead. "And a lot more fun than usual with you around."

Following the celebratory hugs and high fives, Natalie said, "Come on. Lets everyone go to Orene's and celebrate." She looked up at the tree with appreciation. "Someone is going to really enjoy this tree."

Randy looked surprised. "Natalie, wait. I wanted you to have that tree topper. I made it special. For you. Won't you keep that birdhouse?"

She clasped her hand over her mouth. "Yes. Of course. I'm sorry. Yes! I have to keep that one. Take it down." Natalie shot Sheila a look who nudged Tucker to help Randy reclaim the gift.

"Thanks." Randy seemed flustered. "We're all going to Orene's. Tucker, you've got to come with us."

"Sounds good." Tucker pointed to the tree and gave Randy an encouraging nod. "How about I grab that tree topper for you?"

"That would be great," Randy said.

Tucker reached up and got the topper, and Sheila and Natalie and Amanda selected three birdhouses to take down to the senior center. They shifted the rest of the ornaments around, and then moved the bird nest to the place where the topper had sat just a moment ago to fill the gap.

"That looks pretty good," Sheila said to Natalie under her breath.

"It does. We might have to backpocket that idea for another year."

"I agree."

"Are y'all coming?" Randy called to them.

"I don't know why he's so antsy tonight," Natalie said. "We're coming."

They all drove back to Orene's in the separate cars they came to the event in. They were all tired, but enjoying reliving the excitement of the evening.

"That smells like Orene's fresh baked cookies," Tucker said.

Randy sucked in a breath. "This town just gets better and better."

They filed inside, where they were greeted with fresh-baked cookies in the shape of birdhouses arranged on a large white platter, and a punch bowl of eggnog waiting on them.

"How did you do that so fast," Natalie remarked.

"I had a gut feeling you were going to win," Orene told Natalie. "I knew it as soon as I saw your tree, so I got a head start. Let's celebrate." She waved her hands in the air; it looked more like jazz hands than celebration, but it was so Orene.

"You think of everything, Orene." Natalie hugged her. "You're the best family we could have."

"I second that," Sheila said. "You just don't know how much being here with you has meant, especially with my mom . . . well . . ." Sheila's eyes glassed over. "It's just been so comforting to be here with you. My mom would've loved you too."

"Well, if I could've handpicked a bunch of kids to call my own, I'd have adopted you all!" Orene's smile was sweet, and her eyes were misty. "Seriously, you bring this old woman so much joy." She picked up a cup of eggnog. "Get a cup."

Everyone picked up a cup of eggnog.

"Here's a toast to making a big splash at your very first Christmas Tree Stroll." Orene raised her cup high in the air, and the others followed. "Chestnut Ridge is better for having you all become a part of our community. Our family. Cheers."

Everyone took a sip, and Randy swung his other arm around Natalie's waist. "And we are so happy to be here."

"I wouldn't want to be anyplace else tonight," said Sheila. "With all of you."

"I want to go on record"—Tucker shot a playful stink eye in Natalie's direction—"that I have every intention of trying to woo your secret weapon over to my team next year."

There was a collective murmur of interest from everyone.

"Didn't I tell you I can't be bought?" Sheila said with a sassy lilt.

"You did, but it won't keep me from trying. I need to win back my Christmas Tree Stroll title next year."

"Oh my gosh, I'm supposed to help you decorate your tree at your house," Sheila said. "I totally forgot."

"Well, we've been busy."

"True, but I don't want to break the Christmas tree picker primary rule. You pick it, you decorate it." Sheila looked back at Tucker. "That is what you said, isn't it?"

"That is not a rule," Orene said.

"I might have made it up to spend more time with you," he admitted.

"I might have known that when I agreed," she said, tucking up close against him.

Chapter Twenty-five

Sheila couldn't believe it was already the eve before Christmas Eve. Two weeks had sounded like such a long time to spend in Chestnut Ridge, and now she didn't want it to end.

She got up and made her bed, still exhilarated from last night's win.

Christmas is almost here.

She was wearing the pajamas with holiday penguins on them that Natalie had given her last Christmas. It had become their tradition to give each other pajamas, and she couldn't wait for Nat to open the ones she'd picked out for her this year. It was a complete coincidence, but the pattern was called Jolly Good Forest and in muted dark gray and white they looked like a winter Christmas to Sheila, and with the tiny birds amid the snowy limbs, they were sort of perfect following the Christmas Tree Stroll win.

The wooden floors were cold this morning. She pulled warm socks on, then went downstairs.

Orene greeted her. "Good morning. How's it feel to be a winner?"

"Fabulous." She poured a cup of coffee and joined Orene at the table. "You should be exhausted. How do you keep up this pace?"

Orene shrugged. "I just do what I feel up to for as long as I want to, and then I take a nap and do it all over again."

Sheila enjoyed the first sip of coffee. "If only it were that simple. I can't believe how fast the time has passed."

"Maybe you need more naps." Orene lifted her brows. "Could help. Santa will be here before we know it."

"On the bright side, I've been so busy that I didn't give anyone their presents early for the first time in maybe forever."

"Well, not for lack of trying," Orene reminded her.

"True, but you resisted my insisting nature and saved me from myself."

"You are welcome." Orene looked quite pleased with herself. "Isn't this more exciting?"

"I've been too busy to even think about it. I want to do something for Tucker, but I don't want to embarrass him with anything expensive. I mean, we really just met, and he probably won't be giving me a gift. But it would be so nice to do something for him. He's pretty much made my holiday. He deserves some kind of thank-you. Don't you think?" She pushed her fingers through her hair and groaned. "Am I overthinking this?"

"No. I think it's nice that you want to let him know he's appreciated. I'm of the school of thought that homemade gifts are always the best way to go in this situation."

"True. Right!" Sheila nodded. "You are brilliant. Do you always know the right thing to say to everyone, or just to me? Never mind. Doesn't matter. Would you mind if I did some baking today?"

"Not at all. Make yourself at home."

"That would be great. I'm going to bake Tucker something special for Christmas." She got up from the table. "I'm going to take my coffee upstairs. I need to wrap all those presents for the Jacob family that were delivered yesterday."

"I was afraid the UPS man was going to ask to spend the night he was so exhausted after carrying all those packages to the porch."

"They had some amazing sales going on. I stuck to my budget, though."

"It looks like you spent a fortune."

"I didn't, but I do hope it helps them have an easier holiday. It just breaks my heart that they went through that."

"There are a lot of other families going through tough times too. It's too bad more people don't help each other the way you are doing. This world would be in a much better place. Kindness breeds kindness, ya know."

"I know what you mean." She stood. "Actually, 'kindness breeds kindness' sounds like a really good Christmas Tree Stroll theme." She tapped her head. "I'm tucking that away for next year." She pressed her finger to her lips. "Shh. Our secret."

"I told you! You've got the Christmas Tree Stroll bug. You'll have ideas all year long."

"I definitely want to do it again. And I think this lesson in helping others is long overdue for me. I've never really done anything like this."

"Knowing you, that really surprises me, but it's never too late to start," Orene said.

Sheila went upstairs and gathered the gifts she'd wrapped for Natalie and Randy and put them in the fancy gift bag she'd bought at Hobby Lobby last week to carry them over to the cabin on Christmas morning.

She packed some of her things to clear the room enough to get down to the work at hand—wrapping presents.

With the pretty paper spread out across the bed, she began the process, one gift at a time.

It took her nearly four hours to get everything wrapped. She'd run out of store-bought rosette bows, but made do with extra ribbon simply folded over in a one-loop bow.

The gifts looked nice stacked by the door.

After lunch, she went to the store to get everything to make from-scratch cheddar wafers and a big pot of tomato basil soup. Mom taught her to make both. She and Cassie could devour a whole batch of them in short order. To this day it was her favorite winter meal.

Orene wasn't home when Sheila got back, so she got right to work. It didn't take long for the aroma from the savory spices in the cheddar wafers to fill the house. The soup simmered as her first batch of crispy cheese crackers were about ready to take out of the oven.

Sheila watched through the oven window as the edges of the lacy wafers began to brown.

She'd made extras so even after she filled the big mason jar with them for Tucker, there'd be plenty for Orene to enjoy.

The timer buzzed, and the wafers looked perfect. She switched a new baking sheet for the finished ones to let them cool a bit before putting them on the rack.

"What smells so good in here?" Orene walked in wearing a red skirt and white blouse. Her Christmas vest had snowflakes appliquéd on the front. "When you said you were going to use the kitchen, I didn't expect to come home to this. It smells so homey in here."

"It always smells better when someone else does the cooking, don't you think?" Sheila felt at home in the kitchen. Truth be told, ever since she and Dan split, she hadn't done much cooking or baking, so this was a treat.

"You've got a point." Orene wandered in, looking at everything. "I don't remember the last time someone made themselves at home in this kitchen. I love it!"

That made Sheila happy. As lonely as she was for her own mother, she could only imagine how lonely it must be sometimes for Orene. "I made plenty for you."

"May I?" Orene's hand hovered over the cooling cheddar wafers.

"Please do."

Orene lifted one to her mouth and took a delicate bite. "These are so light and crispy. Very nice."

"I made tomato basil soup to go with them."

"My favorite."

"Good. I was hoping you'd say that. I'll serve some up for us right now." Sheila took down two soup mugs from the cabinet. The sweet smell of basil rose from the mugs as she filled them. She carried them to the table and set a small plate of the crackers on the table between them.

Orene reached for her hand as Sheila sat. "I'm so glad you've spent this holiday here with me. It has been so nice having you here. Please know, honey, you are always welcome. Any time, for no reason at all."

"It's special for me too, Orene."

"Tucker has added to a lot to the holiday for you too, hasn't he?" Her lips pulled into a smile.

"I'm almost afraid to admit it." She couldn't deny it, though. "I hope he likes this as a gift. Something simple, but personal." She didn't mention that she had one more thing she planned to put with the gift, as a remembrance of their time together. "I'm meeting him tonight. We're going to set up for the holiday food drive boxes over at the fire station so the team can just assemble them in the morning and get them delivered. He says it'll take all night, but he hasn't worked with someone as organized as me before. I figure we can knock it out in a couple of hours."

"I know he'll appreciate your help. Gifting your time for others is always a good way to spend time together."

"I'm planning to do a lot more of that next year," Sheila said.

"Already thinking about New Year's resolutions?"

"Sort of, except different this year. I want to make tangible ones that I will keep. Maybe I'll just call it a change of pace. Resolutions seem so easy to break."

"If your heart is in it, then I'm sure you will be true to the change." Orene ate her soup, and took another cracker. "These are addictive!"

"They are. I should've warned you." She nibbled on one. "I don't think I've ever felt so fulfilled as I do here. I think a lot of that has to do with the things we've done as a community."

"Well, I won't argue with you there." Taking the last spoon of her soup, she stood. "Why don't you let me clean up these bowls so you can relax before you pull that all-nighter with Tucker?"

"Thanks, Orene." Sheila rose, and stood there watching

Orene begin to busy herself. "Orene. Thank you for being like a mother to me."

"It's my honor, darling. You are a wonderful young woman. I'm sorry your mother can't see you shine right now."

That night, Sheila packed her car full of the gifts she'd wrapped for the Jacob family, then drove over to Tucker's house. She knocked on his door, hoping he'd go with her to deliver them.

She stood there waiting, suddenly wishing she'd texted him first.

He opened the door. "You're early."

"I am." She grimaced. "Is it okay? I'm not interrupting, am I?"

"No, come on in."

She stepped inside. "I was hoping you'd help me with something."

"Sure. What's up?"

"I went a little wild with gifts for the Jacob family," she admitted. "I wanted to kind of sneak up to the chapel house and leave them on the doorstep."

"That'll be tricky unless they aren't home."

"I know." Her confidence dipped. "Maybe it's a silly idea."

He looked like he was thinking about it. "Unless it's not. Hang on." He pulled his phone out and dialed someone. "Hey, Doris. Do you happen to know what the Jacob family is up to tonight?"

He nodded, and Sheila was dying to know what they were saying. "I wondered about that. When will they be back home?"

He glanced up at the clock. "That's actually perfect. Thanks."

"What? What did she say? What's perfect?" Sheila asked.

"They aren't home," he said. "They won't be for about another hour."

"Then let's go. Hurry."

He put on his shoes and they took off in her car.

"I'm so nervous. I feel like I'm breaking the law," she teased.

"Imagine how Santa must feel breaking into houses all across the country on Christmas Eve."

"You're right." She lifted her chin. "If he can do it, we can do it."

"We have plenty of time," he said.

"But we don't want to get caught."

"We won't," Tucker assured her.

They pulled through the gates and drove up the path to the chapel house. All the lights were on, making it look a little heavenly.

"I could live there," she said. "It's so pretty."

As soon as they pulled up to the front she punched the button to lift the falcon-wing doors. "Let's do this."

Sheila raced back and forth toting the pretty packages and piling them near the door. "I feel like I should have worn my black leggings and sweatshirt," she said. "Hurry! Go. Go. Go."

He laughed at her silly antics. "You went bonkers. What all did you buy?"

"Mostly practical stuff for the family, but toys for each child, socks, mittens, the works. Okay, bonkers. Yes, just call me bonkers."

"Is that it?" He double-checked the car.

"Yes. Come on. Let's get out of here."

He hopped into the driver's seat and smashed down on the gas pedal so hard they kicked up dust all the way out.

Sheila held her breath until they cleared the driveway gates and got back on the main road. "Thank goodness." She couldn't stop laughing. "That was so exciting."

"It was!" He tapped the steering wheel, humming "Dashing through the snow . . ."

Lights swept the pavement ahead of them. The car passed them going toward the castle house.

"That might have been them," he said.

"You think?"

He held his hand up for a high five. "Mission accomplished."

Chapter Twenty-six

"That was a blast," Sheila said as they drove back toward town. "My heart is still pounding."

"I'm worried you might be cut out for a life of crime. Fast cars and getaways and all that." Tucker gave her the once-over.

"Don't you worry about that. I'll always be one of the good guys." She crossed her heart. "Promise."

"I'm glad to know that." He looked at his watch. "I think we could head over and get to work on the boxes if you like. The folks bringing in all the food to be packed up should have cleared out by now."

"That sounds great. We can get an early start," Sheila said. "Let's head that way."

"Do you want to stop and switch out to my truck?"

"No. We can drive this. We don't need to move anything, do we?"

"Nope. Everything will be right there at the fire station."

"No reason not to just go straight there, then. I've been looking forward to this all day," she said. "Take me to your leader. Wait. No. You're the leader."

He laughed. "I suppose I am." He drove to the firehouse, and parked her car around back by the second-floor entrance to the community room.

They walked upstairs, and he held the door for her, and then moved past her to turn on the lights. "Sorry it's so cold in here. I'll bump up the heater a couple degrees. They must have had the doors open while they were bringing in the supplies."

"That's okay. It'll warm up." She jogged in place.

Cardboard-box flats lay in a neat stack with a yellow band around them.

On the other side of the room, cases of food lined the wall, filled with all the makings of a full Christmas dinner, from stuffing to green beans to jellied cranberry sauce, and everything in between.

"This is a *lot* of food," she remarked.

"We have a lot of families in need. Our town is small, but the county is big. It's been a hard year for a lot of these people. If it weren't for this effort, they might go without. You'd be surprised this food doesn't go as far as you'd think."

"Let's be sure that won't be a problem this year." Sheila took off her jacket and hung it over a chair. "Where do we begin?" She rubbed her hands together, looking like she was hoping it would warm up fast.

"I have a sweatshirt in my office. I can get that for you. I need to go downstairs and get all the documents anyway. Why don't you cut the band on those boxes and start putting them together, that would be a big help. There are scissors, tape, and markers in the supply locker over on that wall. It's labeled."

"I'm on it, or ten-four or whatever the right lingo is," she said.

He shook his head. It didn't take him long to go downstairs

and gather everything. By the time he got back it was evident that Sheila hadn't wasted a moment.

With the sleeves of her black turtleneck pushed up on her forearms, the table full of supplies, and two boxes already assembled, she smiled when she looked up and noticed him.

"How do these look? Do we pass the quality inspection?"

He acted like it was serious business, pacing up and back, lifting the box, thumping it on each seam. "I believe . . . this is a perfect ten."

She curtsied. "Thank you kindly."

Tucker dragged a chair over to the table. "Okay. This is the list of all the families. There's also one page per family, so we can kind of cross-check and be sure we don't leave anyone out. We'll need to tape one sheet to the front of each box. It has the name, address, and any allergies on this sheet. Then take one of those big, fat, permanent markers and write the last name in block print across the top with this alphanumeric combination next to it."

"What's the code stand for?"

"It's the map grid coordinates. It'll make it easier to assign them for delivery. That's how we'll line them up against the wall over there."

She nodded. "I'd suggest we sort the papers down by code first, then, as we put the boxes together, they'll be presorted. Easier than sorting big boxes later."

"That is so simple, I'm embarrassed to say I never thought of it."

"I'm known for my organizational and planning skills." She pressed her lips together. "Guess I earned my pay today."

"I did tell you there's no pay."

"Maybe I should get a bonus. You think?"

"I'll come up with some kind of compensation, it being Christmas and all." He gave her a wink. "Why don't you sort the papers, and I'll keep making boxes."

"Sure." She started flipping the papers down on the table in piles, shifting them down as she discovered new combinations, but keeping them in alphanumeric order.

He watched her assemble boxes, folding them down, securing the seams with tape, and then doing it all again.

"I'm ready," she said.

"At this rate, this is not going to be an all-nighter."

"But you promised me one."

He couldn't take his eyes off her. "I never break a promise."

He watched her take in a hitched breath, then wipe her brow. It was cold in here, was she sweating?

She lifted her gaze to his. "Good. Me either." With a flirty wiggle, she picked up a box, taped the sheet to the front, and then added name and code and looked to him for approval.

"Very nice." He nodded. "And the box is well put together too."

She eyed it with a sultry smile, looking like she was happy with his comment.

The two of them found a rhythm, working quietly. Sheila was almost as quick as he was at putting boxes together, and he considered himself pretty fast.

"Are you getting thirsty?" he asked. "I'm going to go get a drink out of the machine."

"I'll take water."

He jogged downstairs and came back. He lifted two bottles in the air. "H_2O anyone?"

"Here!" She reached for it, but he toyed with her, raising it over her head out of reach and then swooping the icy-cold bottle against the back of her neck.

She screamed. "That's freezing!"

"Oh sorry. I didn't mean—"

"You are in for it, mister." She took one of the empty boxes and playfully tossed it at him. He juked to the left, laughing as it slung past him.

Then the alarm went off, mind-numbing and wailing. He stopped, still breathing heavily from the game play.

"Gotta run."

"What? What's going on?"

"Fire." He grabbed his radio from the table. "It's at the tree farm." He hit a button on the wall, and the huge garage doors below rumbled up. "Sorry."

"What should I do?" She spun, asking as he rushed past her.

"Keep working. I'll be back."

"Okay. Um, I can do that." But Tucker was already running down the stairs when he heard her call out a goodbye.

Not a minute later, the Bull Mountain Boys were on the road.

Volunteers were already on the scene when they arrived in the tanker truck.

The team dropped to the ground and everyone spread out, working quickly to assess the situation and contain the fire.

Jesse and Joe ran over to Tucker.

"Any idea what happened?" Tucker asked.

"The back gate was compromised. Guessing some kids were hanging out back there. Wish they'd have done it somewhere else. Those are the biggest and most mature trees."

Tucker thought about how much pride Joe took in those few

huge trees he sold each year to shopping malls and private estates. Even the White House that one time.

"We only sell three to six a year from that lot." Joe shook his head. "It's gonna be a huge financial hit."

Jesse patted his brother's shoulder. There were no words that would comfort tonight.

"We'll do our best to get it managed quickly and save them."

"I know you will."

Tucker responded to an update from one of the teams, then waved in the second truck, directing them to the far side. Two vehicles carrying volunteers parked, and Tucker directed them to work the outer perimeter to contain the fire.

Tucker turned just as one of his rookies pulled the hose down toward the trees closest to the blaze.

The team from the neighboring county radioed in their estimated arrival.

Tucker's keen sense caught the unusual movement from the corner of his eye. The rookie was caught up in the ground cover. He was too close to the blaze, and Tucker saw it coming. He darted toward him, hoping to call him off before he fell, but it was too late. He'd fallen right at the base of one of the burning trees.

Tucker raced over and helped him get back on his feet. "Get back to the truck, and take a break. You're okay. It happens."

The rookie jogged off, but the top of the tree broke free and fell across Tucker's shoulder, knocking him off-balance.

Searing pain ripped through Tucker's right ear. Trying to stay focused on the immediate dangers, he scanned the area, and called Tommy Newton on the radio for assistance, then called for the EMTs to meet him near the tanker.

Tucker's heart raced. Despite the pain, he knew he had to

make sure the team stayed in control. He clambered to his feet and ran to the clearing.

Tommy Newton came over. "What's up, Chief?"

"I need you to take over." Tucker lifted his helmet from his head.

Tommy hesitated, then saw Tucker's injury. "I've got it," Tommy said, not missing a beat.

Tucker met the EMT halfway.

"Did it come down on your shoulder?" the EMT asked.

Tucker nodded.

"Okay. Can you walk?"

"I'm fine."

"Well, you're not fine, but we'll get this taken care of." They treated the burn and checked his shoulder.

Tucker gritted his teeth through the pain. It wasn't the first time he'd been burned, but it would've been worse had he not gotten that rookie out of there when he had.

His ear throbbed so badly that he couldn't hear clearly. *I can trust Tommy. They are in good hands.*

"We're going to take you out of here, Tucker. It's not bad, but you know the drill."

"Who has a truck? Leave the emergency vehicle here in case something else happens. I'll get someone to take me."

The EMT made a dash over to talk to Tommy, and the next thing Tucker knew, he was being loaded into Sully's pickup truck.

"You okay, Chief?" Sully asked.

"I will be." Tucker clenched his teeth. As the adrenaline subsided, the true impact of the burn became more painful. The tender skin on his neck and ear felt like it was already blistering away from his skin.

Chapter Twenty-seven

Sheila ran to the windows that overlooked the front parking lot from the second-story community room at the fire station. Several pickup trucks were parked there now, and the other fire truck siren joined in the noisy assault as it revved up and rolled out of the parking lot.

"Holy cow." The noise was deafening. It was incredible how fast it was from the moment of the alarm to the time that first truck moved out. No time at all, and now the second was gone too.

The siren carried off into the distance.

It was a good distance to the tree farm from here. She couldn't see any dark clouds or a glow in the distance. Hopefully, it was a false alarm.

Another fire truck pulled out of the bay below her. Yellow coats and red, black, and yellow helmets raced around on all sides. Probably conducting a quick safety check before departure.

More cars arrived at the firehouse, some of their drivers and passengers getting in the fire truck, others lining up behind it.

The siren moaned, then accelerated until finally the horn

honked followed by the steady sound of the diesel engine filling the night air.

With all the vehicles out of the building, finally, the station alarm quieted.

In the hush, she heard the crackling of conversations. She followed the voices downstairs. In the area next to the garage bays, a radio broadcast the situation.

She made out the words "Joe's Christmas Tree Farm." She froze. They'd just been there. "Not Joe's." She sat, unable to just go back to work, riveted to the garbled radio talk, much of which sounded like a mishmash of numbers and codes.

Her heart pounded. She hoped everyone would be okay.

Memories from the night of the Jacobs' house fire tumbled through her mind. The devastation and how fast the situation changed. The look in the family's faces as they watched.

This is what he does for a living. He knows what he's doing.

Dispatch called in support from neighboring counties.

She sat there with her hand over her mouth.

"Sheila? I thought that was your car down there."

Sheila spun around. It was Doris. "Hi. I was helping Tucker prep boxes for the food deliveries when the call came in. Is it Joe's Christmas Tree Farm? The trees? Or the barn?"

"It's in the farthest field, from what I heard. Lord only knows how that caught fire. Probably kids, or someone homeless trying to keep warm."

"Right." Sheila bit down on her lip. "Are you going over to the fire?"

"Not unless he calls me in. I'll stay here until Tucker assesses the situation to see if there's anything I can help with. If it's the trees, the forest, there won't be much for me to do, except make sure all the communications are followed up."

Sheila's mind swirled. No wonder Orene was so insistent on going and taking food to them at the location of the fire. It was hard to just sit by knowing there was something like this going on and not do anything about it.

"What can I do?"

Doris smiled. "How about finish those boxes, seeing as how Tucker won't be here to finish the job?"

"I can do that. Will you keep me up to date with what's going on?"

"Sure. I'll let you know when I'm leaving."

"Thanks. I'll let you know when I get done." Sheila walked upstairs, feeling alone in the quiet building. Her nerves tingled. *Please don't let anything happen to Tucker.*

She forced herself to concentrate on the task at hand. Putting the boxes together and marking them was mindless work. It was perfect for this situation.

Almost two hours had passed, and Doris hadn't delivered any news. Sheila was done. Had been for a while, just sitting there looking at the window, wondering. She didn't want to leave. At least here she'd know Tucker was okay when he came back in the fire truck.

She paced, watching every swath of headlights that came toward the station.

Didn't Tucker say that Joe's farm backed up to Natalie's property?

She grabbed for her phone. *Why didn't I put that together before?* She dialed Natalie's number.

The phone rang. Sheila prayed everything was alright.

It rang again.

"Hello?" a groggy Natalie answered. "Sheila? It's late. Is everything okay?"

"I guess so. Is everything okay there? Are you at your cabin or Randy's house?"

"I'm at Randy's. What's going on? Are you okay?"

"Yes, I'm fine. I'm sorry. It might be nothing, but there's a fire at Joe's tree farm. Tucker said it backed up to your property. I want to be sure you're safe."

"We're fine. We heard the fire engine pull out from the station earlier. Thanks for letting me know. We'll look into it. Randy's getting dressed now."

"I have this nagging feeling in my gut. Like something is wrong."

"Are you at Orene's?" Natalie asked.

"No. I'm at the fire station. I was helping Tucker put boxes together when the call came in. I've been here waiting ever since."

"I'll come over and sit with you," Natalie said.

"No. Don't do that. You go back to sleep. I just wanted to know you were safe."

"Are you sure? I'll come right over."

"No. I'll be fine." Sheila hung up the phone, wondering how long it normally took to put out the average fire. She really had nothing to compare it to. Maybe it hadn't been all that long at all. The reality of Tucker putting his life on the line struck her. As honorable as it was, it was hard to imagine living with that worry every time the fire alarm sounded.

Chapter Twenty-eight

Sheila walked back downstairs. "Doris?"

"In here," Doris called out.

When Sheila walked in she was doing a word search at the desk. "Any updates?"

"The fire is out. They just called it in. They'll be heading back soon."

Sheila let out a long sigh.

"Oh honey. I didn't realize you were that worried. I'm so sorry. This is business as usual around here. Everything is going to be fine."

Sheila nodded, spotting the coffeepot across the room. "Do you mind if I make myself a cup of coffee?"

"No. Help yourself. There are a ton of cookies and stuff in the kitchen too."

"I couldn't eat. Just coffee, thanks." She poured a cup and added a little creamer.

"I was just getting ready to come up and say goodbye. I'm not needed for anything on this one, so I'm going to head out. Can I give you a lift somewhere?"

"No, thanks. I've got my car. I'm just going to wait here for Tucker."

"Why don't you go home?" Doris put on her coat. "Officially it's Christmas Eve," she said. "You're welcome to stay and wait for him here if you like, but he's going to be beat when he gets back, plus he'll have some paperwork to do."

"I think I'll wait just a little longer." Sheila sipped her coffee and watched as Doris pulled out of the parking lot in her mini-van.

She sat on the edge of Tucker's desk. Everything was done upstairs. She had two choices. She could go to Orene's and worry and hope Tucker would call her, but he might think it would be too late to call, and then she'd worry all night long. Or she could sit tight.

Leaving didn't seem like an option.

Finally, one of the fire trucks pulled into the parking lot and the firefighters got out, rearranging tools and hoses and stuff. She watched, looking for a sign of Tucker.

She went and got her purse and coat from upstairs. Still waiting for Tucker to come in.

The other fire truck rumbled into the parking lot. The backup alarm sounded as it backed up to the doors and the team started doing whatever they did when they got back from a fire.

The firefighters talked as they worked, decompressing as they moved around.

Sheila put her jacket on and walked outside. "Hey, sorry to bother you. Is Tucker back?"

"You're Natalie's friend, right?"

"Yeah, Sheila."

"They took Tucker to the hospital. Nothing too serious. He'll probably call you in the morning."

"Of course. Yeah, thanks for letting me know."

Her heart sank. Her body was pulled as tight as a rubber band pulled around too many books. *Hurt?*

She looked at her phone. No missed calls.

Call me.

She got in her car, pulled around to the front, and got out to talk to one of the EMTs. "Can you tell me which hospital Tucker is in?"

"Yeah. One of the guys drove him over to Christiansburg."

"You think he'll be okay?"

"Definitely. He'll be home before you could get there. Go get some sleep. It's Christmas Eve morning."

So everyone keeps saying. "Thanks for filling me in. I guess there's no reason for me to drive out there then."

"Probably not. He wasn't even going to go to the hospital, but it's policy."

She drove back to Orene's and went upstairs and tried to go to sleep. It was hopeless, though. Her mind was reeling and she was more mad than worried at one point.

She had just fallen asleep when her phone rang at seven thirty in the morning.

"Hey, girl. I hope you got a good night's rest. It's Christmas Eve," Tucker said.

If one more person said that to her, she was going to scream. "I was worried." The words came out clipped.

"I'm sorry. I didn't mean to worry you. I figured you went home when I didn't come right back."

"Well, I didn't. I finished all of the boxes, and then I waited around for hours."

"Oh? I'm so sorry."

"Yeah, you could have called."

"You're right. I could have. Look, this is my job. It's random. The hours are long and things aren't all lined up in a pretty little row. I'm sorry I didn't call you sooner. I'm not used to having someone to check in with. I was waiting for it to be late enough that I wouldn't wake you."

"You didn't." It wasn't quite true, but she was mad, or hurt, or both. Whatever it was she was feeling, it wasn't good.

"I'll make it up to you," he said.

"You'll have to," she said, and hung up the phone. She was mad. Mad at him for worrying her. Mad at herself for being mad. His job was dangerous, and although she'd known that all along, it bothered her that it had scared her so much.

Why am I letting myself get all tangled up in his tinsel? It was flirty and fun, but now it's done. I'm fine alone. I don't need this.

She regretted feeling this way, especially on Christmas Eve.

Better get up now, else I'll wallow in this all day long.

Dressed, and feeling better for it, she walked downstairs. Orene was singing "Rudolph the Red-Nosed Reindeer," scooting around the kitchen doing all the hand gestures and repeats. *Nose. Nose. Nose.*

Sheila leaned against the doorway, enjoying seeing the spirited woman enjoy the season.

Glows. Glows. Glows.

Sheila slid into the kitchen in her socks, like Tom Cruise in that scene from *Risky Business*, to join in.

"'. . . used to laugh and call him names.'"

Like Pinocchio.

"'. . . join in any reindeer games.'"

"Aren't you in a fun mood today?" Orene giggled. "Alexa. Stop!" She pulled her hands on her hips. "Guess you know my whole morning routine now."

"And I thought it was all about the tea," Sheila teased. "If this is your fountain-of-youth secret, I'm going to be dancing with Rudolph every morning the rest of my life."

"It does please me. Don't you tell anyone."

"Your secret is safe with me. As long as I get to join in."

"Any time, dear. You slept in late. I guess the box project with Tucker really was an all-nighter."

Sheila just let the comment ride. "I can't believe it's already Christmas Eve."

"I know. There's always such a whirlwind of activities that it goes by faster than I'd like it to as well." Orene got up. "Get your coffee. Let's sit in the living room and enjoy the Christmas tree."

"I'll follow you."

"Are you going to tell me about your date with Tucker?" Orene asked as they walked to the other room.

"I wondered how long it would take you," Sheila teased.

"I was wondering the same thing. What are you not saying?"

Sheila looked away. "You know, I'm kind of struggling with how last night went. I'm a little upset, and I know I don't have a right to be."

"What in goodness' sake does that mean?" Orene sat forward, balancing her teacup on her knee.

"It started out great. All the time I've spent with him has been . . . well, it's been fun. We both know I'm going back to Richmond, so I shouldn't have expected anything. It's silly."

"What happened?"

"They had a call while we were putting the boxes together last night."

"Right. I heard the siren."

"Yeah, well, I was there for hours. The trucks came back, I still waited, and finally I had to ask someone to find out he'd been hurt."

"Tucker? Is he okay?"

"They said it wasn't critical. I don't know what the bell curve is on firefighter injuries, but he could have called. I was there waiting all that time."

"I see."

"I finally just came back here. Mad, frustrated. Worried."

"Because you care about him."

"Yes and it was selfish. He knew I was there. He left me working on his project. How could he not at least update me?"

"I don't know."

"Me either. Does it even matter? I'm leaving anyway. It was fun for a while."

"Sheila. That is ridiculous. If you didn't have some sort of feelings for him, you wouldn't have yourself all twisted up like this. Have you considered perhaps he thought he was keeping you from being worried?"

"He wasn't doing a good job of it if that was the case."

"He's a man." Orene took a sip of her tea. "Do I need to say anything more?"

Sheila wasn't giving him a pass just for being a man. It was Good Manners 101 to let someone know if you were going to be late, and not coming back was later than late. "Maybe that he should know better?"

Orene laughed. "Honey, their idea of knowing better and ours, well they aren't always the same thing."

Natalie called out from the front door. "Knock, knock. Merry Christmas Eve."

"In the living room," Orene called out.

Randy and Natalie walked in carrying presents. "Thought we'd drop off your presents today, so you can open them in the morning."

"You two are too good to me. Thank you. Come in. Sit down."

Randy stepped wider. "Looks like you two were having a serious conversation. Are we interrupting?"

Natalie tucked the gifts under the tree.

Sheila shrugged. "Good morning."

"How'd it go last night?" Natalie asked.

"He didn't come back."

"At all?"

"Nope. All the trucks came back and he wasn't on any of them. Turns out he got hurt."

"Oh no." She raced to sit next to Sheila. "How is he?"

"Fine. He called a little bit ago. I don't know the whole story, but he sounded okay."

"Wait. That doesn't make sense."

Randy said, "Sounds like it was a rough night."

"For me," Sheila said. "I sat around all that time worried."

Randy withheld comment, taking a step back and sitting in the chair.

Sheila saw the look that passed between them, as if they'd already been discussing it. "What?"

"He's a good guy. He has a dangerous job. An important

one," Natalie said. "This is just part of getting to know one another. Y'all are getting along so well."

"We were." Sheila shrugged. "I'll be leaving the day after tomorrow anyway."

"No. I thought you were staying through New Year's." Natalie looked at Randy. "Tell her to stay."

"She's not going to listen to me," he said. "And I might regret this, but go talk to him, Sheila. At least give him a chance to explain, and you really should stay until New Year's. We've been so busy we've barely had time to really visit."

"I've had fun," she said. "This has been the best Christmas I've had in a long time. I should leave while I remember it that way."

"You have to at least take him the present you made for him." Orene told Natalie and Randy about how Sheila spent the day in the kitchen making soup and cheddar bites as a holiday gift for Tucker.

"Did you make us some?" Randy asked.

"We have plenty in the kitchen," said Orene. "Can I get you some?"

"Yeah. We used to get those things delivered to the police station all the time. I haven't had any in a long time." Randy got up and followed Orene into the kitchen.

Sheila looked at Natalie, who was staring at her.

"What?" Sheila slumped forward.

"I'm sorry you're upset."

"Me too. I didn't sleep a wink last night. I was so worried, and then so mad." She shook her head. "I know I shouldn't have been that mad about it, but it struck me so wrong."

"You should really go check on him. Just because he's not

still in the hospital doesn't mean he doesn't still need some help." Natalie lifted her right arm in the air and flopped it around. "He could've broken his arm, or all of his fingers. He can't hold his coffee cup."

Sheila laughed. "Okay, you don't have to be as dramatic as I'm being."

"Well, if he's like you without coffee, not being able to lift his coffee mug could be dangerous for us all." She laughed. "Go see him." Natalie pressed her hands together. "You should. You'll never know if there's something here worth fighting for if you don't at least see it through. I can go with you."

"No. I've got this." Sheila stood. "I have a right to be mad, don't I?"

"I don't think you're mad. I think you were worried. That's different."

"Okay." Sheila got up and pulled the band out of her messy bun, letting her hair hang long across her shoulders.

"I'm going to wait for you," Natalie said. "You better come right back, or call so we don't worry." Natalie's face showed that she was mocking her, like only a best friend could get away with.

"Don't push your luck." Sheila got up to get the Christmas gift for Tucker from the kitchen, and grabbed the other small gift out of the Tesla on her way out. She decided to walk to his house, to burn off some of her nervous energy, and figure out what she was going to say.

The short walk didn't feel long enough. She was still nervous, and disappointment still hung heavy on her heart.

Chapter Twenty-nine

Tucker's shoulder ached and the painkiller they'd given him at the hospital when they treated the burn to his ear was wearing off. Piercing pain throbbed down the side of his ear and neck. He reached for one of the painkillers. He hated taking pills, but he couldn't bear this level of pain.

"You don't have to apologize to us, Tucker. Sheila had all those boxes ready in record time. She's like her own little production line," Doris said. "The others packed them up this morning. They said it was the easiest sort and load they'd ever done."

"I'm not surprised. She's really something." He'd looked forward to pulling the all-nighter with her.

Doris sat in the chair across from Tucker, shaking her head. "She was working like a fiend to get them done for you when I got there. I feel kind of bad, because I didn't think to set expectations with her. I thought she was fine up there working, but I could tell when she came down and asked that she was worried you hadn't gotten back."

"Worried?" Frank shrugged. "People don't really understand how we work."

Doris nodded. "That's true, but it wasn't just that. I think she was legit worried something might have happened to Tucker." Her eyes darted back to Tucker. "I think she *really* likes you."

Tommy snickered. "All the women always really like Tucker."

Sully said, "She seems nice. I talked to her at the Christmas Tree Stroll."

Jonathan, Tommy, Sully, and Frank all stood in his living room behind where Doris sat on the couch. "Kelly said Sheila asked them about you, too," Doris said. "They told her you'd been hurt, but that it wasn't serious."

Tommy said, "You have been spending a lot of time with her lately, Chief."

"She's nice," said Doris.

"She's very ladylike," Sully said.

"She is every bit a lady," Tucker said. "But she'll be leaving town soon."

Doris shook her head. "Or maybe she won't."

Tucker didn't want to get his hopes up. "Her life is in Richmond. She has a business there. I don't see her relocating up here, and I sure have no interest in going to Richmond."

"If she was upset about you not getting back, she doesn't sound much like fire chief wife material, anyway," said Tommy.

"No one is talking marriage. I just met her," Tucker said. "We've been having fun."

"You looked serious about her. I think there's something there," said Doris.

"Well, if she freaked out over one late night, that would never work." Tommy and Jonathan laughed.

"You got that right," said Tucker. "Well, once she leaves, she probably won't be back for a while. I guess that'll be that. No harm. No foul."

Something clattered out on the front porch.

"What was that?" Doris asked.

Tucker waved it off. "Has to be one of Mrs. Coleman's cats again. Ever since I bought those new rocking chairs, they will not stay off my front porch. The other day, one of them left me a mouse."

"That means they're trying to please you," Doris said. "Maybe they are trying to tell you they like those rocking chairs."

"They ought to be apologizing, clanging around at all hours of the night," Tucker said.

"And you ought to be apologizing to Sheila for not letting her know that you're okay," Doris said. "I know it's not my business, but you've seemed so happy the last couple of weeks. You deserve that in your life, and you aren't getting any younger."

"I'm not that old either. I screwed up not checking in with her, though. I really didn't mean to worry her. I called her this morning. She sounded pretty mad."

"Nothing a little heart-to-heart can't fix," Doris said.

Sully said, "You shouldn't have made her worry. She's a good one."

"I know she is," Tucker said. It came out defensive, and regret was beginning to outweigh the pain from the burn. "She's the best thing that's come into my life. I'll miss her when she leaves."

"Richmond isn't that far to go for the right person," Sully said. "You don't meet the right person without some effort."

"Spoken like a newlywed," Jonathan teased.

"You guys need to mind your own business," Doris said. "Seriously. If you like her, and I think you do, make it right." She got up. "Come on, you gooberheads. Let's let Tucker get some rest." She looked over her shoulder. "Or make phone calls."

She shuffled the guys out, and Tucker sat there wondering why he hadn't called her last night from the hospital. He'd thought about it. More than once. But he didn't want her to worry, and he really didn't think she'd stay up at the fire station all that time.

Truth was, he didn't want to look like a lovesick fool in front of the others, either.

When the alarm sounded and he left, he'd figured they'd be out and back quickly. It didn't seem like the kind of call that would take multiple trucks, but it was a bigger deal than that.

He sat there in the recliner until he heard the guys drive off in Sully's truck.

I need to set this straight.

Tucker picked up his phone to call, then tucked it back into his pocket. He walked out of his house. *Some things are better done in person.*

He headed for Orene's house, his strides long and the words playing in his mind.

He'd just stepped off the sidewalk into Orene's driveway when he saw the back of her.

Sheila was just a few steps from the porch.

"Hey. Sheila?" Tucker waved his arm in the air. "I'm so sorry about last night."

"Sorry?"

"Yeah, I should've called."

"You should have. I was worried."

She seemed upset—not just worried, but a little mad. "I'm not going to tell you not to worry. I work in a dangerous occupation. A little concern is expected, but I promise you I'm very good at my job. I keep myself out of harm's way, and keeping my men and women safe is my priority."

Her gaze went to the big cotton bandage over his ear.

"It doesn't appear you did so good at that last night."

He nodded, even that small motion making the injury throb. "I'm sorry. I really wanted last night to be special."

"Really? I don't think you did. I mean, you know I'm just a city girl in town for a visit. Nothing special."

He cocked his head. Where the hell had that come from?

"Look—"

"No, you look. I might have overreacted. I don't know, but I really enjoyed spending time with you and maybe it was just Christmas magic, but I thought we had something special going. At least I was sincerely enjoying myself, not feeling obligated. You know, I can take care of myself. I don't need a pity date. You're off the hook. No harm. No foul."

"Wait. Whoa." He lifted his hand in the air. "Stop. That's out of context."

"I was at your house, trying to apologize for overreacting and to give you a Christmas present. I had no idea—" She turned and started up the stairs to the front door, then turned again and shoved the packages into his arms.

"Hang on. First of all, that was not the whole conversation! That was you making the noise on my front porch earlier, wasn't it?"

"Doesn't matter. I heard what I heard."

"Let me explain. You're upset. It didn't mean what you think."

"It really caught me off guard, because you seem . . ."

"Seem what?"

"Genuine. A nice guy. Fun. Not a jerk."

"I'm not. Ask anyone in this town. And I can promise you this. Natalie and I might not be related, and we may not have known each other that long, but she was married to my best friend and I would never do anything to upset her. Trust me, upsetting you would upset her. And Orene. And a bunch of other people who have taken a liking to you besides me."

She looked at him. "Well, we wouldn't want you to ruin your reputation."

"It's not about me."

"Isn't it?"

"I screwed up, but I didn't mean to. It does matter. I like you. A lot." He closed his eyes, wishing the pain would subside so he could think clearly. "I know I'm putting my life on the line to save others. I'm trained to deal with the heat, the smoke, and the flames, but there's always the risk of something going wrong."

"I know, but I was worried. No. Really, it's more than that. I don't know if I could worry like that every time you went on a call."

"It's a big ask. I know it is. And I could've communicated better."

"When you left, you said to stay. That you'd be back." She shrugged. "I believed you."

"You can believe what I say." He contemplated. "You're right. I should have called at the first opportunity." He shook his head. "It's been a while since I had someone else to consider. I'm sorry I worried you. In my mind, you'd worry less if you didn't know I was on the way to the hospital, but I see your point. Please don't be upset, and I know what you overheard, but that was in the middle of a discussion. A flippant, guarded remark, because

I don't want my job to scare you off. You're the best thing that ever happened to me, and if you'd come in, you'd have heard me say that."

"Thank you," she said quietly.

He stepped closer. "Were you really that worried?"

She nodded. "I couldn't help it. I know it's your job, and I'm fully aware I don't have any right to feel that way." Shrugging. "It's just . . . how . . . I felt kind of lost, and I didn't like it."

"It's not easy being with someone in this profession. It's a lot to ask. It's not just me looking out for myself. I'm looking out for a huge team of people risking their lives to help others. A whole town. But I sure do like spending time with you, and I am so sorry I made you worried or mad or sad or whatever it was. I'm flattered that you cared that much to worry."

"I sure didn't mean to." Her lips pulled into a straight line. "I tried not to."

"I think we've got something here."

"I don't know. I mean, what you said about me leaving is fair. My life is in Richmond."

"It's worth at least giving a try. I mean, if you dance as good as your mom I'd like to take you out for a spin. And I still haven't seen Virginia Beach. I think I might like the feeling of sand between my toes."

"And I wouldn't mind learning more about the mountains. It's been so enlightening, but Tucker, Christmas is historically bad for me. My mom was diagnosed at Christmas, my marriage fell apart at Christmas, now this."

"This isn't falling apart. It's a speed bump at best. I'm sorry about your mom and I can only imagine how she must've been before Alzheimer's began stealing her away. Sheila, I know that's got to be heartbreaking, and as for your ex: he's the fool." He reached for her hand, squeezing it. "I don't plan to follow in his footsteps."

Orene swung open the door. "I thought I heard voices. Is everything okay?"

They both said, "Yes."

Orene laughed. "Sorry to interrupt." She spun around. "You two kiss or something."

They laughed as the door shut.

"Do you think she's peeking out the window?" Tucker asked.

"Oh, I'd bet money on it."

He raised his brow. "I've been wanting to do this anyway, and this is probably the right time."

She looked puzzled, but when he pressed his lips to hers, she softened in his arms and responded in a way that lifted his spirits.

"Wow," she said, as he opened his eyes and looked into hers.

"If I had to ask Santa for one gift, I'd ask for a chance with you," he said.

"Do long-distance relationships ever really work?"

"I don't know. I'm no expert, but I think if two people are meant for each other, anything can work. Can that be our gift to each other for Christmas? That we'll give this a shot?"

"I gave you a present. You're holding it."

"Yeah. I guess I am. You didn't have to do that. When did you have time to do this for me?"

"I made the time," she said. "It was important to me."

He pulled the soup out of the bag. Around the neck of the mason jar she'd hung the ornament from Joe's Christmas Tree Farm. "From when we got my tree?"

"It was a really special moment for me," she said.

"I'm glad. You should keep the ornament as a keepsake."

"I want you to remember it too."

"I will." He pulled her into his arms. "See. This is what I love about you. You're sweet and thoughtful. Genuine."

"And still a little hurt. I am. I can't help it."

"I'm going to make it up to you."

Chapter Thirty

Sheila practically floated back into the house. It was amazing how this visit with Natalie, which Sheila had considered a favor to her best friend, had turned into so much more. This town, these people, they brought an energy back into her life that had been missing. All the big houses, fancy cars, and money didn't hold a candle to the simplicity of the joy she felt right now. Tucker was an unexpected gift. Even if it went no further than friendship, she wouldn't have missed this for the world.

Sheila walked inside, her stomach still doing elegant ice-skater spins from that kiss. Breathing in the last itsy bit of his aftershave that lingered on her cheek, she stopped feeling as guilty as a teenager sneaking in after curfew when she saw that Orene was sitting on the stairs smiling at her.

"You were eavesdropping." Sheila pretended to be shocked.

"Flat-out watching through that side glass window. That was one heckuva kiss!" Orene held her hands to her heart. "I love the two of you together. That wasn't just a mistletoe kiss. You saw fireworks, didn't you?"

Sheila let out a breath. She was tempted to play it down, but she couldn't. She raced over to the stairs and plopped down at Orene's feet. "Saw them and felt them all the way to my toes!" *I look forward to doing that again. Soon.* She covered her face, giggling and almost embarrassed at how incredibly elated she was. "It was so nice."

"I could tell from here. Honey, I'm so happy for you. Couldn't happen to two nicer people. This is turning out to be the most precious Christmas in all my years," said Orene. "One I won't forget, the way we've all pulled together to help the Jacob family, the best Christmas Tree Stroll in the history of this town, and love. So much love."

Sheila sat, realizing she'd passed a lot of judgment and jumped to a lot of conclusions over the past few years. She couldn't blame Dan for all of that. It was her doing. Too much focus on work and material things. Had she been hiding from life?

"You know, Orene, I used to think it was a huge mistake that Natalie was putting roots down here. I judged her and that wasn't how a good friend should react. I wanted her to come back to Richmond. That was selfish. I missed her, but as her friend, I couldn't be happier with how things are going with her and Randy, and I do understand why she's here in Chestnut Ridge now. I never really listened."

Orene patted her hand. "Don't be so hard on yourself. You're a wonderful friend. We're all on our own journey, and they happen at different paces."

"Randy and Natalie are so perfect for each other, and I honestly can't see them anywhere but in this wonderful town. With you, and Paul and Nelle and all of these wonderful people."

"Thank you, and we can see you here in our lives too."

"There's something special about Chestnut Ridge."

"I like to think so," Orene said. "I mean we have fairy stones, that's pretty special, and the Blue Ridge Mountains treat us to an ever-changing landscape that is beyond imagination every single day."

Sheila thought of the night Tucker drove her up to see the lights from the parkway.

Orene said, "Some things you can't teach or explain. They have to be experienced so that things can work out the way they should."

"You're so right." It was like suddenly the air around her was lighter, things made sense, and it made her heart dance. "It sure does. I've got to do something." She leapt to her feet.

"What? Is something wrong?" Orene's brows pulled together.

"No," Sheila said. "Things are very right. I gotta go!"

"Where are you going? It's Christmas Eve. You can't leave now."

She lifted her hand. "Right." She looked outside, and then back at Orene. "There's something I have to do. I don't know how long it's going to take, but I'll be back in time for you to open your present. I promise."

"Where are you going?"

She grabbed her purse. "If Natalie comes over, tell her I had a last-minute Christmas emergency to take care of. Everyone is meeting here in the morning, right?"

"I've already got my breakfast casserole made up and in the refrigerator."

"I'll be here for that."

"But it's Christmas Eve, we'll be celebrating that too."

"And that's what makes this perfect." Sheila hugged Orene and then ran to her car and sped off.

Sheila made one phone call, and it went exactly as she thought it would. "Yes. I'll meet you at my office in two hours. Merry Christmas." She dropped her phone into the passenger seat and settled both hands on the wheel and turned onto the main road. It wasn't all that far to her office.

"Oh what the heck, drive yourself," she said to the Tesla as she pulled the cruise stalk toward her twice in quick succession, and let the self-driving mode engage.

The car continued down the road. Sheila kept her hands hovering just above the wheel, unwilling to give up complete control to the car, but it stayed right on course, which was pretty cool. "That's enough." She tapped the brake and then pressed the right scroll wheel on the steering wheel. "That was pretty exciting, but I think I like being the one steering my life these days."

Although her heart was still racing from the little experiment, she was right on schedule when she hit the city limits.

Traffic snarled in front of the mall. Last-minute shoppers were out in full force. Thank goodness what she had to do didn't involve any shopping.

Richmond history had always fascinated her, but learning the background of Chestnut Ridge had been interesting too. Shopping most certainly was head and shoulders better in Richmond than Chestnut Ridge, but in the age of online shopping, how could that even be an argument? Richmond was a cultural hub in comparison, but there was something enchanting about the rugged range of mountains, craggy peaks, and stunning vistas.

Cassie is right. It's just geography. It's not where we live, it's how we choose to live.

Seeing all this traffic and all these people in a hurry made her think of the view of the mountains and homes nestled among the trees, looking down from the Blue Ridge Parkway overlook for what seemed like miles and miles. It had taken her breath away.

Maybe some of that was because of Tucker too. Yes, Tucker, you lift my spirits like I've never felt before.

She recalled Cassie's comment. "And what's more important? Population or the perfect relationship?"

"Thanks, Sis. I'm working on it." Sheila drove across town to her office. Glancing at the clock, she saw that she'd calculated the timing of this exchange nearly to the minute.

An hour later, she walked out of her office with satisfaction flowing through her. She tapped Enter in the app on her phone and stood there waiting.

Something was about to change. Like a caterpillar transforming into a butterfly, she felt as if she'd just earned her wings. *I'm flying now.*

I've spent my life chasing career goals. How did I miss that there is so much more to success? Looking back, she saw that her career had cost her a marriage, the chance to have children, and all those vacations she'd always dreamed of but never taken. *My priorities are shifting.*

Deep down, she yearned for something more, and maybe she'd known it all along. *Maybe expanding and bringing on the team was in preparation for this new phase in my life. A chrysalis.*

Nothing is tying me to Richmond.

She'd been born into city life, but she had no family still living here.

Since Natalie had moved, she'd felt disconnected. How could she judge Natalie for leaving town, when really she missed her? It wasn't a bad decision for Natalie. *Is this routine I've made my life really living?*

She'd been on a path to this reckoning ever since getting to know Tucker and seeing how committed he was to his neighbors, how he put his life on the line for the Jacob family and helped them get through the devastation, even helping his team find them safe shelter for their family—all the things he did that were beyond the parameters of his job.

Tucker's very spirit was built on a foundation of gratitude and giving.

I want that.

She couldn't ignore the pull she felt toward Tucker, or the satisfaction that came from working as part of a team in a community that operated on a mission to uplift one another.

Could she leave behind her life in Richmond and follow her heart?

She stopped and turned back to look at the office building and the fancy logo on the sign in front of it.

I can try to run things from Chestnut Ridge for a few months. Worst-case scenario, I come back. No harm. No foul. She could see where those words could mean something else now. It meant she could take a chance.

The Uber pulled up to the door. "Sheila?"

"That's me." She climbed into the back seat, and the driver pulled off, following the route on his GPS.

It was like looking at her familiar surroundings in a whole new light, and it was exciting. She let out a long breath as she leaned back in the seat. It might just be her best Christmas ever.

A few minutes later the car entered her neighborhood. She couldn't even name her neighbors. She wouldn't even have to say goodbye to anyone.

"Here we are," the Uber driver said.

"Thanks for the ride." She got out, clicked a five-star rating for the driver, then checked her watch. She went inside and packed a suitcase, and went through her mail, most of which was junk anyway. The Christmas cards she tucked inside the top of her suitcase to take with her. *I'll put them in my room at Orene's.*

She wheeled her bag out to the garage and loaded it into the trunk of her Mercedes. She pushed the garage-door opener and backed out into the driveway. Before backing into the street, she looked at the overstated home. *It's too big for one person anyway.*

"Here I go! Goodbye, house. I'll be back, but maybe not for long, if I'm lucky."

Chapter Thirty-one

Sheila noticed antlers protruding from both side windows of an old red pickup truck in the right-hand lane. Smiling as she pulled alongside, she noticed that the man in the front seat was dressed like Santa, white beard and all, and darn if he didn't have a giant red ball like Rudolph's nose on the front of that red sled.

"Merry Christmas," she shouted, and waved as she passed him. "How fun is that?"

She started singing "Here Comes Santa Claus," and was pleasantly surprised to find that she actually remembered all the words. It was another story when she tried to count off "The Twelve Days of Christmas," however, hiccupping on what her true love was supposed to give to her each day, so she just made it up as she went along—and laughed when for lack of a better idea for the tenth day she sang "Ten perfectly manicured fingernails!" Tapping them on the steering wheel, she sang on, quite pleased with herself.

The Chestnut Ridge sign welcomed her back.

Passing through town it was a different situation here. Main Street was quiet, and there was a bustle of activity at the big church, where they were setting up a live nativity.

Not ready to answer a lot of questions about where'd she been, she parked on the street and walked down to Orene's. Randy's and Natalie's vehicles were both parked out front.

She left her suitcase on the front porch and walked inside. "Hey. It's me," Sheila shouted.

"Sheila? Where have you been all day?" Natalie rounded the corner from the kitchen. "Orene is being really evasive about it all."

"No, she's not. I didn't tell her where I was going. I had some things to take care of."

"That's what she said."

Sheila shrugged, a teensy bit of snicker escaping. "Well, that's all there is to it."

"She said you might not even be back until morning. Why do I think you're leaving something out?"

"Is there anything to eat? I'm starving," Sheila said.

Orene piped up. "You know there's always something to eat! Spiral-cut ham and sweet potato biscuits. They should still be warm."

"Perfect," Sheila said, purposely ignoring Natalie's questions not just to torture her bestie a little but also because it would make her announcement that much sweeter. "Aren't we supposed to deliver our Christmas Tree Stroll tree tonight?"

"We are," said Randy as he walked into the room. "It's about time for us to head over to the stadium to pick it up."

"That's exciting," Sheila said. "Do you know who it's going to?"

Natalie pulled a piece of paper out of her back pocket. "A Ms. Ferebee. She's a widow who lives near the old mill. I've got the address right here."

"Oh gosh. Yes," Orene said. "It's her first Christmas alone. Her sister asked to put her on the list even though the deadline had passed. She was so worried about her when she found out she hadn't decorated."

"First Christmases without your husband are the hardest," Natalie said.

"I know." Sheila hugged her. "So hard."

"Eli and I will meet you over at Ms. Ferebee's house to unload the tree and set it up," Randy said.

"That works. They'll load it up for us at the stadium. You riding with me, Sheila?"

"I wouldn't miss this for anything."

Natalie and Sheila headed for the stadium. A line of trucks was already forming at the stadium gate. They watched the volunteers load the trees.

The line moved surprisingly fast.

Natalie edged up for her turn, handing a red-haired boy in his teens her form with the information on it.

"Be right here, ma'am," he said with a big smile.

"He called you 'ma'am,'" Sheila said with a laugh.

"That sucks. We are not that old." Natalie pursed her lips. "I don't feel that old."

"We're not. He's just that young. And brought up right!"

"The Chestnut Ridge way," Natalie said.

"Yeah. It's a whole different world up here." She sat back in the seat and watched as two men in red firefighter T-shirts carried a tree out to the truck. "Did they wrap our tree in plastic, or did they just chuck a dead body into the back of your truck?"

Natalie laughed. "It's that clear moving wrap. They said it

keeps the ornaments mostly in place so we can just unwrap and voilà it's perfect again." Natalie crossed her fingers.

"It looks like an alien," Sheila remarked. "Hopefully it works, and it'll fluff back out nicely. It looks menacing. I hope we don't scare this old lady to death when we show up on her doorstep with it."

"They do it every year." Natalie handed Sheila the sheet of paper with the address on it. "Can you put this address in your phone?"

"Got it."

They drove to the other side of town, up a winding road. Natalie's headlights came on as dusk began to fall and the clouds hung low like fog ahead.

"It should be up here on the left," Sheila said.

The GPS announced their arrival, and Natalie stopped and texted Randy to see where they were.

RANDY: Coming up behind you now love.

She glanced in the rearview mirror, then turned in to a driveway marked with blue reflective markers on each side of a black rail fence. The porch light was on, but only one light in the house glowed.

"Think she's home?" Sheila said.

"Hope so." She put the truck in park. "Let's see."

They waved to Eli and Randy, who were getting out of their truck and dropping the tailgate on Natalie's by the time Natalie and Sheila reached Ms. Ferebee's door.

Sheila knocked.

Randy and Eli wrestled the tree out of the truck and lugged it to the porch.

"You're right. It really looks like a dead body," Natalie agreed. "Maybe we should ring the bell. She might be hard of hearing or something."

"Or not home. It's Christmas Eve. She could be at church."

"True." Natalie reached over and rang the bell.

Finally, a white-haired woman in a red robe opened the door, and peered around the edge. "Can I help you?"

"Hello, Ms. Ferebee. We have a special delivery for you," Natalie said with all the glee of a rock-star elf.

"Oh?"

"May we come in? I'm Natalie, and this is my best friend, Sheila. I live up on the mountain."

"Best friends? How sweet. But I didn't order anything. You must have the wrong address."

"No ma'am. Actually, we're here to see you. We have a little surprise for you." Sheila hoped Ms. Ferebee wouldn't have the same first impression of the mummified tree that she'd had.

"We won the Christmas Tree Stroll," Natalie piped up. "And you, my new friend, are the winning recipient of it."

Randy danced the tree behind them catching Ms. Ferebee's attention.

Sheila couldn't hold back the laughter. "I promise it's a beauty under all that cellophane. We were just trying to keep all the ornaments in place for you. You don't have a Christmas tree, do you?"

"Oh my goodness. No, I didn't put one up this year. Please, come in." She opened the door enough for them to enter. "This is such a nice surprise."

"Merry Christmas," they said as they stepped inside and the guys shuffled the tree in behind them, then moved a chair out of the way to make room for it.

Sheila pulled a pair of scissors from her purse and started cutting away the clear wrap, straightening the ornaments as she went. "See! It's beautiful! Did you make it over to the Christmas Tree Stroll? It was my first year."

"I didn't go this year. First time in my life I didn't." She looked sad. "I probably should have."

"You missed one glorious night," Natalie agreed.

A tear slipped down the woman's cheek. "You have no idea how nice a surprise this is for me."

"We're glad you like it," Natalie said.

Randy whispered goodbye, and he and Eli left to help the next folks tote and set up their tree.

Ms. Ferebee pressed her hands to her heart. "Birdhouses?"

"Yes. We called it the Feathered Friends Home for the Holidays tree," Natalie said. "Do you like it?"

Through tears in her twinkling blue eyes she said, "Did you know that my husband was a bird-watcher?" She reached for one of the birdhouses. "This is my first Christmas in fifty-seven years that I've been without him."

"I'm so sorry." Sheila took her hand. "We'd heard you've had a difficult year. Can I give you a hug?"

The woman stepped right into her arms. "Sometimes we need hugs," Sheila said as she held the tiny woman tightly.

Ms. Ferebee stood there a long time before she stepped back, and patted Sheila's hand. "I've been really struggling." Tears fogged the woman's glasses. She tugged them from her face, wiping them clear on her robe. "He would've loved this."

"Oh gosh, I hope this is a welcome addition to your holiday. If it's not—"

"It's as if you knew I needed a reminder, or a sign, that he is still with me in a way."

"He always will be," Natalie said, pressing her hand to Ms. Ferebee's. "He will be in your heart always. You take your time. It's hard going through the holidays without the ones we love."

"It is." She stood quietly staring at the tree. "There are good memories though. So many of them."

"Cling to those."

Ms. Ferebee smiled.

Sheila said, "I bet he loved your smile. I hope you enjoy the tree."

"Bless you. This really couldn't be more perfect," Ms. Ferebee said.

"Merry Christmas," Natalie said.

"And to you both."

"Hang on, I want to get one more thing." Sheila jogged out to the truck and came back. "This is my business card, but my cell phone is on it. I'm going to be in town pretty often. If you need something, please call me. We're sort of new in town, it'll be nice for us to make some new friends, and I have a feeling we can help each other have some better days ahead."

"I'd really like that. Thank you. That's so kind of you." Ms. Ferebee placed the card on her mantel and looked at the tree. The guys had plugged the lights in. She reached out and touched one of the birdhouses. "The bird nest as the topper is such a unique choice. Makes me think of new beginnings. Quite appropriate for this year. Thank you."

Natalie edged toward the door. "We'll let you get back to your Christmas Eve. Merry Christmas."

"And Happy New Year," Sheila added.

Natalie and Sheila held hands as they walked back to the truck.

"She's so sweet," Natalie said.

"I know. Bless her heart." Sheila sniffled. "I can't believe how well replacing the real topper with the bird nest worked. We couldn't have planned that better." She sniffled. "Oh my gosh, I'm crying like that first time we watched *P.S. I Love You.*"

"I know. Me too."

"Fifty-seven years. She was married her whole life!" Natalie got back in the truck. "We should plan to visit her."

"Definitely," said Sheila. "I want to do a lot more things like this."

"It feels good, doesn't it?"

Sheila suddenly wanted to tell Natalie about her plan. At least part of it. "Natalie, I sold the Tesla."

"What? When?"

"I drove to Richmond this morning. Sold it to one of my clients. He was beyond thrilled."

"Did you make a profit?"

"A huge one. I'm going to loan the Jacob family their insurance deductible money."

"What?"

"It's the right thing to do. I know it might sound a little crazy, but I really want to do this."

"I know they'll appreciate it."

"I'm going to give it to them tonight when we take the presents over."

"You sure you want to do this? It's a lot of money."

"It is, and I realize there's a risk that I might not see it again, but I think they'll pay it back. I'm offering them zero interest, but they've got to have the money to get started, else they could be stuck for who knows how long."

"I know. I've been racking my brain over it too. I think it's a good thing."

"Good. I was hoping you'd think so. I'm going to see if Orene would mind if I come up to stay more often."

"Really?"

"Yeah, I was thinking today that I could run my business from here, it would kind of force me to take my hands off the wheel a little—"

"And quit micromanaging?"

"That too. Plus, being here with you, and Orene, it just feels right."

"That's exactly how I felt about Chestnut Ridge when I came here. It felt safe, even though I didn't know what all the pieces of the puzzle looked like."

"I understand that now. I'm really sorry I wasn't more supportive about your decision to move here. I knew it was out of necessity at first, but I didn't recognize the peace that you gained being here until spending time here with you."

"It's hard to explain." Natalie pulled over in front of the church where the nativity was set up.

"It is."

"Want to go see?" Natalie's eyes were filled with hope.

"Heck yeah!" They bailed out of the truck and walked over, listening as the children dressed in robes told the story they all knew so well. One of the lambs was sort of stealing the scene, probably calling for its mother, who called back in an annoyed "baaa-aa."

"No wonder they didn't want live animals on the stage. What is the saying, never act with kids or animals? Scene-stealers . . . all of them!"

The lamb suddenly spotted its mother and nosed right under her belly, practically lifting her right off the ground. Luckily, the focus shifted to the star of Bethlehem, which had just been lit high above them on the tallest tree.

"I wish we'd picked up Orene to see this," Natalie whispered.

When the play ended, it was with quiet jubilation that they walked back to the truck.

Natalie's phone buzzed in her pocket. She smacked her pocket trying to quiet it and answered.

"Hey, babe," Natalie said into her phone. "Yes. We're on our way back now. Is everything okay?"

She glanced toward Sheila and rolled her eyes. "Yes. We'll see you there."

"He's dying for us to get back to Orene's."

"He misses you. Isn't that sweet?"

"It is." Natalie started the truck and drove the short distance back to Orene's.

When they got there, Tucker was sitting on his tailgate with packages in a blur of colors and patterns stacked up behind him.

"Hey there," Sheila said.

"Hi. Thought you two might want to deliver presents to the Jacob family with me." He gave Sheila a wink. "A little less co-vertly than before. I told them we're coming."

"I'm going to run in and see Randy." Natalie ran up the porch steps, calling his name before she even hit the door.

"Count me in." Sheila patted her coat pocket, where the check and note were safely tucked inside a little Christmas card. "Can you give me a minute, though? I just need to talk to Orene. It shouldn't take long."

"Take your time," he said. "I'll be right here."

"Great."

Sheila went inside. It always smelled like home here. She could hear Natalie talking up a storm to Randy about the visit with Ms. Ferebee. "Orene, can I talk to you for a minute?"

"Sure, honey. What's on your mind?"

"I have a favor to ask of you, but promise me you will say no if it's not convenient."

Orene chuckled. "Well, that's an intro. What do you have up your sleeve?"

Chapter Thirty-two

"Ready?" Tucker said as he slid off the tailgate and closed it.

Sheila said, "Yep." Then walked into his arms. "I am very ready."

"Nice."

He and Sheila drove up to the chapel house and quietly helped the Jacobs pile the presents under their tree.

Then Jack and Diane walked with them out to the truck. "I don't know how we'll ever thank you for everything," Diane said.

"You'll pay it forward," Tucker said. "That's how things work."

"I have one more thing." Sheila pulled the card from her pocket and handed it to Jack. "I want to help. I wish I could just give you this money. I can't, but I *can* loan it to you. Interest-free. You take however long it takes. It's the deductible for your insurance."

"No. That's too much. You can't." Jack pushed it back toward her.

"I can. I am. You will get through this. Sometimes we just need a hand up and I want to do this for you. Please allow me to."

"But you don't even know us," he said.

"This is too generous," Diane said.

"Please. We'll work out the details over the next few months, but you need to be able to pull the trigger with the insurance company and not worry about this one part of all the recovery ahead of you."

"Thank you."

Diane hugged Sheila. "Thank you. So much. We will make this up to you. I promise."

"You're welcome. I know you will." She stepped toward the door. "We've got to run. We've got family waiting for us, and you've got to get some sleep. Those babies are going to wake you up at the crack of dawn to see what Santa brought!"

"You've got that right," Jack said. "Thank you. Sincerely. We really appreciate this."

"Merry Christmas," they said as Sheila and Tucker hopped back in his truck.

Tucker stared at her for a long moment before he started the truck. "You are amazing. How did you come up with that so quickly, over the holidays?"

"Sold the Tesla."

His mouth dropped. "You didn't."

"I did. I was going to anyway. I knew someone who could afford it and made a call. He was delighted. Treated himself to it for a Christmas present." She shrugged. "It seemed like the right thing to do. I'm so happy to be able to help them." She choked back a sob. "I'm so grateful to be able to be a part of this."

He kissed her on the cheek. "I'm so glad you forgave me. I'll never make you worry—well, I guess I can't promise that, but I won't do it on purpose and I'll always be there for you. Forever. Always. All the ways possible."

"That's a lot of always and forevers."

"I'm serious. I know it's fast, but I believe that with all my heart."

"I feel it too." She let out a breath. "I've never been this happy. I have a feeling I'll be spending more time up this way."

"Really? You just gave me the best Christmas present ever." Tucker nodded. "This is great. I'll come to Richmond too. It'll work out."

He reached over and put his hand on top of hers. They drove back to Orene's in comfortable silence, sneaking occasional smiling glances, and he picked up her hand and kissed it.

She squeezed the kiss closed in her hand.

They got out of the truck.

"What's that?" Sheila stopped tilting her head and leaning in to get a better listen.

Tucker paused. "It's the church bells. They ring them at midnight on Christmas Eve."

"It's beautiful."

He stopped and pulled her in front of him, hugging her. "It is."

Orene walked outside. "Yes, they are ringing. It's officially Christmas." Natalie, Randy, Eli, Amanda, and Paul all walked outside and joined Orene on the porch. Tucker and Sheila walked hand in hand to join them.

"It's so beautiful," Sheila said.

"Merry Christmas, everyone." Orene raised her hands in the air.

Words of merriment and joy were passed among them. Tucker chimed in glancing over at Sheila. "The Merriest Christmas I've had in a very long time."

"I guess that means we get to open presents now," Sheila said with delight.

Orene laughed. "Well, I guess that's true."

"Come on, y'all!" Sheila led the way, and everyone followed into the living room and gathered around Orene's beautiful tinsel tree.

Sheila dove for the present wrapped in the pretty toile paper she'd brought for Orene. "Open mine first."

Orene held the package in the air. "She tried to get me to open this on the thirteenth. I made her wait."

"That was almost two weeks ago, which was pure torture for me." Shelia sounded extremely dramatic about it, which Tucker found endearing.

"I shouldn't be the first one," Orene said. "Randy, why don't you give Natalie hers?"

Randy shook his head. "You go first. Then Natalie can open hers from me."

"Fine by me!" Orene ripped into that paper like a hungry beagle with a steak bone. "Oh my goodness!" She lifted the holiday teapot for everyone to see.

Sheila was tickled by Orene's reaction.

"I've never seen one like this! No wonder you were so excited for me to open it. Thank you so much. It's perfect! It's going to be a special addition to my collection." She hugged the teapot.

"I knew it would," Sheila said. "I thought of you as soon as I saw it." She was all smiles and clapping like a youngster still filled with the magic of Santa and wishes come true. "This is so fun." She turned to Randy. "Can you two please open my gift to you before Natalie opens yours?"

Randy didn't say anything, but Natalie did: "Yes. I know how you hate to wait."

Sheila handed them the package. "Goody, thanks!"

Natalie removed the paper, slowly just like always, and then let Randy take the top off the box.

Before they could even see what was inside, Sheila was spoiling the surprise. "I wanted to be the first to give you ornaments as a couple, since this is kind of your first official Christmas together as a serious couple."

Randy held a turquoise-colored ornament up. "These are like the ornaments my grandmother used to have on her tree. Thanks, Sheila. This really is a special gift. Perfect for this Christmas."

Natalie hugged Sheila. "Thank you so much."

"Now it's my turn." Randy handed Natalie a small package. He let out a long breath, and Tucker wondered if he might pass out.

"I can't wait." Natalie hunched her shoulders in excitement. Inside, there was a small photo album. The cover was wooden, with an etched image of her cabin on the front. "This is exquisite." She grazed her fingers across the indentations. "How did you do this?"

Randy nodded to Tucker. "Tucker made the photo album and did the engraving."

"Really?" Natalie said.

Sheila swung around and looked at him. "What other talents are you hiding from me?"

"Wait and see." Tucker blushed. "I'm no expert. I mess around. It turned out pretty good, though. I'm glad you like it."

"So sweet." Natalie held the album close.

"Look inside," Randy insisted, glancing over at Tucker.

"Oh. There are pictures inside?" Natalie opened the cover, and Sheila huddled closer to see them over her shoulder.

"Oh gosh, this is when we visited your sister at Giddy-Up and

Go when she was at the art festival." Natalie turned the picture for everyone to see. "And the first time we ate at Trout and Snout together."

Randy explained, "My sister opened a coffee shop in a horse trailer that she moves around. It's called Giddy Up and Go."

"It's so cool, she built it out of a horse trailer," Natalie said. "The coffee and tea are wonderful, but she's a baker too."

"Cute idea," Tucker said. "We should hire her to come up for one of the festivals."

"We should," Randy agreed.

Natalie giggled and commented as she flipped through the pictures, and then she stopped. "Whoa."

"Another giddy-up-and-go moment?" Sheila teased.

Randy sat there bobbing his head with this weird expression on his face.

The sudden silence caught Sheila off guard. "What's going on?"

Natalie lifted the photo album and showed the last picture to them. It was a picture of the tree topper he'd made for her, and next to it, in script, Randy had written,

> *Natalie,*
> *Will you be my wife?*
> *With all my love,*
> *Randy*

"Yes!" Natalie leapt from her seat.

Randy swept her into his arms and kissed her. He spun her around in a circle, kissing her on the forehead, the nose, and then the cheek. "I love you madly."

"I love you too."

"Your ring was in the birdhouse tree topper the whole time," he explained. "I was afraid the tree was going to be whisked off with your ring inside! I was going to propose during the Christmas Tree Stroll but there was never a good time."

"But it wasn't." Orene pulled the two-story birdhouse tree topper out from behind the couch. "It's right here. The bird nest you put on top of the tree you delivered wasn't quite as fancy, but I don't think Ms. Ferebee will ever know the difference."

Randy picked it up and held it in front of Natalie. "Lift the roof."

Sheila watched, with tears in her eyes, as her friend lifted the rooftop. Engraved in the wood was "I love you. Be my better half forever. With all my heart, I want to make you happy every day of your life." Inside, a Tiffany Blue box. Natalie's hands shook as she retrieved it and handed it to Randy.

Orene, Natalie, Sheila, and Amanda were all crying.

Randy popped the lid open, and lifted the diamond ring from the box; then he took a knee. "Let's make this official. Natalie, I've already talked to Paul and asked for your hand in marriage, and we have his blessing. Will you marry me and make me the happiest man in the world?"

She said, "I will," and her hand still shook as he slid the ring on her finger.

Tucker reached for Sheila's hand and squeezed it.

"Merry Christmas, Nat," Randy said. "And to all of you, who make living in this town so wonderful. I can't wait to see what happens in our next chapter in Chestnut Ridge together."

Tucker whispered into Sheila's ear, "It's going to be a really good year. I can feel it."

"I'm going to follow the stars," Sheila said.

"What exactly does that mean?" Tucker asked.

"Following the stars instead of a schedule. I'm going to live my life according to the natural rhythms that come my way, rather than adhering to a strict schedule."

"That sounds promising."

"I think so. You know, more spontaneous."

"Like playing catch in the grocery store?" he asked.

"Excellent example. It seems to be working for me already. I'm happier than I've ever been."

"I'd like to help you with this whole following-the-stars thing."

"I was hoping you'd say that."

Randy and Natalie were showing the ring to the others.

Tucker walked Sheila into the next room, and out the back French doors. "This has been a Christmas to remember," he said. "It's beautiful back here."

"It is. This has been such an amazing Christmas."

"You don't think it's possible that all this, you and me, is just Christmas magic? I'm not going to wake up tomorrow and you're going to have forgotten me?"

"Not on your life." She shook her head, taking a breath, almost afraid to speak from her heart and break the spell. She understood what he was feeling. She was afraid too. "I don't think so, because I'm honestly counting the days and the ways that we can experience wonderful things together in the new year."

He turned toward her. "This doesn't happen by accident. I wasn't looking. Neither were you. We just—"

"Fit. So perfectly."

"Yes," he said. "My job is important to me, but I want to experience life too. I can see that with you."

A whirl of excitement pushed through her. "I know. I didn't even know that's what I wanted. But I do."

"The timing and the stars just finally lined up for us. We owe ourselves the chance."

"Yes. You're right." She slid her hand down his arm, then laced her fingers with his.

He rested his body against hers as he looked to the sky. "What a special night."

She followed his gaze, and at that moment a shooting star zoomed across the sky. Instinctively, her hand reached for the sky.

Tucker said, "Tell me you just saw that too."

"I did."

"My mom always told me that a couple witnessing a shooting star together means they've found their soulmate."

"This is better than snow," she said.

"I'd follow you anywhere," he said.

"You won't have to," Sheila said. "I'm going to be right here in Chestnut Ridge with you."

"Well, that's good, because even if it snowed three feet, I could snowshoe to come see you."

She froze. "Wait a minute. You don't really get that much snow, do you? Please tell me you don't own snowshoes."

"I don't, and you won't need any either."

"Thank goodness, because that might be a little too much snow for me."

"No such thing. We'd just have to build more snowmen to clear the sidewalk, and how bad could that be?"

"Not bad at all as long as it's with you."

Epilogue

Sheila rang in the new year with Tucker at the Ruritan Club celebration with Randy and Natalie, and all of her new friends. It wasn't exactly the lavish affair she was used to, but it was a lot more fun. People brought their families, and even Paul made an appearance at the party, and was a hit handing out silver dollars to all the kids in the crowd.

Jack and Diane brought the children, and he was already making progress on the rebuild of the house. It was moving as fast as if it were an old-fashioned barn raising, according to Paul. Orene's house smelled of salty ham the whole following week after she fed half the county all the things that were supposed to guarantee a good year, and just about every bit of it was cooked in some kind of pork fat.

There was cornbread fried in a skillet until it was crispy around the edges and with the slightest sweetness to make it only narrowly escape the cake category. According to Orene, the golden color of the cornbread was supposed to bring extra spending money to those who ate it on New Year's Day.

There was a mess of collard greens, the color of money, and

another huge pot of black-eyed peas that she'd shelled and frozen over the summer just for the occasion. "The more you eat," she said, "the more you luck you'll have." That was the week Orene taught Sheila how to make Hoppin' John by using leftover ham fried to a crisp, black-eyed peas, collards, and spices mixed into rice.

On Valentine's Day, Tucker surprised Sheila with dinner at Primland, a fancy resort not too far from Chestnut Ridge. It was an evening in fancy clothes with music and dancing, and they ended it in the observatory looking at the stars.

Sheila wasn't sure if it was all the good-luck rituals that made the difference, because this was the first year she'd done all of them.

By spring, Tucker had made as many trips to Richmond as she had to Chestnut Ridge. They spent most of their free time together, and things were only getting better and better. Richmond was losing its luster as her friendships in the mountains grew stronger.

Sheila knew her life was in Chestnut Ridge with Tucker, and she couldn't imagine spending it anywhere else.

Sheila tapped lightly on Tucker's office door. "Do you have a minute?"

He got up with a lazy smile and walked over and kissed her on the nose. "I always have time for you."

"You looked busy."

"Paperwork."

"You should tell them the dog ate it. Or better, it caught on fire and was destroyed."

"Only since I'm the guy requiring it, that would just mean I had to start over."

"Right. Not a great plan."

"Everything okay? You seem . . . I don't know . . . anxious?"

"I made a decision," she said.

"Okay. What did you decide?"

"I'm going to put my house on the market." She pressed her lips together. "What do you think?"

"I think you aren't spending much time there. It makes good financial sense." He settled his hands on her hips. "I *could* give you a key to my place."

She laughed. "No. I like things the old-fashioned way too. I'm not rushing things. But, thank you. I am considering buying the old bank building on Main Street."

"It's been empty a couple of years. It was a restaurant. It's a neat building. What are you going to do with it?"

"Well, I wanted your opinion first. But I thought I'd make a satellite office up here for my business, maybe rent out office space to someone who doesn't need much room. I'll focus on the luxury homes up here in this region. If we build out apartments upstairs I can rent them out during leaf-peeper season, and there'd be a place for me to stay in."

"Moving here? Full-time." His eyes lit up.

She nodded.

"I love it," he said. "Let's go look at the space. I'm pretty handy, and between me and the guys at the firehouse, we can do just about all the work ourselves."

She lifted a key in the air. "I already got the key from the real estate agent."

"I love you, Sheila. I can't wait to get you moved up here. Don't for a minute think I want you staying in an apartment on

Main Street for long. I see us in a house with a white picket fence, two kids, and a dog. Maybe even a cat. A little garden."

She sucked in a breath. "That sounds so perfect, but . . . I don't know if I can get pregnant. I told you about—"

"That was you and Dan." He looked into her eyes. "This is you and me, and if we don't have our own children, we'll adopt, or foster, or borrow a couple of kids to hang out with us a couple of days a week like a time-share."

She started laughing. "You're sure? I'd never want to disappoint you."

"Children don't have to be of our flesh to be of our heart. I want to share the experience of family with you. No matter what it looks like."

"Me too." Her heart was so full. *Thank you for this man. This love.* "This town is amazing. I'm so thankful Natalie's journey brought her to Chestnut Ridge, and because of it . . . me to you."

"You know," he said, "I never thought this town could get any better. But it just did."

Recipes

SHEILA'S CRISPY CHEDDAR WAFERS

Ingredients

1 cup unsalted butter, softened
½ pound block of sharp cheddar, shredded and
 softened
½ teaspoon salt
¼ teaspoon red pepper
¼ teaspoon paprika
1½ cups flour
4 cups Rice Krispies

1. Preheat the oven to 375°F.
2. Beat together the butter and cheese until creamy, then mix in the salt, pepper, paprika, and flour, and form a large ball.
3. Work in the Rice Krispies by hand.
4. Roll the mixture into one-and-a-half-inch balls, pressing down with a fork so they will be thin

enough to crisp up, and place on an ungreased cookie sheet.

5. Bake for 8–10 minutes, watching carefully so that they don't burn.

6. Try desperately to not eat them all before you're finished!

Makes about 100 crisps. Enjoy.

SHEILA'S BUTTER PECAN SNOWBALL COOKIES

Ingredients

1 cup salted butter, softened

½ cup powdered sugar

¼ teaspoon salt

1½ teaspoon vanilla extract

2¼ cups all-purpose flour

¾ cup pecans, finely chopped, the finer the better!

Additional powdered sugar, for dusting

1. Preheat the oven to 350°F.

2. In a mixer, cream the butter and powdered sugar together until light and fluffy.

3. Turn the mixer to low and add the salt, vanilla, flour, and finely chopped pecans.

4. Using your hands, roll the dough into one-inch balls.

5. Place the balls on parchment-covered baking sheets a few inches apart.

6. Bake for 8–10 minutes or until very lightly browned. Do not overbake.

7. Remove from the oven and allow to cool just enough to handle them.

8. Pour 1 cup powdered sugar into a medium bowl. Drop each cookie in the powdered sugar to cover, then use a fork to lift it and shake off the excess and place it on a cooling rack.

9. Once completely cooled, roll each cookie in the powdered sugar one more time.

Makes about 3 dozen cookies.

Acknowledgments

Every book is a unique journey. For this special Christmas story, I had the chance to return to Chestnut Ridge, and I thoroughly enjoyed hearing readers' stories and suggestions while researching this one.

Huge thanks to Eileen Rothschild and Lisa Bonvissuto. I'm so grateful for the continued stories we bring to life together, and to the entire St. Martin's Griffin team, for helping get them into the readers' hands.

To my agent, Steve Laube, for being my safe harbor no matter what the tides bring in.

Most importantly, to my dear friend Pam, who helped manage my move in the middle of this book, giving me the time to create and finish it on deadline. Who knew I'd sell my house in just twelve days and then move within thirty? None of this would have happened without her help and kindness.

And to friends who gave me that calming "you've got this" when there were so many book signings, edits, deadlines, and things going on that I wasn't quite sure which way was up. Thank you. I needed that!

And to my neighbors in Patrick Springs, Virginia, I'm thankful and grateful for your kindness and sense of community so much that it inspired the town of Chestnut Ridge. I treasure the friendships we've made and hope to pay it forward with the books in this series.

About the Author

Adam Sanner

USA Today bestselling author **Nancy Naigle** whips up small-town love stories with a whole lot of heart. Several of Nancy's novels have been made into Hallmark movies, and most recently *The Shell Collector* was adapted as the first Fox original movie to stream on Fox Nation. A native of Virginia Beach, Nancy now calls the Blue Ridge Mountains home.